NO MARKING IN L

A
CRUEL
LIGHT

A CRUEL LIGHT

A NOVEL

CYNDI MACMILLAN

CROOKED
LANE

NEW YORK

Published in the United States by Crooked Lane Books, an imprint of The Quick Brown Fox & Company LLC.

Crooked Lane Books and its logo are trademarks of The Quick Brown Fox & Company LLC.

Library of Congress Catalog-in-Publication data available upon request.

ISBN (hardcover): 978-1-63910-325-6
ISBN (ebook): 978-1-63910-326-3

Cover design by Nicole Lecht

Printed in the United States.

www.crookedlanebooks.com

Crooked Lane Books
34 West 27th St., 10th Floor
New York, NY 10001

First Edition: April 2023

10 9 8 7 6 5 4 3 2 1

To
My husband, Colin, my anchor,
and
our daughter, Verity, my sail

PROLOGUE

June 12, 1957

THOMAS MACGOWAN KNEW he was being watched and exactly who was watching him. He stopped crossing his front yard, lit his pipe, and took a long, thoughtful puff. Maybe Robin could clean out the garage instead of missing out on their weekly father–son fishing trip. The boy had been caught sneaking his first beer with two of his buddies in a neighbour's sugar shack. MacGowan wondered if he was being overly harsh. Naw—his own father would have tanned his hide, made him stand on a stool for an hour, then ordered him to bed without a bite to eat.

Frustrated, almost angry, he kept his head down. Better not look up at that dormer window, or he'd be swayed by those sad, puppy eyes. He was already too soft with the boy. Misbehaviour required consequences. Dammit, life had lessons! MacGowan marched to his Chevy, jumped inside, and motored toward the river, smoke billowing around him like fog as the sun pierced the horizon.

It would be a good day. Bess had woken up early, too, and offered to fry him bacon and eggs. He'd given her a long kiss and told her he'd already had a large bowl of porridge. She shared a pot of tea with him and added a hunk of banana bread to his lunch pail. Before returning to bed, she once again reminded him about the family of mice in the crawl space. His tender-hearted wife had no stomach for things like traps or poisons.

He'd forgotten how still the world could be at dawn. Robin had a bad habit of whistling, frightening away the fish. The boy barraged him with questions and knock-knock jokes while those gangly limbs of his swished about, to and fro . . . yes sir, a little time alone would be nice for a change. Perhaps he would actually catch something.

He tromped through the high grass, passing the tree that Robin said looked like a funny old gnome. An owl perched on its highest branch and swiveled its head to glare at him, as if annoyed by his intrusion. The sunrise was picture-postcard material, too pretty for words. He made his way down the path, frowning at a string of lights. They shouldn't be there. His stomach tightened at the unmistakable metallic stench that brought him back to Dieppe, to a bloodbath.

A part of him wanted to run in the opposite direction, run like hell, and yet he continued heading toward the river, preparing himself.

But when he saw the body, he sank to his knees. Too young. Oh God, too young for such a horrifying death! He squeezed his eyes shut and moaned, filled with a guilty relief this child was not his.

Robin was at home. Safe. For now.

1

October 2, 2019

Felicity Street was mostly what I'd imagined it would be. Its pebbled driveways swelled expectantly with canoes and ATVs—sundries for cottage country. I'd anticipated the neatly stacked woodpiles and cheery flagpoles, the browning lawns peppered with Adirondack chairs and scraggily hedges. But some things cannot be foreseen. Besides, people in my line of work are never called out to crime scenes. Ever. So, when I reached my destination, only to find it boxed in by four police vehicles—one being a forensics van—I stupidly kept gawking, bumped the curb, and nearly flattened a cat. It streaked away in an orange blur as I straightened the wheel and parked the car, posthaste.

I continued to sit there, ogling the lanky constable who was planted like a signpost at the same address that I had typed into my GPS eleven hours earlier. Wary and more than a tad agitated, I polished off my water bottle before hauling myself from my seat. The drive from Montreal to Northeastern Ontario had been draining, and I was becoming tetchier by the minute, the brusque autumn air doing little to improve my mood.

Why the police presence? Without the barricade, I'd have guessed vandalism, could imagine bored teens embellishing portraits of retired pastors with Godzilla-sized genitals. After all, I'd been forewarned the job required discretion. Lilith had cautioned me this wouldn't be any run-of-the-mill art restoration, like such a thing existed. She'd said—actually, she'd said very little, but her uncharacteristic vagueness did what she'd meant it to do: lured me here. It would have served her right if I'd hopped back into my lemon of a vehicle, chucked a U-ey and hightailed it to the nearest motel, but I stood there, shivering in the cold, feeling both puzzled and miffed.

I leaned back against my SUV and scoped out the property. The lofty Victorian appeared to be in duress. Tape cinched the former parsonage's wrought iron gate, barring it with a cautionary yellow, and heavy equipment had rutted its yard. Wind stirred up damp leaves, sending them slithering between my feet, and though I could detect the roil of the river as it snaked through the town, the water itself remained elusive, as if it did not want to be found.

The building sprawled, and something about its dark windows reminded me of a Charles Burchfield painting . . . intimidating, almost sinister. Ironic, considering it had once been owned by the church. I stared at the house, and the house stared back.

Something flashed just out of my line of vision. Curtains had parted behind me. The neighbours were curious too. Had they seen something? Maybe they'd been subjected to the buzzkill of construction for so long that they'd paid no mind to suspicious activity. A building permit was taped to a window, and the contents of a dumpster in the parsonage's drive had all the markings of an overhaul. A turquoise toilet balanced on rotting two-by-fours, and a hill of peach carpeting displayed a bewildering number of stains.

A valuable painting must be at stake . . . must be. One casement window provided me with glimpses of a much leaner Lilith, pacing as she chewed at a thumbnail, something she only did in public when distraught. She'd drawn blood at her father's funeral, had worn bandages for weeks, and she'd later developed an equally bad habit of gnawing at pens.

We'd stayed fair-weather friends, as we had little in common except a love for the arts, but we trusted each other, and if your old Delta Phi sister—who happens to be the mayor of a small town—pleads for your help, you pack two duffle bags, fill up your tank, and drive 'til you drop. I rolled my neck, attempting to loosen a stubborn kink. Thunder grumbled in the distance, and the wind pawed at the hem of my duffle coat, prickling my thighs. I burrowed my hands deeper into my pockets, wishing I'd packed gloves.

The two-plus story building lorded over the street's humbler bungalows. Its intricate gingerbread trim reminded me of the wares of a lacemaking shop I'd visited during my short stint in Belgium. Slight colour variances showed where loose or crumbling red bricks had been replaced, but only the pricey, black metal shingles strayed from historical accuracy. The blue-grey woodwork had been left half-painted, and the abandoned paint trays littering the broad porch clattered with each

strong gust. Another officer flung open the maroon front
door. He stepped outside and called out to me, "Annora
Garde?"

I jaunted across the road, glad I'd worn my com-
bat boots. Two police personnel exited the building and
headed toward the van. I waited until they drove off, then
plotted my way down the short, potholed driveway. Muddied timber formed a sort of wobbly boardwalk, offering a
makeshift passage over the muck of the yard. Everywhere,
there were piles of topsoil and landscaping material.

The officer met me on the porch, but his half-smile
seemed forced. Something about his square jaw, brawni-
ness, and stance reminded me of a boxer, and his intense,
grey gaze was downright disconcerting.

Without warning, Lilith flew out the door, greeting
me with one of her fierce hugs. "I'm so glad you came."
The bags under her eyes were dark. "This is Inspector
Scott MacGowan—"

"—but he goes by Mac," the constable by the fence
yelled.

"Shut it, Johnston!" The inspector's smile relaxed.
"Thing is, most do call me Mac." His warm hand shook
my icy one as he casually dropped a bomb. "Thank you
for coming. I'm told you can shed some light on this
case."

"I'm lost. What case?"

Thick auburn brows rose and knitted together. Mac
said to Lilith, "You didn't tell her?" I could almost see
him counting to ten. He turned toward me. "Ms. Garde,
I hope we haven't wasted your time."

Lilith nudged an ash-blond wave behind her ear.
"Really, it's not as bad as all that." Thunder sounded
again, and she flinched. "Let's head inside."

I nodded and tried to keep my expression mild. We stepped into a vestibule that reeked of new paint and tile adhesive. I started to remove my boots.

"Best to leave those on, Nory. But may I take your coat?"

Mac's sharp sideways glance made me nervous. I handed her my jacket, which she hung on an antique hall tree. We remained in the cramped space, and my suspicions grew.

"Many wanted this building to be demolished," she said. "The church sold it decades ago. It became a rooming house, then a tavern. It was boarded up for years. We had our work cut out for us—rot, pests, bongs." She kept us at the entrance, bottlenecking the doorway. "But soon it will be a multipurpose art museum—offer exhibits, residencies, weddings, and—"

"Lil, I'm losing my patience."

Finally, she moved. I veered past her, rounded a corner, and froze. So, this is why she'd been stonewalling me. Plastic sealed off the room at the end of the short hall. Taped to the clear barrier, a large sign warned, "'Danger: Mould Spore Hazard."

"There's some water damage, and the double parlour is infested—nasty toxic stuff. A remediation team came out, but—you'll see, after we put on these suits and masks."

A formal archway divided one long, empty shell of a room. The right parlour wasn't the problem. I peered through the left parlour's transparent shield. Thick, dark mould had swallowed most of the back wall. I bit my tongue, inwardly fuming. I'd worked with fungus before, of course. It didn't daunt me, wouldn't affect my decision. Still, a head's-up would have been nice.

As we slipped into the hazmat coveralls, Lilith continued to sell me on the commission. "The town's centennial is next month. The museum's grand opening will be the highlight of the celebration. But we came across something . . . hidden." She frowned as she unzipped the plastic closure. "Now, Mac and I are at odds about how to proceed with this find."

The "find" was a three-and-a-half-by-four-and-a-half-foot mural located above the fireplace on the back wall, the one with the extreme infestation. From the one-inch blocks that cornered the painting, it seemed the imposing over-mantle—removed from its place above the hearth—had concealed the mural. The elaborate piece had not been in direct contact with the old wall, creating a thin gap between the back of the mirror and the painting. The cushion of space had failed to protect the mural. Instead, it had formed a microclimate, a breeding ground for destructive white blooms. And black and green blooms too. Possibly *Aspergillus*. Fungus all but obscured sectors of the art.

Mac and Lilith stopped speaking. They stepped back, allowing me to assess the damage, to take in the scope of the work.

I eased up to the fireplace and tipped my head back. Layers of grungy mould veiled a young girl. She wore a drab summer dress . . . a tainted yellow, perhaps. Behind her, a jaundiced river swelled, burdening unnaturally pallid banks. From March until June, I'd been told, the town held its breath, waited out flood warnings and hoped the water wouldn't reach low-lying homes. The setting suggested a pastoral theme, probably whimsical, but I could just make out the church steeple in the background—its presence too Sunday-best for a portrait of a young child playing by a riverbank. Impossible to tell if it was a day or night scene. Maybe twilight? *What a jewel this would be, once cleaned.*

Even in its neglected state, from what I could see of it, the artwork was astounding. The artist could very well be renowned for her or his body of work. Or not. The bottom right corner held the hidden answer. Fungus had made the signature indecipherable, but it was there.

I frowned at the wall. "Lath and plaster?"

"What! Yes, plaster," Mac repeated. "The mural stays where it is!"

"First, I need to do a condition report!" The respirators muffled our voices, so we needed to shout to be heard. "Before I touch a thing, I'll record the state of deterioration—in this case, mostly mould damage. I'm not seeing any flaking or aging cracks, but I may need to stabilize it. I'll run it through cleaning tests, experiment with different solutions. Next, I would carefully—inch by inch—clean off all the accumulated fungi and ensure it won't resurface. When we pass that point, we can begin to address repairs, true restoration, and conservation." I still felt somewhat bamboozled, but the prospect of restoring beauty to the piece thrilled me. I could hardly wait to return it to its original splendour.

"How long will it take?" Lilith bellowed.

"Three weeks?"

"Three? Not any quicker?"

"Hard to say." I grew tired of enunciating each word. "It all depends on the extent of the damage. It's helpful this area is already contained. So, your crew should be able to finish the other rooms while I breathe life back into this little girl."

Lilith and Mac shared a startled look. I didn't like the look one bit.

"I've issued a stop-work order." Mac stepped closer to me until our masks almost touched. "We need your help. The girl in that mural has waited over sixty years for someone to ID her killer. There's a slim chance he may still be alive."

"Someone killed her?" My stomach churned. "You're telling me *her killer* is the artist? But—but it's signed!"

Lilith's shoulder brushed mine. "Her name was Rosemary."

Mac handed me a photo sealed in a bag. Plastic shielded a lovely, oval face, heartbreakingly young. Her innocent smile dazzled. She seemed so alive. The room began to spin, and four hands steadied me.

"How many stops did you make? When did you last eat?" Lilith went into mother mode.

"You can both let go of me now. I'm fine. But I'd like to revive myself." *And get my bearings.* "Is there a washroom I can use?"

"Yes." She paused. "Unfortunately, the downstairs powder rooms are still a work in progress. The one upstairs hasn't been touched yet. It has everything, but it's scuzzy." Her forehead wrinkled. "This shouting is ridiculous! Let's finish this discussion elsewhere."

Mac said, "Good idea. She's travelled a long way."

"Nine hundred kilometres?" I took pity on the man. "Pftt. *She's* driven from Toronto to Montevideo."

"Bet there's a story there."

We left the contained area, took off what we had put on and regrouped in the second parlour. Despite all the Canadian Association for Conservation conventions I'd attended, I couldn't recall a single presentation on

"Challenging Law Enforcement" or "Hints on How to Restore Incriminating Evidence." Note to self: Should a friend say a new museum requires my expertise, ask for details.

Mac's expression turned serious. "We just need the signature. It's a confession, right? If it's there, we're done."

"As I said, *first* I complete the report."

"We're talking about an area smaller than a gift tag."

"So, you or other officers didn't take notes or document the evidence?"

"Yeah, sure, we have protocols that must be followed. To the letter." He sighed. "I get what you're saying. And obviously, conservation has its restrictions and procedures too. I'm asking you to break some rules. We're one step away from naming a killer."

"Isn't this a cold case? Would another hour or two make that much of a difference?"

He shot me a harsh look. "What if this was your hometown? What if Rosemary were your great-aunt or a relative of a good friend? If this was personal, would you feel the same way? Would you tell family to wait another two hours?"

I turned away, struggling to keep my composure. He had no idea what he'd just said to me, but Lilith did. Her eyes shimmered.

"Okay," I huffed. "What I'm about to do goes against a code of ethics. Documentation safeguards cultural property. It's essential that I examine the art and record my findings. So, I'll take a few snapshots, then I'll clean the signature, but I'll need access to the mural so I can complete a report."

"Cultural property? This? We'll have to disagree on that point."

"They canonized Saint Catherine of Bologna in 1712. Victorian Richard Dadd was committed to Bedlam for stabbing his own father. They've both had their paintings restored and preserved by experts in my field." I lifted my chin. "We don't discriminate. I've sworn to treat all art with equal care, just as you've sworn to preserve the peace, even for those found guilty of violent crimes."

He barked a laugh. "Alright, alright. You argue like a crown attorney."

Lilith slowly exhaled.

"I'd like to wash up. I wouldn't normally ask, but could one of you get my kits—the aluminum briefcases—from my car, please?"

"Sure thing." Mac took my keys and walked away.

His absence did an odd thing to the atmosphere; the energy in the building drastically changed, curdled like milk, deepening the gloom.

I WAS NOT AT all happy with Lilith. In fact, I was peeved, but I kept my thoughts to myself. She may have realized what this commission would do to me, shown her concern, but she hadn't backed me up during the whole report debate.

She checked her phone. "Darn. I have a meeting. The downtown business association etcetera, etcetera. Are you okay?" She touched my arm. "Are *we* okay?"

Had she been intentionally elusive or deliberately misleading? "You're forgiven."

She laughed. "How about dinner at the pub where John's playing tonight? They have a decent menu, and the bartender is hot."

"Single by choice, remember?"

I gazed through the clear plastic. What could be seen of Rosemary's elfin face loomed above us, holding me spellbound. What colour were those big eyes? And an oil lamp? Symbolic? Best to focus on her, not on the artist or on what he might have done . . ."

"Nory?"

"Sorry. Distracted."

Her frown disappeared. "It'll work out. You've always been so level-headed. Sensitive, yes, but even earthquakes don't shake you."

Two decades of being friends, and she didn't know me at all.

Lilith tightened the belt of her plum jacket, and the move emphasized her new hourglass figure. "Our guest room is set up. The work side of your visit should be done in a few hours, right? While here, perhaps you can take a much-earned mini-vacation. Bliss River may be Lilliputian, but we do have a fabulous spa."

"We'll see."

"Call me as soon as you can."

The door closed, and the odd quiet expanded, hollowing out the room with a voraciousness that had me grabbing my purse and hurrying down another barebones hall. I couldn't help but compare it to my small, cluttered home. I'd squeezed paintings from floor to ceiling, until my condo looked like an art salon. Pastel portraits snuggled against impasto landscapes. Most were the works of new artists who survived on pizza and idealism, not quite starving artists, but close. Bliss Rivers' Artist Residency Program would be a dream come true for many of them. Maybe Lilith would be open to suggestions. I thought of Boon-Mee's pointillism series and Genevieve's ink-and-water sketches as I plodded up a set of stairs which didn't creak. The steps hadn't yet been stained, but they had been restored.

The washroom's tub was indeed horrid. The toilet seat had been left up, and the bowl needed a thorough scrubbing. On the counter, two paintbrushes had been left in a boggy mason jar, explaining why the room reeked of turpentine. I turned the taps, relieved the water wasn't brown. The face in the scarred mirror grimaced. Two days prior, I'd been in Amsterdam, and jet lag had mottled my skin. People have told me I look like a younger Sandra Bullock. I glanced at my reflection and saw only my father's espresso-hued eyes, toffee-brown hair, and cleft chin. Quickly, I washed up and straightened my ponytail. Maybe, just maybe, I'd help solve a decades-old murder. The thought energized me and squared my shoulders.

On the way back to the parlour, I checked out the study. Walls sported a trendy taupe, and the gas fixtures had been replaced with modern knock-offs. Someone had set up two vintage lawn chairs. A large portable radio burdened a pocked card table, and a bag of toiletries leaned against one of its legs. Mac must have shopped for me. His thoughtfulness made me uncomfortable. I'm accustomed to fending for myself.

I turned toward the bay window across the room. It had a padded tapestry seat, and the cozy spot called to me, but I had no time to rest.

I put on the hazmat suit, strapped on the headgear and entered the isolated room. My kits lay on a long worktable that had been placed close to the mural. I walked the parlour's perimeter. Half a century's worth of wallpaper had been peeled away; a ribcage of lath showed through numerous holes and cracks. Both heating vents were properly sealed off. Good. The set-up couldn't be better. I'd been gifted with full containment, a zippered access, negative-pressure ventilation, and air scrubbers.

As far as the mould went, I easily spotted the causes as rain, melting snow, humidity, and frost. Two small windows on either side of the fireplace were boarded up with new-looking, plywood squares. From the water stains and the degree of decay around them, I'd say the original glass panes had been missing for years. The room was uninhabitable.

In contrast, the picture window framed a lively, bucolic view. St. George's Anglican Church and parsonage topped the hill, while below, Bliss River curved like a well-rounded hip. The bright fall colours jarred with the stormy sky. Scarlet leaves flounced in the wind, ruffling a tall oak that dominated the center of the backyard.

A massive over-mantle leaned against the opposing wall. Black spots and a large web of cracks marred its hefty mirror. Within the distorted reflection, Rosemary's image split apart, her shrouded features crosscut by shards. The horrific collage effect left me all the more uneasy.

Decisively, I approached the table, opened the kit, and unpacked my supplies. I'd come prepared and had pre-rolled dozens of six-inch cotton swabs. I'd also lugged along a variety of non-ionic detergents and neutralizers, empty squeeze bottles, my head-mounted magnifier, three clean smocks, my laptop, and a partridge in a pear tree. My stock of cotton was running low, but I wouldn't need more. The task should be straightforward compared to the work involved if I'd been commissioned to restore and preserve the entire mural. Though it deserved full treatment, cleaning a few inches of the portrait felt as if I were disturbing a grave. For the first time in my career, I wondered if I was doing more harm than good.

I wished I had time to get my phone and scroll through my playlists. Classic rock can normalize any situation, an embalmer once told me. A memorable date that had been.

I took my camera out of my kit and photographed the mural from different angles and different heights, zooming in on several areas and taking multiple shots of the one zone I'd tackle. I also took a few snaps of the back wall.

I should have brought a vacuum cleaner. I'd have to make do. I poured a solution of tri-ammonium citrate into the bottle, diluted it with distilled water, and squeezed a few drops of the solution onto a swab. Gently, I rolled the cotton just above the signature. I did this again and again, new swab after new swab, checking each to see if any paint had been removed with the mould. What had been a putrid off-white morphed into a vibrant cobalt blue. I rolled neutralizer across the cleaned surface to prevent paint from dissolving.

Satisfied with the results, I started on the signature, rolling swabs across the concealed writing. The chalky scrawl changed into brushwork of searing crimson. Too lengthy for a name. Perhaps, it was hyphenated. Dab by dab, at a slug's pace, I revealed the letters, thrown by the illuminated words. It wasn't a signature.

"You're done?"

I jumped about a foot. When had he returned?

Mac leaned over my shoulder and squinted. "So, three weeks, then?"

Shaken, I bolted from the room, tore off the suit, crammed it into a garbage bin, and kept moving until I found the kitchen. I rested against the apron sink and stared at the massive faucet, so new its box still lay on the counter. The professional gas range wore protective plastic film . . . *it* had never been touched. I remembered Lilith's tight face and clipped tone. The mural was just some unwelcome interruption to her, an inconvenience. The thought made my skin crawl.

The thunderstorm had missed the town, but the wind remained torrential; it yowled down the stove's vent and made the walls groan. I flinched when a door slammed somewhere upstairs. A window must have been left open on the second floor. The kitchen light flickered, once, twice, and then grew brighter, as if it had dug in its heels.

Mac entered the kitchen and placed a paper bag on the table. "You were so deep into your work you didn't even hear *me*. And I'm loud." He reached into the bag, pulled out a sandwich, and motioned to me. "Sit. Eat."

"I've lost my appetite."

"Sit anyway." He caught my expression. "Please."

I settled onto a pleather chair. He took a bottle of Perrier out of the double-door fridge and put it on the table. No doubt he'd seen the multitude of empty green bottles littering the Jeep's floor. I alternate between caffeine and fizz but never combine the two or I get jittery. I opened the bottle and chugged half its contents. His lips twitched.

He rummaged through cabinets until he found a tin of coffee and a bag of filters. An odd disquiet filled the room as coffee sputtered into a decanter.

"*Us?*" I finally said. "He actually wrote, 'May God forgive *us*.' He had a partner!"

"He might've had an accomplice. Or he could have used *us* in reference to Rosemary, as if she'd participated in her own murder. Best to avoid mindset, how he justified the killing."

My temple began to throb. "The date is the day she . . ."

"My grandfather found her that morning. Pops liked to hunt but fished on Saturdays." He wiggled a mug at me, and I shook my head. "Dad said Pops changed. Kept a closer watch on him, became a vegetarian. Claimed dead things could look clear through a person."

A memory stirred. Dead eyes. I blocked it.

Mac's gaze softened, then he turned away. He poured himself a coffee and frowned at the jar of whitener. Nevertheless, he stirred a heaping spoonful of the powder into his cup, sat down, and continued, "If you find gruesome images under the dirt—and I believe you will— they could haunt you for years." He took a sip, scowled, and put the mug down. "One inspector I know studied a kill journal. It contained explicit details of what a psychopath did to each of his victims. Two years later, the cannibal was released from a mental health facility, but my friend still sees a counselor. If you take on this job, you need to know the facts."

My headache intensified. "Hold that thought. I'll be right back."

I retrieved my purse from the second parlour and rifled through its pockets for the travel-sized container of acetaminophen tablets. Mac had mentioned counseling. What toll would this particular job take on me? The mural needed me. No, *she* needed me, and if I could help her find justice, I'd somehow cope with the fallout. I returned to the kitchen and downed two pills, thinking "extra strength" better mean *extra* strength. Not truly prepared for what I might hear, I sat down, steeled myself, and waited.

CHAPTER

3

He placed his phone on the table and settled back in his chair. "In the fifties, people managed to keep their dirty little secrets to themselves, carefully hid domestic abuse, addictions, prostitution. But they promptly paid their taxes and went to church."

Mac didn't so much as blink when a severed twig slapped the window behind him. It glued itself to the glass, slowly inching down the pane as the kitchen became draftier.

He continued, "Fayette Green—a widow—moved here in the fall of '47. The following spring, she gave birth to a baby girl. Fayette worked as a seamstress and struggled to make ends meet. Rumours quickly spread, started by women so riled up by their husbands' infidelities that they popped Miltown, a pre-Valium tranquilizer. Men noticed Fayette, so the ladies' auxiliary had it out for her from day one."

The temperature continued to drop, and I longed for a sweater, something thick and soft and oversized. I hugged myself, wishing I'd accepted his offer of coffee. A warm cup to wrap my hands around would have been comforting.

"Rosemary inherited her mother's good looks. Teachers described her as creative but shy. She had friends, but this was long before anti-bullying campaigns. Kids tormented her. Once, an older boy pulled off her skirt, said he'd been dared."

I blurted, "Was he a suspect? Wait, no, no—of course he wasn't. Obviously, a grade school boy didn't paint the mural. Sorry, Mac. Please, continue."

"The police questioned every resident. The population in the mid-fifties was half of what it is today. Our most notable resident, Kingsley Boyland—"

"Boyland! From the patches I can see of the mural, it's obviously characteristic of a Boyland portrait; the subject's neo-classicism has been juxtaposed against an impressionist background. And symbolism! Yes! Boyland!"

"Whoa, air bubbles hit you hard, don't they?" Mac chuckled. "I think I got about half of what you said, but yeah, I immediately thought of Boyland. He'd been in Ottawa, painting the prime minister's family portrait that spring, so his alibi is rock solid. Boyland is innocent. Thing is, he'd started an art school. Student enrollment exceeded a hundred."

A professor would have rapped him upside the head. "Students do *not* duplicate work."

"I know. Could you please stop scowling at me? Anyway, Boyland was a man ahead of his time. He started a troubled teen's program that kept a few kids out of juvie. It was called The Guiding Light Project. He mentored four pupils. Three became permanent residents and are still alive. The fourth used a wheelchair and died in his early twenties. Brain tumor or something. Anyway, Boyland didn't do it. But one of the three may have."

"If you already have three suspects, why is cleaning the mural so urgent?"

"You mentioned symbolism. I think the mural's chock-full of it, and those clues could lead us to the killer. The painting's our star witness. And you're its interrogator." He pressed his forearms to the table. "Annora, the animal brutalized her. Forensics has advanced over sixty years." He paused. "She'd been sexually assaulted with an object. They couldn't tell whether the rape was post-mortem. The assault fractured her skull and shattered two ribs, a femur, and her pelvis. Clothing helped identify the remains, though she'd been missing less than eight hours."

I felt sick and hoped he was done, but he wasn't finished.

"Her mother collapsed, needed to be hospitalized. Battery-operated Christmas lights were found at the scene. Will-o'-the-Wisp, she kept saying. Rosemary loved fairy stories. The SOB knew her, duped her with twinkling lights. This wasn't a crime of opportunity, and yet he doesn't fit the profile of a child predator. The murder had been methodically planned," Mac said. "They found someone guilty. An indigenous teen. And it took thirty-seven years for DNA to prove him innocent. Thirty-seven. Years."

I mentioned a similar case that had garnered national outrage.

"Thing is the media didn't run with *this* story. Non-indigenous folk weren't that interested in First Nation news, back then. And that hasn't much changed."

He stopped talking, and the silence lengthened. The fridge's hum seemed loud. Outside, someone cursed out a dog. Mac didn't rush me. He sat there, patiently waiting.

"I'm onboard, but here's what I require," I said. "I want twenty-four/seven access to the mural. No motel, no B&B. A blow-up mattress will do. I need good lighting, minimal disruptions, and both your guidance and input. Tonight, I'll stay at Lilith's, but I want to get an early start."

"I have one of those bring-your-own-beds. A leftover from my daughter's sleepover phase. I could set it up in the study."

"Is that an office through those doors? Can I use it?"

"Whatever you need." He looked down at his phone. "It's getting late. Tomorrow I'll get you a set of keys."

"Thank you. The next three weeks will be about methodology."

"Two things: One, I've shared privileged information with you, so, please, don't discuss this with anyone else. Not even Lilith. And two, it's unprecedented that evidence cannot be processed by one of our own." He stood up. "This building isn't the scene of the crime, but it's still off-limits to the general public. You, of course, being the one exception."

"What? No toga parties?" My stupid attempt to lighten the mood failed.

He walked me to my Jeep. I drove off, wondering if I should have taken the commission.

The sun had lowered, and the sky quilted itself in deep pinks and purples. It took effort to concentrate on the road. What had I'd gotten myself into? My mind grappled with the whole awfulness of the undertaking as I passed a hair salon, two boutiques, an auto repair shop, and the post office—all closed for the day. Above the provincial blue "H" for hospital sign, a faded banner promoted a fundraising masquerade. Roadwork had me making a detour down a new subdivision of adult lifestyle homes where doors wore leafy wreaths, and pumpkin displays promised future cornucopias of sweets for trick-or-treaters.

Small-town life was foreign to me, more foreign than Cairo or Ankara or Lima. I stopped for a freight train and winced at its blaring whistle, but as I caught sight of the lumbering boxcars with their end-to-end graffiti tags, I felt more at home.

Years ago, I'd visited Bliss River for Lilith's and John's tenth anniversary celebration. Their then-five-year-old son and eight-year-old daughter had taken advantage of the occasion, running wild with cousins. John's fiddle had kept the gathering lively. The following night, once the house had quieted, Lilith and I had shared a bottle of wine. We gabbed for hours, sniggering over the past.

We'd both achieved our dreams. She governed a small town, illustrated children's books, and gardened. As a freelance art conservator, I travelled the world and preferred to live in a studio condo. She'd been happily married for seventeen years, while I remained contentedly single, despite being thirty-six, as my mother liked to remind me. Often.

I pulled into Lilith's driveway and parked beside her day-glow, lemon-hued Mini Cooper, amused by the personal plate: MYBLISS. The house hadn't changed. The kids, however, had me doing a double-take. Her daughter, Katie, opened the door and informed me she was now "just Kate." Her eyes were rimmed in black,

and she'd straightened her naturally wavy hair. She went
back to texting before I'd even sat down. Five minutes
later, her date arrived; she paused at the entry and sent
me a bafflingly sympathetic look, which set me even
more on edge.

Lilith and I sat in what felt like a staged room. She
told me that Parker, twelve, was on a two-day field trip
to Ottawa. She excused herself and disappeared around
a corner. Sliding glass doors framed a lovely view of their
property, and I admired the maples tenting their enormous lot. The trees shaded their pool and patio in the
summer, but I did not envy the yard work they created
each autumn. John puttered outside, raking and bagging
leaves, pausing to guzzle more beer. Stubble covered his
jaw, and his hair could use a good trim. I watched as
Lilith approached him and said something. He stormed
off, and her body tensed.

I turned away, giving her privacy.

She returned and led me to the guest room. I
tossed my travel bag into a corner, glad I had my own
en suite. Though a hot bath would have relaxed me, a
quick shower would have to suffice. Keeping it casual, I
dressed in leggings and the flowing tunic I'd purchased
in Morocco.

A vendor and I had had a wonderful time haggling,
so after she met my price, I'd surprised her by paying
hers. I dabbed on sandalwood oil perfume and left the
room.

"Ooh," Lilith said. "You always could carry off
boho."

To simplify things, I rode with them in John's truck.
As if roles had reversed, John barely spoke a word while
Lilith chattered non-stop about everything from the cost

of fresh vegetables to local tourist attractions. The ten-minute drive felt much longer. I bit back a sigh of relief as we pulled into the parking lot of The Cheeky Monkey. The pint-sized pub bustled with townies. A banner of mini Union Jacks hung above the bar, and the stucco walls were covered in lions rampant. Three muted TVs showed various sports.

A table had been reserved for us. A busty millennial server handed us menus and shouted out the specials of the day. The ruckus of locals unwinding from their week soothed me. I like the sound of people enjoying themselves.

Conversation at our table did not flow. Meals were ordered, and Lilith prattled on as if she believed that, should she stop, even for a second, somebody might say something *he* shouldn't.

I hated being right.

Out of nowhere, John leaned toward me and muttered, "You know something? This isn't a goddamn movie of the week. The case won't get solved. Meanwhile, carpenters and plumbers are stuck at home, twiddling their thumbs as bills pile up."

I'd forgotten that, as Bliss River's only contractor, the art museum must be his project, his bread and butter. I lowered my voice. "I can't discuss the case. Even with you. Believe me, everyone wants this resolved as quickly as possible."

I let them know I would be staying at the parsonage, as I wouldn't be keeping banker's hours and didn't want to disturb them with my comings and goings. John tersely nodded. Lilith chewed on a stubby nail and sank lower in her chair.

Our meals were brought to the table, and we ate. Lilith said little for the rest of the night.

We sat and listened as John played his fiddle on the five-by-five stage. All around us people relaxed or tapped their feet. I had intentionally ordered a pot of herbal tea. Meanwhile, John tossed back whisky shots, and Lilith studied the tablecloth.

We returned to the immaculate side-split, and I told them I needed to get an early start, excusing myself. Lilith had the decency to look guilty, flushing as I headed upstairs.

She'd made the guest room as welcoming as she could. An embroidered sachet lay on the pillow; a jar of French hand cream prettified the marble-topped nightstand; and my favourite art magazines had been placed on a chair. A perfect orchid decorated the dresser. It fooled me. I thought it real, but it was artificial.

I set the alarm clock and punched the feather pillow. My last stay had come with an awkward moment; the sounds of restrained lovemaking had travelled through their bedroom wall, softest sighs followed by throaty murmurs and sensual chuckles.

My mind continued to race. Lilith and John walked up the stairs and shut their door. I didn't want to eavesdrop, to interpret the low hiss of whispers as livid. Tonight, the wall gave off a different kind of heat. The people of Bliss River still knew something about keeping up appearances, and despite two decades of friendship, it seemed I did not know Lilith either. I pulled the comforter to my ears and willed myself to sleep.

Something woke me around midnight. I sat up and listened but heard nothing. Deciding a bit of fresh air might help me relax, I quietly dressed, tiptoed down the stairs, and grabbed my boots, grateful the door didn't screech. I quickstepped toward the sidewalk, again wishing I had gloves. Increasing my pace, almost jogging, but not quite, I soon discovered another bridge. It was half the size of the one on the main road.

I began to cross it and stopped halfway, intending to lean against the railing—until I noticed all the large spiders there, busy with their webs. The Bliss's strong currents rumbled below me as they made their way to the lake. An unexpected burst of reflected light startled me. The sky had erupted in undulating ribbons of green. I'd never seen the Northern lights before, and the sight amazed me. I reached into my jacket pocket for my phone.

Quickly, I snapped several photos, wondering how long the show would last. The candescent emerald mist meandered between constellations and had a sort of living rhythm that slowed my heart rate. Long ago, as a child, I'd been given a book on Cree mythology, wondrously illustrated. I remembered reading that Cree people believed the aurorae borealis were made of the spirits of dead loved ones, silently speaking with lights, always watching over them. It was a beautiful notion.

Fifteen minutes later, the colours disappeared, and I sighed as a falling star blazed a small trail. Calmed and centered, I approached the house, surprised to find John sitting under the front porch light. He was hunkered forward on the edge of a wicker chair, and his stiff posture had me guessing he'd been there for some time.

He cupped his hand to light a cigarette. Did Lilith know he'd started smoking again? She'd told me it had taken him two years to wean himself off his pack-a-day habit. I hastened down their garden path but hesitated at the porch's steps. His arms rested on his thighs, and he looked washed out but wired. One wrong word and he'd either lash out or self-combust. He stared blankly at the street and blew a large smoke ring toward the banister, as if all were right in the world, though hostility radiated off him. I said nothing, hurried inside, and dashed upstairs.

The guest room was India-ink dark. I stumbled toward the bed. The pitch-blackness pressed down on me—a long-time city dweller—who was used to around-the-clock illumination, all those high-rises and highways twinkling.

A childhood memory stirred, of a monster in a closet, how I'd convinced myself that night gave it strength, making it invincible. Feeling like a preschooler, I reached for my phone and scrolled through the photos of a radiant sky, trying to remember light has power too.

CHAPTER

4

A̲T DAYBREAK, I penned a thank-you note and
escaped through the side door. The air held more
than a hint of winter. My Jeep cooperated, starting up
without so much as a hiccup. I set out for the only coffee
shop with a drive-thru and ordered a large latte. Both
grocery stores wouldn't open for another hour, but the
Kwik Mart kept their shelves well stocked. I filled a
small cart with the necessities, which included five bottles of Perrier, cream cheese, frozen dinners, a chocolate
bar, and ten cans of soup. The cashier had actually asked
if I needed a bag.

I pulled up behind the empty Ontario Provincial
Police truck a little after eight. Single-mindedly, I
reached behind the passenger seat and snatched the
bag of bagels I'd purchased before leaving Montreal.
Wood-fired ambrosia is an absolute necessity, as far as
I'm concerned. I slung my travel bag over my shoulder, grabbed the rest of my supplies and again trekked
through the front yard's muddy terrain. The door was

locked. I managed to transfer the bags to one hand and knock.

The sound of geese grew louder; they blew overhead in a misshapen "V." A straggler blasted at the others as Mac opened the door. "Figured you'd get here in another hour or two. Need help with your luggage?" He slipped the travel bag from my shoulder, his nose twitching. "Mmm. What is that smell?"

I narrowed my eyes. "I'll let you have one. Just one."

We walked past the parlour and moved toward the kitchen. In the fridge, I found a casserole dish filled with a salad—obviously not purchased from a grocer. I thanked him but added that it wasn't necessary.

He shrugged. "Most businesses in town don't open until nine and close around eight."

The top drawer held an assortment of plastic utensils, a can opener, salt and pepper packets, and one less-than-sharp knife. I sliced two bagels, turned on the conveyor toaster, and adjusted the speed to "Light."

"Huh. You know what you're doing, there."

"It takes plenty of part-time jobs to get a master's in science, a minor in art history, and a fine art degree. Stop gawking at the egghead. It's rude."

"Honest, you don't look like an egghead. But you sure talk like one."

We ate at the counter, said not a word more until we'd finished every bite. I swiped at the crumbs with a sponge and asked, "Ready?"

He'd made the parlour more work-centric. Floor lamps lit up the mural, and another folding table provided a place for notepads, pens, and a digital clock. He'd also hung barrier sheets across most of the back wall, so the only fungi that were exposed were the ones on the mural. For a man who seemed fixated on speediness, the taped corner and seams showed me he'd been vigilant, had taken his time. How early had he arrived at the parsonage?

We approached the containment area.

"I want you to start there." He pointed to an area two feet above the words I'd revealed the day before. "He painted it wrong. They found her body on the other side of the river." He gestured toward the backyard of an impressive brick home . . . beside the church . . .

Goosebumps rose on my arms. "The murder took place *behind this building*?" I turned to stare out the window. I could see why a girl would be drawn to the riverbank and trust it to be a safe place. Painted turtles basked on a fallen log. Through the respirator's plastic shield, I saw a barn swallow flit from cattail to cattail, causing them to sway. It all seemed so tranquil, so peaceful, as if nothing evil had ever happened on that piece of land. A distance of forty feet can close in on you. I shivered and turned my back to the river.

"Yes. This property is the primary scene. Which is why that area of the mural should be tackled first. Investigative priorities."

"Look, treatments aren't applied haphazardly—a bit here, a bit there. I usually work from the top down. A cleaned area is more vulnerable and could be accidentally damaged."

Mac frowned, and we walked back to the study. He sat down at the table, grabbed a pad of paper and pen, then sketched a grid, numbering the areas. "I don't want to see evidence destroyed. But there's a million in one chance he painted *himself* into the primary scene. My choices aren't in any way random either."

I assessed the grid, feeling more and more stressed. "Care to make this job even harder? Blindfold me, tie one hand behind my back?"

"Can you do this?"

"It'll be tricky." *Understatement.* "And costly." I gave him a rough estimate.

He nodded. "I figured about that much. All's good. If you need—"

I jumped as a voice spoke from his radio. "Sorry, Mac. Wild pigs broke through the Smits fence again. They want you. Only you. And yes, the goats have been rounded up."

He hung his head and answered, "I'm on the way." The look he threw me was wry. "Don't ask." He placed a key and business card on the table, then moseyed toward the door.

"Good luck," I called.

After he left, I wrote a short list and headed out, making sure to lock the door. The radio's weather forecast warned of yet another storm. To be on the safe side, I'd pick up candles and batteries. The GPS guided me to the local hardware store. I parked the car, noting the closed sign with disappointment. Before I could drive off, the owner good-naturedly waved me inside. "Business hours aren't set in stone." He locked the door behind us. "Need anything, just ask."

I went through all the vacuum cleaners they had in stock, relieved to find a lightweight one with a HEPA filtration system. I picked up two packs of replacement bags. Though the dusting brush was soft, I decided I'd better safeguard the mural, so I added a screen repair kit to the cart. The screen would act like a buffer between the vacuum and the wall. Fieldwork requires resourcefulness, finding alternatives. I already missed the conveniences of a lab.

I bought emergency supplies and a pair of rubber boots. The lack of any line-up was a bonus. Bob, the owner, beamed with delight as he rang me up. I swear, I heard my credit card groan. The grocery store was across the road. In less than half an hour, I'd completed my shopping and felt better equipped for the week ahead.

I drove back to the parsonage. A patrol car was parked in front. I grabbed half the bags and walked up to the black and white sedan. Constable Johnston rolled down the window. His fingers fiddled with the steering wheel as if he didn't know what to do with them.

"You pull the short straw?"

He gave me an enormous grin. "Nope. My wife's overdue. Whenever the phone rings, I start to blather. It's driving everyone at the station nuts, so . . ."

"Baby number one?"

"It's that obvious?" He chuckled. "I've been told my eyes keep bugging out."

I laughed and searched through one of the bags, opened a box, and passed him a granola bar. "Here. It'll be a long afternoon for both of us."

He helped me with the rest of the bags, showed-off an ultrasound picture, and told me they'd decided to keep the baby's gender a surprise. He ambled toward his car in a charmingly giddy daze. Thinking of my father, I blinked back tears.

I used the study as a staging area and went on autopilot as I rolled swabs, recognizing I'd need to place an order for more cotton and wooden applicators and pay the exorbitant price for express delivery. Light streamed through the narrow panes of the front window. The wavy glass distorted my view of the street, acting as another barrier.

White noise has made me more productive at times, but the drone of the air filtration system would soon grate. The parlour had become a mausoleum, and I was about to peel back a pall. Music could anchor me, but the bump and grind of the top forty had no place in this room. Vocals would be discordant, no matter the lyrics. So, I scrolled through my playlists. Classical music felt more commiserate or—at least—less apathetic.

I slipped into my gear and strode to the parlour. I studied every aspect of the mural and filled out the condition report, carefully describing the major degree of mould infestation as well as some minor bleeding and patches of insect detritus. Dirt and bulges were negligible. The over-mantle had mostly protected the mural from tobacco and soot. Fortunately, its peculiar location had also saved it from the blanching effects of sunlight.

I took more pictures and made a quick sketch, mapping each area. I decided on what treatments I'd try first and gathered all my supplies. After I'd arranged my workstation, I tentatively placed the window screening over the mural. A fellow conservator had recommended the technique to me last year, but this would be the first time I had tried it. I vacuumed a small area of the mural, using the lightest pressure possible. Happy with the results, I cautiously vacuumed the rest of the mural, removing a thin layer of mould from the painting. To the naked eye, nothing much had changed, but it did prepare the surface for further cleaning.

I stepped back. Rosemary stood in the foreground, holding a lit oil lamp. An exaggerated flame illuminated the background—my area of focus. All the barbarism of the murder would be spotlighted, but first, gradually, cattails, water willow, and reeds were revealed. Swab tips began to fill the jar.

I sucked in my breath as one by one the decoy Christmas lights appeared. Red, pink, and blue bulbs glowed like harmless fireflies. Once I'd cleaned the small area, I took a short break.

The containment area was chilly, but the airtight suit kept me warm. I decided to use disinfecting wipes to clean the suit—although the coveralls were disposable, I refused to be wasteful or inconsiderate. The costs for the commission would quickly add up.

Next, I deliberately brightened the lantern's wick and restored translucence to its chimney. A pale form took shape. A body other than Rosemary's lay by the river.

The room grew darker as the sun moved out of the window's range. I continued to work, dabbing in a circular pattern, forcing myself not to hurry, not to apply too much pressure.

Was it a dog? A white dog? The head was too large. It had a muzzle and a long face, but its brow was more pronounced than a dog's. Two swabs exposed a forelock. Four more revealed a mane. A pony. A dead pony.

Hours passed.

In the golden sphere of the lantern's light, a white pony bled out into the river. Its legs were curled beneath itself, as if in a fetal position. The poor animal had been garroted with something thin and grey, perhaps a barbed wire. I'd also managed to expose the other weapon. Beside the pony lay a baseball bat. Around it, crimson dew clung to trampled rushes.

My gaze shifted to Rosemary's sweater. There was an embellishment. Embroidery or a brooch? I pulled off my mask and put on my head-mounted magnifier. The clue was emblematic. What was it? A badge?

I phoned Mac. "Forget to tell me something?"

"Ah, hell, hope not," he said. "You sound shaky. What's up?"

"Did Rosemary own a pony?"

He groaned. "Damn. I'm sorry." Paper rustled. "Rosemary owned a miniature pony named Misty. The killer slaughtered it first." He hesitated. "No idea how her mother could afford to pay for its care. She boarded it with Mrs. Reece, a sympathetic senior. A week after the murder, Mrs. Reece died of a stroke."

I turned toward Rosemary. "Mac? There's something on her right shoulder. Did her sweater have an embroidered crest? Had she been wearing any jewelry?"

"What? No! I've spent two days pouring over the old reports. The crocheted sweater had an eyelet lace pattern. Here it is—pink, short-sleeved, no ribbons, no buttons. One fastener had been torn off. They never found it."

The lump in my throat wouldn't budge. "So far, I've finished an area about the size of a DVD case. You wanted me to clean Rosemary next, and I'll do that. I'll start with the insignia—or whatever it is. But I've barely stopped since you left."

"You've been at it for nine hours. You'll burn yourself out. You're more than a consultant on this case. We're partners, in a way. I got your back. Understood?"

The tension in my shoulders relaxed. "Understood."

I agreed to call him when I'd discovered more. Between Mac's even-headedness and my sensitivity, we made a good team. Timing is everything. I turned toward the back window just as a little yellow bird flew into it. It slid down the glass, leaving behind a grisly streak.

I took off the gear, walked out the front door, and started toward the back of the building, passing another entrance in the process. The bird had been a wild canary. The poor thing didn't move, and its neck appeared to be broken. Squirrels nattered at me from the branches of an old elm as other birds flitted between shrubs.

The thought of carrion crows had me trudging back inside. I found a trowel by the pantry, lying on a pile of tiles. The rudimentary tool would work. I took another set of gloves from my briefcase and resolutely marched down the other end of the hall, locating the side door. The stiff lock finally turned, and I stepped out onto a cracked, mildewed stoop.

I decided to bury it under the largest hedge. The earth there was soft and accommodating. It only took minutes. Afterwards, I peeled off my gloves, stood, and inhaled the fresh air. Not a cloud in the sky, but it was as dismal a day as I'd expected it to be. The mural was a memento mori, both tragic and terrible. I brushed the dirt off my knees, but the memories of other small graves would not be shaken.

Conservation resuscitates and defends. Some have said I take things far too seriously.

They're probably right. I'd chosen my career intentionally: I save whatever I can, whenever I can. It's a single-mindedness that only a few understand.

I walked across the tawny lawn and found the overgrown path that led to the riverbank. A distant train wailed and drowned out the sound of rippling water. If I allowed myself to surrender to the peace around me, I'd have better understood Rosemary's attraction to the area, but I became aware I wasn't alone. An old man watched me from the other side of the river. His companion, a black Scottish terrier, sat by his feet. He lifted his hand and gave an almost imperceptible wave I politely returned. He turned toward the path, but the dog refused to budge. It cocked its head side to side, eyeing something a few feet from me. The dog started to wiggle, barked, and made a dash for the river.

"Zibi, stop!" The man called. "Come here, boy."

The dog glanced at its owner, clearly torn, swinging its head back in my direction, fixated. The man grabbed its collar and tugged. Eventually, the dog obeyed, sitting back on its haunches and licking its master's hand. Moments later, they both wandered back into the dense woodland, but the stillness did not return. Something rustled.

Beside me, leaves lifted off the ground as if being kicked. *Great, just great.* I scrambled up the hill and, once inside, straightaway called my supplier. He's a stolid type of guy who could ground even the most active of imaginations.

"A bit out of the way for you, isn't it?"

"It's a tad closer than Helsinki, Eddie." My laugh sounded phony even to my ears, but as I'd predicted, our chit-chat had a calming effect. It not only cleared my head, it had me shaking it too. I needed to recharge more than my phone. It was after six, my eyes were gritty, but I hadn't so much as plugged in my laptop.

I peered into the room I'd claimed as mine. From the size and location, I guessed it had once been a butler's pantry. Mac had managed to squeeze the cot under the window.

Pillows and bubblegum-pink sheets had been placed on a wooden chair. A slim desk took up the opposing wall. I noted the Wi-Fi password tacked to a bulletin board.

I retrieved my bags and organized the room. One email required an immediate reply. It nearly broke my heart to turn down a job at the Museo de Prado, the museum where I'd interned. There are times I envy those who have less integrity, who go back on their word without any qualms. Resentfully, I sent the curator my regrets, made the bed, set the alarm, and crawled between the girly-girl sheets as images of Madrid danced in my head.

After a long nap, I trekked upstairs with a towel and fresh clothes. The door to the walk-up attic was open. I considered exploring the space but hesitated. Cold hit my cheeks, but the air smelled stagnant—faintly of mothballs—and I retreated from the stairwell as goosebumps rose on my arms. I firmly shut the door. Yet another draft wafted from a small bedroom, but its scent was clean and seasonal. A window had been left slightly ajar. As I struggled to close it, I couldn't help but admire its view of the river. It all seemed so picturesque. A blue heron waded through the shallows gawkily. A fish jumped and managed to escape the bird, and the sight had me thinking of haiku, of my year in Japan.

I peeked into another room. It reminded me of an old *Twilight Zone* episode, with its half-filled Styrofoam cups and open box of uneaten doughnuts, as if the crew had simply vanished into thin air. My peace of mind vanished too. Nothing rested in this museum-to-be. Nothing could be taken at face value, as if rooms bore smokescreens.

Though most of the lower floor had been renovated, the second floor was very much a work in progress— sawdust and stripped wallpaper covered the floor. I zeroed in on the ladder-and-plank scaffolding. Surely, the crew wouldn't mind if I moved it downstairs, especially if it hastened my departure. I wasn't looking forward to lugging the heavy wood and metal down the stairs, but I like healthy challenges. And I didn't want to bother Mac or the other officers.

I made my way to the bathroom, wanting a bath but unwilling to take one in that tub.

The tiles were rank, but at least the shower had me thinking more clearly. Moonlight streamed through gaps in the filthy mini blinds. I peered outside as I dried off and dressed, feeling like a squatter.

The majority of my days would be spent indoors. Such is the life of a conservator. Although the parlour provided ample natural lighting—deadly for art—and the luxurious kitchen made most museums' staff lunchrooms seem primitive by comparison—the parsonage came with its own set of warts. All the exposed wiring made me nervous. Dust is my enemy, and it was everywhere. The temperature fluctuated too.

I headed back downstairs and took Mac's salad out of the fridge. He'd separated most of the ingredients. Inside the bowl, he'd placed individual bags of cooked chicken breast, bacon, cheese, cashews, and croutons. It could be that someone in his family had food allergies or was a vegetarian. I mixed everything together and ate each delicious morsel.

As I walked down the hall, it occurred to me Mac hadn't mentioned a wife, though he wore a wedding ring. The more time I spent with the inspector, the more curious I got about his history. His grandfather had been a townie, which suggested Mac had been born and raised in Bliss River. Local boys seldom stayed local. He was a nail-tough cop with old-school gallantry, and the fact he couldn't be pigeon-holed reassured me. I trust complexity.

The parlour was too dark. I switched on all the lights, appreciating the room's wall sconces but missing the brightness of museum labs. The mural, though smaller than some televisions, seemed to fill the room. It saddened me that my efforts had illuminated carnage instead of her winsome face. I could almost hear my counselor: *"Any feelings of negligence are unwarranted. You can't save the world."*

I moved closer to the painting, a promise forming in my mind that I may not be able to keep. I could only hope to help her, hope the killer had painted himself into a corner.

Apprehensively, I kept to Mac's grid system and began to work on Rosemary's sweater.

Could the hidden object be a corsage? I wondered.

Because I'd been alone so long, I jumped when I heard voices. The neighbours across the street had turned off their porch lights, but not everyone was asleep. I watched as a small pack of teen boys quickened their steps and egged a garage door. Two weeks 'til Halloween, and high jinks were well underway. Though I doubted they could see me, I froze as one boy pointed toward the parsonage. Another shook his head. Two shoved him forward, pushing him toward the old building. He held up his middle finger and stalked away with shoulders hunched. One rushed after him, and they talked. The others caught up. They huddled there for a bit before heading back down the street.

I continued to work, making progress, keeping my hands moving, but I needed to be cautious. I'd mixed a new cleaning solution almost devoid of any detergent. The . . . artist . . . had used gold leaf in an intricate motif. If I rubbed too hard or used too much detergent, the clue could crumble apart. This might be the one tell-tale admission of guilt. I finished cleaning the tangerine-sized area, relieved I'd kept damage to a minimum.

My arms ached, but I was excited. The cleaning had revealed a gold Celtic knot with two jewels: a diamond and a ruby. I didn't recognize the knot, but I did recognize the symbol in its center—the claddagh.

Right away, I called Mac.

"MacGowan," he drowsily mumbled, "this better be good."

I turned to look at the clock and winced. "Sorry. Didn't realize—"

"Annora? It's okay. You found something?"

As coherently as I could, I told him about the knot. "Whatever this symbol is, the use of gold suggests it has value."

"Good work. I mean it—I'm impressed. But it's three in the morning. I'll drop by around nine to take some photos. Now, get some sleep."

I promised I would, turned off my phone, and stretched. I thought about the museum in Prado, about the masterpiece I had let slip through my fingers. The restoration project would have been a game changer, would have opened other doors. Already, little Rosemary had come to mean more. Tomorrow, I'd be able to lavish *her* with attention.

I shut off the lights, all but one. She'd been kept in the dark long enough.

5

M AC FOUND ME in the converted study, sitting on my yoga mat in the Sage pose, slowly twisting the tension from my lower back. His white shirt and tie surprised me.

"Spiffy," I said.

"Meeting with the chief superintendent." He shrugged self-consciously before patting his camera bag. "I need to document the changes made to the evidence. Won't take long." I was rolling up my mat when he returned.

"You're right. Whatever it is, it has meaning. You'd have made a great investigator."

I could have told him art conservation *is* detective work. But I didn't. "Next, you'd like me to concentrate on the foreground, Rosemary's head, neck, and upper body, right? I think something has been placed behind her left ear."

"I want to know what it is as soon as you do. So, keep plugging away, but slow down now and again." He slipped the camera back into its case. "And call me day or night, okay?"

"I'll be picking up some staples later. I may even take a walk."

"Good. The butcher on Main carries fresh perch, if you like fish."

෫~෮

I drove into town almost sheepishly. The library was still closed, but a nearby thrift store turned on its "Open" sign and provided me with an excuse to stock up on a few comforts. I scored a cardigan, extra blankets, and some kitchenware. The pots and pans would help lower food expenses, and the woolens would ward off the ever-present chill at the parsonage. Its furnace seemed iffy at best.

At ten o'clock, I scooted over to the library, which I found to be well laid out. The children's area livened up the left side of the building while the adult section, with its air of reticence, ran the full length of the right. I wandered the nonfiction aisles and found the one for local history. As I'd expected, one shelf was reserved exclusively for Kingsley Boyland.

There were biographies, thick art tomes, and archived files, as well as books about the Boyland Art Academy, including yearbooks and course catalogues.

One comprehensive study of Boyland's paintings also included some personal correspondence, so I added it to my growing pile. I brought six books to the front counter, set them down, and asked about their town-guest loan policy.

The librarian looked at the books and scowled. "I'm sorry, but you must be a resident to take books from this library, Ms. Garde."

"Excuse me, but how do you know my name?"

She held up a small newspaper: *The Bliss River Independent*. Its front page showed a picture of the mural—untouched—and a smaller photo of Rosemary. The headline was a cocker and actually read, "Mural of Murdered Girl Kills Project Deadline." I winced at another photo, further down the page. It was of Mac and me shaking hands.

The librarian sniffed. "Why all this interest in the Boylands? They are and have always been generous to a fault. Why, Jane Boyland is an award-winning artist, a philanthropist, a hospital volunteer, and the president of the historical society."

"Mavis," a Rubenesque, elderly woman called out, marching toward us. "You know very well she's entitled to her own library card whether she's a resident or not. But don't bother." She clapped a library card onto the counter. "Here, as a board chair, I say she can use mine."

Mavis scanned the books but snipped, "They're due back in two weeks."

The woman turned to me. "Do you have everything you need, dearie?"

I nodded.

"Good. Let's chat outside."

I picked up the books and followed her out the door. She put her card back into a large tote bag that held several hardcovers and a few DVDs.

"Thank you," I said. "I will return them."

"I couldn't care less if you keep 'em. I'd happily pay for replacement copies." She lowered her voice. "I'm Barb Martin, by the way. Rosemary Green was my best friend. I've hoped and prayed to live long enough to see her murderer found." Her eyes filled with tears. "I thought it would never happen."

I jumped as a very old Ford drove by and backfired.

"There goes my crazy brother, the former mayor, in his blasted Model A coupe," she said. "He just got back from Belize yesterday, and he's already bored stiff. Don't fret. You'll get used to the noise."

No. I wouldn't.

We made small talk for ten minutes, and at her request, I added her phone number to my contact list. She encouraged me to visit, patted my arm, and maundered down the street. Once she'd disappeared around the corner, I dug coins from my purse and slid them into a newspaper box. I hotfooted it back to my car and called Mac. He'd read the article.

"Easton damn well knows better."

"The picture must have been taken by someone working on the renovation." I tossed the paper onto the passenger seat. "How serious is this?"

"You mean, what are the consequences if evidence has been compromised? Before we've laid a single charge? The commissioner isn't happy, but we didn't break the chain of custody.

Someone snapped that shot before we were called. If the murderer is still alive, we've given him your credentials. Until you're finished, the mural's under police protection."

Great. "But the murderer must be in his late seventies or older, right?"

"Serial killers Ray and Faye Copeland were in their seventies when they knocked off men in their twenties. A centenarian recently axed his wife to death," he said. "And Charles Manson lived to be over eighty. Tell me, could you imagine being alone with him in his cell, ever? Even for a minute?"

I stared out the windshield. "Okay, okay, enough."

"Someone threatens you, you run, and you run fast, hear me?" He stressed each word. "Annora, don't engage the killer. He'll win."

I sighed but didn't mention my self-defense training, figuring it would lead to another lecture. The ride back to the parsonage took four minutes. In small towns, everything is so close by and seems impossible to miss.

The parsonage moaned like all old buildings do, but Mac's hypervigilance had left me jumpy. *The power of suggestion,* I told myself as the hairs on my neck stood up. Nobody else was in the building. I stopped putting away the groceries, detected a trace of something floral or fruity in the air. The candles I'd tucked into a cabinet were scented. That explained the smell.

Though I longed to flip through the library books, I laid them on the cot. I tossed the newspaper onto the window seat and went into overdrive, trying to work my way through an unshakeable apprehension.

It took an hour to troop up and down the stairs, taking apart and reassembling the scaffolding. I positioned the plank a foot and a half off the floor. The difference would help prevent neck and arm strain, and the new height put me face to face with Rosemary, but I still needed to stretch in order to reach the very top edge of the mural. The killer must have been tall . . . or he'd used a stool or ladder. The realization did nothing to sooth my nerves.

It wasn't yet noon. I taped up the too-long sleeves of the hazmat suit and arranged my workstation. I dipped the swab into the solution, poised to apply it to the mural, but something about the colour of the swab tip froze me in mid-motion. I pulled back my arm as if I held a torch, and quickly marched out of the room. I tore off the mask and slowly brought the swab closer to my nose, inhaling the unmistakable scent of orange.

I walked to the doorway and dragged the swab down an inconspicuous spot by the frame. Anger replaced disbelief. I put down the swab and marched across the hall. Fit for a fight, I threw open the front door and frantically waved to Constable Johnston.

He leapt out of his car and jogged down the path. "Is something wrong, Ms. Garde?" "That's putting it mildly," I said. "We've been ambushed!"

CHAPTER

6

M AC ARRIVED AS I reached my car. "Ambushed?
Johnston was ready to call in SWAT." He put up
a hand. "I get it. This is big."

The books in my arms were getting heavier by the
second. "Someone broke in and messed with my sol-
vents," I spit out. "My mixture was exchanged for indus-
trial paint stripper. I would have skinned her!"

"Pardon me?"

"'Skinning' in conservation means to over-clean a
painting. If I hadn't caught on, parts of Rosemary would
have . . . dissolved. How did he do it? Mac, I swear, I
locked both doors."

"We're dusting for prints, and we've sent the solution
to our lab." He gave me a once-over. "Morris said your
chemicals were secure in your briefcases. And Johnston
checked the back door. It was locked. You did everything right."

"Someone tried to sabotage your—our—investigation.
Let me back in there."

"It shouldn't take long. I'll call you when we're done."

"You can find me in my SUV. Reading and stewing."

He grinned. "Ornery, aren't you?"

I considered telling him where he could stick his "ornery." Instead, I crossed the street and got into my ole unreliable. The frigid seat made me shiver, and the windows immediately fogged up. I let the car run, hoping the few minutes of heat would last. Resigned to my short-term eviction, I flipped open *Mystery in Plain View: The Kingsley Boyland Collection* and scanned photos. Boyland had been an attractive man, with a lanky build, deep-set eyes, and dimpled chin. My mother would have called him eye candy.

His father had been a doctor, well-to-do. Though his parents encouraged his creativity as a child, they were disappointed with his choice of vocation, a fact that surprised me. The family had cut him off for several years. Quaint sketches kept him out of the poor house until portraits brought him fame and fortune in his late twenties. He went on to become the country's leading portrait painter. His infamy made him the prodigal son and—again—an heir.

I studied two of his most well-known portraits; one was of the sixty-first governor general, and the other was of an infamous silent film star. I flipped up the collar of my jacket. Angry grey clouds had scratched out the sun, and neighbourhood chimneys puffed wood smoke into the bleakness. A truck drove past me, slowing down when it saw the patrol cars.

I continued to read. Boyland had served in the Royal Canadian Armed Forces and come back from the war with a Victoria Cross. Home just one month, he fell head over heels for Delphine Wallace, a glamorous heiress.

They were married within the season, and in less than nine months, Delphine gave birth to a girl: Jane. She had been the light of her father's eye. Black-and-white snapshots showed him as a doting, attentive father.

Another baby arrived. A son. The photo of a baby's casket hit me hard. I read the caption: *Edmond, four months, tragically dies of natural causes.* Shortly after, a despondent Delphine took her own life. The graveside photo violated the family's right to privacy. Yet another funeral sensationalized by the bloodhounds of the era.

I flipped to the next chapter. There were photos of the Boyland Art Academy. His prepubescent daughter had cut the ribbon at the opening ceremony. I'd reached 1957.

At last, pay dirt, a full-page spread of Boyland with the students from The Guiding Light Project: Ricky Elwes, Floyd Kent, James Powell, and Len Warriner. The quartet was so very young, fourteen to seventeen, but each possessed an air of self-assurance, wearing brash smiles and slicked pompadours. The picture also included Jane Boyland, perhaps thirteen, at most.

One of Len Warriner's arms hung around her small shoulders, and his air of possession seemed out of place. Had she wanted him that close? She looked cornered, somewhat resentful.

Two officers walked out of the parsonage as Mac waved to me from the porch. I pointed to the side of the house and footslogged it to the second entrance.

"We found the point of entry," he said as I took off my new boots. "The attic has a fire escape on the church side of the building. He must have taken off his footwear on the landing. We found no impressions."

"I'd forgotten all about the attic."

"It'll be temporary living quarters for the town's new artist-in-residence program. A new floor is half laid. Guess someone opened a window. It is rank up there."

I zipped to the kitchen and put the books down on the counter.

He followed me at a leisurely pace, picked up one of the books, and read aloud, "*Shadowing Light: Painters Influenced by Kingsley Boyland.*" His eyebrows met. "So, you're leaving the legwork to me?"

I grabbed water from the fridge. "In for the penny."

"Here's a rundown of the suspects: One has domestic abuse charges pending; one's a manifesto away from being the Unabomber; and one taught at the academy until sexual misconduct got him terminated. Keep your penny out of this." Mac crossed his arms. "Stick to the plan, Annora."

"Don't you want my professional opinion?"

"Sure, I do. And I also want you to stay away from the art academy. Bliss River seems down-home, benign, but it's no place for an amateur sleuth."

"But—"

"No."

I wasn't giving up that easy. "Is there a gallery where any work from The Guiding Light Project is being exhibited? I'd like to study the student's art. Hear me out. An artist's body of work is as unique as a fingerprint—unless forgery is intended. I can perform a type of psychological aesthetics profiling—in essence, I'm talking about art forensics."

"You've got my attention."

"It's called a Morellian analysis. It takes into account colour palette, brushstrokes, the use of light. How masterfully were faces and hands rendered? Proportions, themes. Even habitual shortcomings are telltale and can identify the artist."

"Like how a scar can break up a fingerprint?"

"Exactly. In a few more days, I will have exposed more of the mural. The more I reveal, the more I can study it, not just for content, but for technique. I'll be able to compare it to other attributed paintings, put them into an artist line-up, so to speak."

He snorted. "Okay, okay, Miss Congeniality, I'm sold. Boyland's daughter was the primary champion for the art museum." He zipped up his duty jacket. "She has an extensive art collection that includes the work of former academy students. She's a bit uptight, but I'm sure she'd let you view the collection. Anyway, I'm late for a meeting."

"Miss Congeniality?" I bristled.

"You feed Johnston, gave O'Neil a blanket, and made coffee this morning for three cops. So, someone said you're a bona fide Miss Congeniality. What? It's a compliment," he said. "Oh yeah, and the others think you look like Sandra Bullock. But much shorter."

"There be dragons." *Always the short jokes.* "Wait. You don't think I look like her?"

"Your face is heart-shaped, and her eyes aren't as big or as—" He cleared his throat.

I quickly asked, "Have you discovered the meaning of the Celtic knot?"

His expression changed in a heartbeat. "He may have got the idea from the Holocaust. The yellow badge. A faith symbol twisted into a mark of shame." Mac hesitated. "This particular knot represents an abiding love between father and daughter. The birth certificate shows Fayette's marital status as single. Rosemary was, in fact, illegitimate. A big deal in the fifties. The killer may have targeted her because she was fatherless."

I wrapped my arms about myself.

"It's biblical. He, appealing to God. She, 'born out of wedlock' in a town full of corrupt believers. The body found on church property. This points us in a whole new direction.

"But motive is something *you* shouldn't even contemplate. Leave the why and the who to us," Mac said. "Let the mural show you the what and the how." He sighed. "Those facts will be hard enough for you to uncover."

The furnace sprang to life. I stared at the vent by my feet, willing it to blow warmer air.

He moved toward the door and spoke over his shoulder. "I tried to reach Barb Martin. She's visiting family and should be back in a few days. You've got good instincts. So, you dig, and I'll sift through the rubble. But keep the doors locked."

After he left, I made myself a sandwich, tidied up, even swept the floor, delaying the inevitable. I'd run out of excuses, so I left the kitchen. I'd known the parlour would feel strange.

The intruder had taken measures to leave no prints behind, and yet traces of the invasion remained—a soundless echo, a residual malice. I did my best to shake off the jitters.

I cleared off my workspace, physically and mentally. The Celtic knot had become ugly to me. It would take less work to wash it clean off her, but I couldn't, so I unlocked my briefcases and measured out all the surfactants I found worked best. Again, I tested areas, ensuring the solution was neither too strong nor too weak. Satisfied with the results, I went to work. I took one break and pushed through the afternoon into the evening. A shower invigorated me, and I pressed on. Sunup had me crawling into bed, where I power-napped for two hours, caught in a loop of work, eat, work, sleep.

By mid-morning, I was back on the scaffolding. With upmost care, I returned the luster to Rosemary's strawberry-blond waves. I washed the mould off her fair skin, freckles, and button nose. When I unveiled the forget-me-nots tucked behind her ear, I dropped the swab. My mind reeled from all the implications. The sparkle in her green eyes, the perfectly formed lips, ears tenderly shaped, all spoke of an artist's gentle affection for his subject. My gaze shifted back and forth between the bloody area over her shoulder to her unflinching gaze and sun-kissed cheeks.

The sudden blare of Nazareth's "Love Hurts" had me grimacing. My ringtone needed to be changed. I left the containment area, pulled off my mask, and answered the phone.

"Hi. I'd like to take you out to lunch today," Lilith said.

"How about I meet you tomorrow for brunch instead? At the diner?" I patrolled the room. Even through the plastic enclosure, Rosemary almost glowed. Her eyes followed me, and the effect seemed more pitiful than eerie. "I'm finally getting somewhere."

We arranged to meet at the local hotspot and said our goodbyes.

I continued to work on Rosemary's face, cleansing her jawline, polishing her delicate chin, but I went into panic mode as I shifted to her neck. I kept checking my swabs, ensuring I hadn't skinned her. I hadn't. There were gaps in the pigments. It wasn't flaking. It was that the paint had never been applied. The odd line around her neck filled me with a sense of dread, a sudden awareness that I didn't know her exact cause of death. I looked at the clock, realizing I'd barely slept in twenty-four hours.

My vision blurred as I called Mac. "Hey."

"You sound beat."

"And you sound like a mother hen." I parted the study blinds. It wasn't Johnston in the patrol car. I gave the constable a thumbs-up. She waved back. "Was Rosemary beheaded?"

"What the hell! Why you asking?"

"Was her throat cut? Was she strangled, choked, garroted? "

"I'm on the way over."

"I'll be on the window seat, comatose." I yawned. "But you do need to see this."

How close did he live? He showed up in minutes, out of uniform. Well, out of his OPP uniform, anyway. "You look like a hockey coach."

"I am a hockey coach. You look like the lab rat that lost the race."

"Gee. Thanks."

He left the room, made a beeline for the parlour and returned, still suited up.

"Impressive. You've finished so much. Forget-me-nots? How warped can a mind get?" He moved closer, leaned against the window frame. "I'd expected blood or bruises around her neck. I'm confused."

"At first, I thought the cause lacuna—"

"Lacuna?"

"Sorry. It means an area where paint has flaked off due to damage or decay. But I don't think that's the case here. I think the void is intentional. The shape's too perfect. Here." I handed him the magnifier. "Use this and take another look."

"Cool gadget!"

"They're only for lab rats." I walked with him but remained outside the sealed room.

He slipped on the magnifier and studied her neck. "I see what you mean. What's he showing us? Silence? Mind and body separation? What?"

"I don't know."

He left the parlour and stood beside me. "It's telling us something. Good call."

Things weren't adding up. "You'd said she didn't have any jewelry."

"No, *her mother* said Rosemary didn't own any jewelry," Mac clarified . "There were notes in the case file. The staff sergeant asked about other belongings that could help identify Rosemary, any missing personal effects, and the mother was slow to answer. The question needed repeating. We're trained to watch for giveaway reactions." He turned back toward the mural and squinted. His brow wrinkled. "She stuttered a 'no.' But her response felt so off, the sergeant included it in his report."

"I hate to think Fayette hid something."

"Everyone has something to hide, something painful."

"Mac, the shape of that void suggests a necklace or a chain. A stolen object."

His eyes widened. "A trophy? But if he did take a necklace, and even if we manage to find it, we can't link it back to her."

"There are no other pictures of Rosemary?" I asked. "Wait. What about Barb Martin? I met her at the library. She said she'd been Rosemary's best friend. She may have some photos or remember if Rosemary owned jewelry. It's worth asking, right?"

He'd have patted me on the back, I think, if plastic hadn't separated us. As soon as he left, I dragged myself to bed. Even the backfiring of the old jalopy didn't faze me, but I woke from a nightmare; the sound of exploding glass replayed in my ears. Mac had said we all hide things, keep certain agonies private. I gazed at the ceiling, thinking about forget-me-nots and trying to forget how easily a small neck can snap.

7

THOUGH I'D MADE considerable progress, I wished either the morning would slow down or I could speed up. I'd cleaned most of the book that Rosemary clasped, and it was as enigmatic as the Celtic knot. Why would such a young girl hold a leatherbound edition of *King Lear*? I wasn't finished with the cover—embossed with climbing roses—and I hadn't yet touched the small hand clutching the book, so I put off phoning Mac. I considered asking Lilith if we could postpone our brunch. Instead, I decided to keep our get-together to under an hour. Considering how quickly she wanted the work done, Lilith wouldn't mind if I ate and ran.

Lear dwelled on themes of insanity and betrayal. I kept returning to the relationship between the King and his daughter, Cordelia. She'd remained steadfast in her love, despite her banishment. I'd seen the play as a fifteen-year-old. An odd choice for a school trip. My classmates had jiggled their knees and fidgeted at the most heartbreaking of scenes, but I'd sobbed when Lear had cradled Cordelia.

I hurried out of the parsonage, upset, then readjusted my thinking. This job wasn't about me; it was about Rosemary.

Halfway to the diner, it started to rain—the squall had finally arrived. I dashed from the car to the restaurant as the sprinkle turned to a downpour.

Lilith waved from a booth, looking contrite. "I'm sorry about the other night," she murmured. "John had a little too much to drink."

"It happens," I said. "So, did Parker enjoy the trip?"

She lowered her voice. "He got sick on the bus. Humiliating for a tween."

The conversations around us were kept to a low buzz. The jukebox worked, sort of. We enjoyed our meal, right up to the point a burly man marched up to our table and growled at me, "Shouldn't you be getting on with your job so I can get on with mine?"

I bit back a retort, knowing it would make matters worse.

In an instant, the atmosphere changed. The other patrons collectively held their breath, and the clanking in the kitchen stopped.

"Mark, you're being a total ass," Lilith said coolly. "Go home."

"Sure. My apologies. Afternoon, Ladies." The door slammed behind Mark the Snark.

Chit-chat around us resumed, but the general tone was more animated. One man, in his early to mid-fifties, had taken quite an interest in our little drama. I took note of his short beard and even shorter hair. His tattoo caught my eye. Three inked words stretched across his wiry, lower arm: "A Thousand Words." The last part of the quote about "a picture painting" struck me as bizarrely coincidental . . . or was it?

Our gazes locked. His conveyed recognition but showed no hint of aggression. And yet something felt off. He broke eye contact first, took a twenty out of his pocket and laid it on the table. He left the diner noiselessly, as if to draw less attention to himself.

"Nory? What's wrong?"

"Do you know him?"

"Mark? Yes. He, uh, he works with John."

"No. The other man. Mr. Thousand Words."

Her forehead crinkled. "Who?"

"Never mind." I glanced down at the bandage around Lilith's thumb. "I do need to get back to work," I said, somewhat grateful I'd been given an out.

She insisted on footing the bill. Knowing it would help her feel more in control, I let her. We left together, huddling under the small awning. We agreed to touch base later in the week, before dashing off toward our vehicles. Lilith gave a friendly honk and drove off. I finger-combed wet hair away from my face and turned on the wipers.

I could see the river, and it did not look blissful. It looked dark and deep and treacherous as it sped toward Lake Huron. Worryingly close to its bank, a fisherman stood on an uneven boulder, unruffled by the deluge or the torrent before him. I took a mental picture of his patched yellow slicker, his unflappable stance, his scruffy boots toeing a wooden tackle box. I rarely have time to work on my own art, not anymore, but I often find inspiration in unlikely places.

The rain refused to abate. I'd been meaning to repair the rip in my soft top. A steady drip wet my passenger seat, further dampening my mood. I decided to make a pit stop, despite the weather—or maybe because of it.

I pulled up in front of the florist shop. Though small, it sold calla lilies, birds of paradise, and belles of Ireland. The simple bouquet of pink carnations seemed the best choice. Hope Cemetery was close, just another three-minute drive away. From what I could see though the drizzly window, the groundskeeper took his job seriously. Perennials had been readied for winter, and fall mums bloomed in ornate cement planters. Sentinels of pine and tamarack surrounded the property, guarding the quietude. I grabbed my umbrella and the flowers.

A few graves bore arrangements, but most did not. I know headstones. The newest ones gleamed. The luster of those marble and granite slabs had not yet faced decades of ice melts, so I searched out markers stripped of polish. Crumbling sandstone belonged to those gone for a century or longer. I sought the patina of sixty years, stone weathered to a bleak matte grey.

I strolled between plots, eyeing names and dates. Though I found some markers with cemetery art, her gravestone would be basic, I presumed, something dolefully affordable for a disadvantaged single mother. Below a balding oak, a stone cherub watched over a four-foot monument. Drawn to it, I walked up the slight hill. I should have felt surprised it was Rosemary's grave, but I wasn't.

Flowers and birds had been etched into the stone. The small angel held its hands to its face, weeping for the unfathomable loss of a child. Someone else must have recently visited her. A single peach rose fluttered against the stone's base, anchored there by a large rock. I placed my bouquet beside the single bloom, tucking the stems under the same rock. The dates engraved into the memorial stunned me. Rosemary had been killed the day after her birthday. She'd just turned eight. I closed my eyes, wondering if I should have come.

My umbrella blew inside out. I gave up, closed it, and let the heavy rain do its worst. I braved the knoll, using it like a crow's nest, saddened by the sight of peach petals flying from a newer grave. More peach roses? I tramped through puddles and crossed the graveyard.

Realization dawned as I read the marker: "Kit Mac-Gowan, March 17, 1975–March 27, 2017, Loving Wife and Mother. *I am the soft stars that shine at night.*"

Mac was a widower. I'd inadvertently poked into his personal life, and he had as much a right to his privacy as I had to mine. We hadn't known each other long enough to share raw personal information.

On the way back to the parsonage, I turned up the heat in the SUV and willed my teeth to stop chattering. My thoughts may have raced, but I drove well below the speed limit, heeding a "Slippery when wet" road sign as I crossed the bridge. Bliss River had suffered many sorrows. I pitied Fayette and Barb; Boyland's tragic loss of a baby and wife touched me deeply; and I ached for Mac and his daughter. We are all eventually motherless, but she and I had experienced the loss of a parent at too young an age.

Every twelfth century write-off I resurrect is my personal Lazarus. I bristle at the term "obsessive"; I prefer being thought of as driven or persistent or—better yet—accomplished. The Bliss River commission was unlike any other I'd experienced. Though I'd worked on religious and mythical paintings, conserved gruesome magnum opuses, the work had left me mostly unmoved. But if I unraveled this monster's masterpiece, I felt I'd in some small way be rescuing Rosemary. She'd no longer be his. She would be set free.

I hurried past Constable Andrews. He blinked at my sodden clothes and sopping-wet hair. Rain blurred my vision. I dropped the house keys, swore, and dug them out of the mud. Then, though I'd used the correct key, the lock refused to budge. It took considerable key jiggling to get the door to open. It did—abruptly—and I tumbled into the entry before I dripped my way to the back room. With a sense of resurgence, I toweled myself dry and threw on a tee-shirt and jeans, grumbling. I was running out of clean clothes.

I'd been too busy to read the "Killed Deadline" story. The article could fill in some missing pieces. After making a chai tea and slipping on a thick sweater, I settled onto the window seat in the study and unfolded the weekly paper. The story opened with Rosemary's body being found. Few details were disclosed other than the fact she'd been severely beaten. There was no mention of the pony.

Reverend Knapp and his wife, Emily, had accepted the charge of another parish. An interim pastor travelled to St. George's for Sunday services, so the parsonage had been uninhabited for several months prior to and several weeks after the murder. Rosemary took piano lessons from Emily until the Knapps moved. Rosemary's modesty delighted the pastor's wife, so Emily provided the lessons free of charge. The neighbours grew accustomed to seeing the girl skip down Felicity Street and did not think it at all strange that she continued to frequent the area, though the Knapps had moved, and the parsonage was vacant.

Mig Daybutch was a quiet fourteen-year-old boy who liked nature. He'd spend hours hiking along the river. A six-year difference between Mig and Rosemary did not prevent them from becoming casual friends. The two were often seen together, catching minnows or skipping stones, walking side by side.

A neighbour reported seeing Mig near the parsonage on the night Rosemary was murdered. The next day, a constable fished a jacket out of a dumpster. Bloodstains were found on its collar and sleeves. Mig acknowledged the coat was his. He insisted he'd tossed it out a week earlier and admitted some of the bloodstains were his but most belonged to Joe Belmore. He said he'd been involved in fisticuffs with the older boy. Joe, a stand-on-his-head goalie for the Bliss River Bears, denied the fight had ever happened and said a puck to the face had caused the split lip. Two friends backed up his testimony.

I disliked the long aside about Joe Belmore's hockey career, his standing as one of the greatest goaltenders of all time. Why include that he'd played for the National Hockey League for eighteen seasons or his induction into the Hockey Hall of Fame in 1981? The paper even stated that a year after his retirement, he'd died of liver failure.

I used a lap blanket as a shawl and flipped the page. The article veered back to Rosemary. She had confided in her best friend, Barb Martin, that she had other, older friends. But she wouldn't divulge names and insisted they were "nice and treated her well."

Mig Daybutch was taken into custody on June 2nd, 1957, one day after Rosemary's body was found. His trial lasted less than two weeks. He was found guilty, sentenced to life imprisonment, and released twenty years later. However, it had taken another seventeen years for DNA to prove his innocence and for his wrongful conviction to be overturned.

The article went on to describe how mould had led to the mural's discovery. Toward the end of the story, a connection between the mural and the art academy was implied, with several notable artists who'd attended the academy being listed.

The journalist went further, perhaps too far. He tagged an artist who'd attended the academy in 1957. In 1958, Randal Vize had moved from Bliss River to Vancouver, where he became a serial rapist who targeted pre-adolescent girls. The '60s media had dubbed him "the Painterly Pervert." Vize had slathered dyed lard on his victims and ordered the girls to hold certain poses or die. He'd been killed in a shoot-out that also took the life of a young officer.

It is an odd thing to read about yourself in a newspaper. The article mentioned my contract with the OPP. The reporter had done his research. He listed my credentials and notable paintings I'd "rejuvenated." A lead conservator had made one too many romantic advances toward me—though I'd repeatedly asked him to cease and desist—and so I'd reported him for sexual harassment. It's a smaller planet than I'd imagined. The newshound had quoted Gabin Charpentier as saying that I was "a quirky loner." The next time I saw Gabin, which I hoped would be never, I'd be hard pressed not to whoop his bony, misogynist ass.

I heard an alarm, so I looked out the window. Constable Andrews stepped out of his car and sprinted across the street. He saw me at the window and motioned for me to stay inside. Andrews said something into his radio, a word or two, and disappeared from my view.

I moved away from the window and glanced at the clock. One twelve. The alarm went on and on. While it wailed, I preoccupied myself with rolling more swabs and prepping for another seven-hour stretch. My shoulders relaxed when the alarm stopped. My reaction felt overblown. Alarms constantly sounded in the city. Usually, it was some sensor gone haywire or a family member forgot the code. Robberies seldom happened in broad daylight.

Someone knocked on the door. Thinking Andrews wanted to let me know that the coast was clear, I turned the lock. A stranger pushed the door open and stepped inside. I was able to identify him by his square jaw and Roman nose. Len Warriner closed the door behind him. I backed away, wondering if he was the wife beater, the crazed hermit, or the sex offender.

His shoes squelched as he followed me. "Don't scream," he said. "I just need to see it."

"What? The mural?" I heard myself asking. "Is it yours?"

He shook his head, suddenly looking very much his age. "No. And I'm praying I don't recognize the work. I want to stand an inch from it and say, no, it wasn't painted by someone I've known my whole life. Family."

"You've crossed a police barricade. There will be serious consequences." I trusted my intuition. "But I can't stop you from seeing it."

His weak smile wobbled. "Thank you. Two minutes and I'll be gone."

Rain trickled off his long, dark coat, and a stream trailed behind us. He unzipped the containment area and stepped into the parlour.

I followed him, watching as he approached the mural, noting he walked like he was in a trance. His gaze lifted, dropped, and rose again. "Holy mother of God." His raspy moan was almost inaudible. He turned from the painting and stumbled toward the back door, hesitating as he twisted the knob. "You should have run for the constable, you know. I could have hurt you." His gaze held onto mine. "Be careful, Ms. Garde. Bliss River *is* dangerous. Trust no one."

Before I could form a reply, he leaned into the wind and vanished around the river bend.

Rain sleeted the windows, hazing the world. His words hung in the air, far more disturbing than any alarm system. I returned to the parlour and fixed the plastic separating me from Rosemary. Her face seemed paler and those big eyes even wider.

I'd revealed something after all. But I had no idea what it was.

8

T HE RAIN STOPPED as quickly as it had started.
I waved over Constable Andrews and told him
what had happened. While he called Mac, I went out
back to clear my head. Droplets fell from balding
trees, and a double rainbow ribboned the horizon. I
contemplated the swollen river. A school bell sounded
somewhere quite close, and I heard the unmistakable
clamour of the young, all their vitality and enthusi-
asm. I wondered when the school had been built and
if Rosemary had been one of its students. Children
are so vulnerable. We think we can protect them. We
cannot.

Mac found me feeding birds. "You alright?"

"I feel stupid."

"Funny. Andrews said the same thing. The rock-
through-a-window is a classic diversion." He rubbed his
forehead. "Look, Len Warriner was a respected dean
who got caught with his pants down. The adult student blackmailed him. Student–staff fraternizing broke

outdated academy regulations. Len lost his job. And his standing in the community."

"So she seduced him, and he was punished?"

"No. *He* seduced *him*, and the twenty-year-old hustler faced extortion charges."

"Oh. Poor Len."

"Even more so now. He's about to be charged with unlawfully entering restricted premises and causing property damage. Doubt he'll do time, but the fines will be hefty. The guy's almost destitute, as it is. This is a mess."

"Why is he a suspect?"

"People change. In his early teens, Len had anger management issues, started fights, stabbed someone in an arm with a pocketknife. Art became his outlet. Boyland fostered him, took him under his wing. In turn, Len idolized him. The kid reformed, but it took a year. There'd also been some mischief charges."

"Still . . ." I'd run out of bread. Birds are so fickle. Off they flew.

"Anybody who had direct contact with Rosemary was and is under suspicion." He moved closer to me. "Len's community service involved teaching art to other underprivileged children. Different era, different sentences. Rosemary took the class."

"You didn't see his face, Mac. He's not the killer."

"Never said he was. But we're searching for him all the same."

I pocketed the bread bag. "You were wrong, you know. I'd make an awful cop."

"Could be." His mouth pursed, as if he had more to say on the subject but wouldn't. "So, how much allegory can be shoved into one image, anyway? Lear? What the hell?"

"'*This heart shall break into a hundred thousand flaws.*' Act two, scene four, I think."

"Bah! Psychobabble. Just give me an hour in the interrogation room with him."

"I don't get it. He commits murder, goes on to paint a mural of his victim in a vacant building, and hides it? It's not like he could admire his handiwork whenever he wanted."

"Child killers have vivid imaginations. He may have walked by these buildings night after night. And he would have rested beside a streetlamp, stared through these windows and *remembered*. Bliss River could still be his home. He might be dead, or tonight he may watch the news, wondering how close we are to finding him."

I received a stern warning to only open the door for uniformed officers. I promised to be more careful. Mac went one way, and I went another. Once again, I was alone in the parlour. I chased away stress with Pachelbel Cannon in D Major, which also drowned out the whine of the air scrubber. I calmed and then got down to work.

It took hours to remove the bloom casing that hid her pretty sweater. I moved on to her dainty hands, wrought in perfect dimension. I reached her right pointer finger and frowned. I'd need to change my emulsion again. More gold leaf. Painstakingly, I dabbed the area below the petite knuckle. An emerald ring slowly took shape. It was large and far too sophisticated for a young girl. My mother had turned sixty last spring, and I'd bought her a pair of emerald earrings. The birthstone for May is emerald. Rosemary wore her birthstone. Diamonds framed the exaggerated jewel. If the ring actually existed, it would cost more than I made in a year.

I decided to carry on and call Mac in the morning. What if I could give him more? And so I pushed on, finished revealing Rosemary, from the top of her head to the bottom edge of the mural. I took several breaks but kept them short. There had been too many delays, too many interruptions. That being said, my roll of cotton continued to shrink. I followed Mac's grid, worked on the parsonage and church, a four-by-six-inch area.

The buildings were silhouetted against a disappearing sun. It felt redundant to literally wash the windows, return the depth to each miniscule black pane. At least, I thought so until a swab revealed a candle. I gasped as I noted the gleam from eyes the size of sesame seeds. Someone peered out through the glass. Witness or killer?

I gazed across the street. The neighbour with the smashed window had hung a string of sneering pumpkin lights along a cedar hedge. Corn stalks had been tied to the front porch columns, and a scarecrow grinned ghoulishly, seeming somewhat passive-aggressive.

My ringtone startled me. Sheepishly, I retrieved my phone and perched on the window ledge. "Good timing, Mac."

"Call it a night, would you."

"I could be up to my ears in bubbles, for all you know."

"Turn your head and wave."

There he was. In his truck. "Johnston got *the* call?"

"We wish. He got *a* call. Just another false alarm."

"Ah. The baby's in no rush, I see." I rubbed my eyes. "Go on, ask what I've dug up."

"It's after midnight. You've had a long day. I was trying to be nice."

"You are nice. Now, since you're here anyway . . ."

Minutes later, he met me at the door, carrying a parcel. "Yours?"

"My conservation supplies! Sorry, I forgot to tell you I had them sent to the station."

"More gadgets?" He looked at the box as if it were a birthday present. His.

"No. Cotton wool, mostly."

He almost pouted. He went off to suit up, taking his camera and the magnifier with him.

He returned to the study and grumbled, "Eyes? More damned head games."

"So, next you'd like me to fill in the space between the parsonage and where she was found? You wouldn't prefer me to focus on the water or the woods over her left shoulder?"

"Go ahead and connect those dots." He cleared his throat. "Off topic, would you like to join my daughter and me on Sunday? Thanksgiving? She's home from York for the weekend and heads back on Monday."

"The YU? I lectured there a few weeks ago."

"She told me. This is Grace's first year in their art's program. She said, 'Annora Garde is a genius.' With you as our guest, I'll be her hero, again. It's been a while." He waggled his brows. "C'mon. Say yes."

I cautioned, "You realize Grace and I will talk shop. You'll end up nodding off and miss our discussion on artificial saliva."

"Saliva? Get outta town."

"The non-synthetic kind works best. It contains mild enzymes that can clean away a build-up of dirt, and it's a safe bet."

"Spit?"

"Famous art has been bathed in gobs of it. I'm a champion horker."

He belly laughed as he walked to the door. "I almost forgot. You've been granted an audience. We have an appointment with Jane Boyland Powell tomorrow. Two o'clock. Look for the estate on Boyland Avenue. You can't miss it. I'll meet you there."

∽∾

At daybreak, I gathered my dirty clothes and towels, crammed them into bags, and headed to the laundromat, hoping it wouldn't be busy. I filled a double loader and kept my back to a wall. Within minutes, a young mother arrived, looking frazzled. She had her hands full with a toddling girl and a preschool-aged boy. Soon she was giving chase and trying to negotiate a truce, but the boy scowled. Something in me softened when he finally apologized and hugged his baby sister. I have a biological clock, but its hands move very slowly.

So, I played peek-a-boo with an imp in pigtails until the old man appeared out of nowhere. As he sat down in the chair beside mine, I realized how much Len's warning had affected me. Without provocation, I nervously shifted my position. It took a moment to place him. It was the man with the terrier, the one I'd seen walking by the river.

"It's good you are here." He leaned back in the chair. "I'm Mig Daybutch."

Nearby, a washer started its rinse cycle. Outside, a motorcycle roared down the street.

I've never been able to hide my emotions. I don't do poker face.

His chin lifted. "No, I don't want pity. I leave the past in the past. Life has been good. I married, had children, and I'm a grandfather." His eyes held such sadness. "Rosemary was kind, an old soul, all heart and hope and goodness. Things were hard for her too. I lost time, but she lost everything, will never know what it is to grow up, get married, rock a grandbaby." His voice deepened. "I found my peace long ago. Please, help her find hers."

I exhaled. "I'll do my very best. It's all I can promise."

"It's all we can ever do."

He pulled a travel-sized game board out of his pocket and asked if I played. It was dreamlike to be in that curiouser and curiouser town, playing chess with a man who'd come out the other side of a wrongful conviction. He humbled me.

Mig Daybutch left as unobtrusively as he'd arrived. I went to take my clothes out of the dryer, and he disappeared while my back was turned. I drove back to the parsonage feeling both lighter and more burdened.

The morning flew. It's possible to squeeze six hours of work into a four-hour stint. The mural continued to disclose its embittered code. Apples do not grow on silver birches, and the serpent twisting around one tree gave me a queasy feeling. Bliss River has never been and will never be Eden.

I dressed in my favourite meet-the-client outfit—a brushed jersey burgundy dress and a rose-patterned vintage blazer. I put on my business face, tamed my hair, and slipped into my pumps. *I'll do my very best,* I'd told Mig. I drove toward Boyland Avenue, wondering if my best was good enough. Would the collection include anything remotely similar to the mural? I felt pressured to find something, anything. But what if there was nothing to be found?

THE CENTURY HOME was grandiose with its two tow-
ers, wrap-around porch, and outbuildings, but I
wasn't sure it would qualify as an estate anywhere south
of Sudbury. Mac stepped out of his vehicle, and I hopped
out of mine. We met at the arched trellis.

"Don't ask too many questions, and don't let on if
you ID the artist," Mac cautioned. "Jane's protective
of her lifelong friends. Len lives in her coach house,
and he's vanished into thin air. James Powell is her ex-
husband, a drunk, but they're still close. And she stood
behind Floyd, believes his current wife lied. Spousal
abuse would nullify the pre-nup."

"Seriously! What else haven't you told me?"

"One more thing: you're convinced the killer is an
unskilled hack. And you're here to prove any connection
to her father is a fabrication."

"Mac! How am I going to look her in the eye!"

"Just smile and do your professor thing."

"Wow. We should talk about your communiqués."

"You wouldn't be crossing that posh threshold if I'd told her the truth." He opened the gate for me. "Fibs catch criminals. Consider yourself egghead on a mission. Lab rat undercover. Annora, the academic spy. "

I burst out in laughter. "Sure, sure. Sell it, why don't you?"

"You'll do fine."

We walked up the pretty, curved pathway. My steps slowed. The woman who opened the door possessed a timeless beauty. My mother said she didn't fear growing older because seventy was the new fifty. She was right. Jane Boyland Powell reminded me of a retired prima ballerina. Her silver hair was pulled back into a low, tight bun, and the severe style emphasized her long neck, inexplicably firm. I had catty thoughts, wondering if she'd had work done or had been gifted with good genes. She smelled like Shalimar and gestured like a Hollywood expat.

Jane invited us into her expansive foyer. The entry walls pulsed with art. I tried not to rubberneck as we walked down the corridor. Awestruck, I passed an original Tom Thomson and sucked in my breath when my shoulder nearly brushed an Emily Carr. The estate was a candyland with bonbons by Kurelek, Savage, Colville, and Lismer. Torture, to not stand and gawk, but the proprietress sailed us down the lengthy hallway. Even Mac struggled to keep up.

The dining room sprawled. Nothing competed with the art—the furnishings, floor, and drapery were as bland as porridge. The featured work did not disappoint.

"Your expertise is truly welcomed, Ms. Garde," she said. "Our little group tires of conjecture and gossip. With your help, all this endless speculation can end."

She sent us a warm smile and pointed out that refreshments had been left on the bar, encouraging us to help ourselves. She left and Mac, sensibly, stayed out of my way.

I started with Len Warriner. He dominated one wall with several large canvases and half a dozen smaller sketches. His strokes were long and free flowing. The compositions captured mood, a soulful atmosphere. His subjects' features were fuzzy, as if not a one could keep still. The effect had appeal, tricked the eye. I stood and admired the work longer than necessary, intrigued by the unique style and what he'd borrowed from Boyland: the magic of light.

Floyd Kent had taken symbolism into darkest sur-realism. A skeleton operated on a surgeon without anes-thesia. A hot air balloon landed in a hell filled with voluptuous women wearing red stilettos. And watery flames engulfed a forest, blazed with turquoise drop-lets. A firefighter hosed it down with a liquid inferno—a reversal of nature. I thought about the long table behind me, wondered if her grandchildren had asked about bloody entrails as Jane had carved the turkey. Surreal indeed. Boyland's influence was only evident in its balls-out, representational composition.

Poor James Powell. Like a cook who had all the right ingredients, he knew how to mix this with that, and a little something about presentation, but what he offered lacked mastery.

Though better than mediocre, his pieces did noth-ing for me. I moved closer and studied flat brushstrokes. What had Boyland made of his son-in-law? The two had little in common, artistically, save for an appreciation of classicism.

Mac and I were alone. "Nothing," I mouthed. He looked ready to bang his head against a wall. We walked into what must be the great room. I froze. Jane was an artist in her own right. She took her inspiration from flora and fauna, but her paintings also contained a considerable amount of symbolism. Each animal possessed a humanistic quality that I couldn't quite put my finger on. The effect mesmerized me.

Mac moved toward the sliding glass doors, frowning, lost in his own thoughts. His plan had backfired, and I understood his frustration. He had to find a brand-new needle in an even larger haystack. My insight hadn't been helpful. And what had Len spotted in the mural? His shock had seemed genuine, as did his concern for my safety. I needed to finish my work, return the mural to its original condition. But impatience gave in to enthrallment. The wildlife paintings were incredible. While Mac ruminated, I let myself escape into the natural world, put the true reason for visiting Boyland Manor on temporary hold.

I started with *Den Mother, 1988*. Jane had managed to instill a hunted look in the wolf's eyes as it nursed its cubs. It took a moment to spot the missing paw. It must have chewed its own leg off in order to return to the lair. Leisurely, I made my way toward *Waylaid Wanderers, 2002*. The wild horses of Alberta nestled together, ears flattened, nostrils flaring, as if they were being circled by enemies. A band of brothers both terrified and consigned to battle.

The next painting, of a snowy owl, fascinated me. One of its wings was missing a large part of its tip. Maureen, a dear friend of mine, is an obsessive birdwatcher. I asked her one summer if she'd spotted any snowy owls, and she'd said absolutely not. They travelled south for the winter, she explained. Come spring, they could only be found in the arctic. So, the bird's perch on a lilac branch in bloom puzzled me. Regardless, the white feathers against the vivid blossoms had a stunning effect, almost bridal.

"*Ghost Story*. It's dedicated to my father," Jane said.

I'd heard her approach, but her comment startled me all the same.

"He loved owls. I'd like to imagine I had something to do with it. But I didn't."

"It seems so real."

"Actually, it is—was—real. It had a nasty tussle with a golden eagle, and the larger bird managed to pinion it. The owl survived, but it would never fly again. It haunted the west side woods, where locals kept it well fed." Her expression saddened. "My father called it a ghost story waiting to be painted. So, I obliged him."

"It's exquisite. What a gift you have."

"You're far too kind. Any talent I have stems from my father. I miss him so much some days . . . " She glanced away. "I need to remind myself that he had a good, long life. Still, what he could have done with a few more years."

I'd avoided the portrait over the fireplace. Boyland had a rock-solid alibi, couldn't have murdered Rosemary, but the painting had been calling to me since I'd stepped into the room.

Even from this distance, its splendor beckoned. I'm a sucker for chiaroscuro, all that yin yang dark and light, the razor-sharp contrast.

"May I?" I glanced toward the massive painting. "Please?"

She nodded indulgently. "It's a bit contemptuous, yet there it stays."

The closer I got to it, the harder it was to hide my goosebumps. It was a life-sized portrait of Jane as an adolescent. She sat at her dressing table; the setting was feminine and highly intimate, but the wall had been kept dark, almost obscure. Moonlight and an oil lamp provided mood lighting. No wonder she disliked the painting. It was akin to having one's tween diary on public display. Boyland had captured his daughter's rebellion with a lifted chin, compressed lips, and narrowed eyes. She wore a black, formal dress. Her direct gaze expressed both pain and triumph. I looked at the slender hands, *wrought in perfect dimension*. Jane wore a large ring . . . too sophisticated for such a young . . . oh my God . . .

I projected myself into the painting, stepping into the scene like Alice through her looking glass. I honed in on the tabletop, inspected what lay in the trinket box and noted a lovely cameo. My gaze kept returning to the oil lamp with its exaggerated flame, another sphere of gold honed with a technique I'd been appreciating all week. And in that light, upon that table, lay an elegant leather book . . . the title . . . the embossed roses . . .

I dropped my purse to disguise my shock. The magnetic snap popped open, and the purse's contents spilled across the floor. I crouched and let my hair hide my face. The ruse worked. I composed myself as I picked up loose change, credit cards, and my phone. Jane stepped closer as I snatched the last item and said, "This bag has had its day."

Mac crossed the room, looking like a whipped dog. "Thank you, Jane, for allowing us access to all this artwork. We appreciate your cooperation."

She saw us out, seeming to suspect nothing. I held in my excitement. When we reached the sidewalk, I whispered, "Bingo."

"Not yet, not here," Mac warned. "Follow me to the station."

The drive took us to the highway. I passed a small white cross with a bright wreath of flowers. One of those roadside markers erected after a tragic accident. The marker put things into perspective. I couldn't wait to talk to Mac.

Bliss River's OPP detachment was larger than I'd thought it would be. The building also housed the Fire Department. We got out of our cars, and he held the door open for me.

"I'm in a meeting," he said to the constable in the reception area.

Mac led me to his office and gestured to a chair. He leaned against his desk. "You look like you're ready to explode. Spill."

"Boyland may be innocent. But the mural is his."

"You're certain?"

"Forget his unique style, those distinct markers. Jane's portrait? It doesn't just employ the same painting techniques, it has the same elements—the gas lamp with its high flame, an oversized jewel. Didn't you see the identical volume of *King Lear*?"

He raked his hands through his hair. "Dammit! Should've paid more attention to the art. I'll need a warrant next time. Just a hunch."

"I'm sorry. Undercover rat fails."

"What are you talking about? You were amazing!" He folded his arms. "So, the mural isn't a confession . . . it's a condemnation? Boyland knew who killed Rosemary and didn't go to the police? It makes no sense . . . unless . . ."

"He was protecting the killer," we said in unison.

"Who? An uncle? A brother?"

"You're getting warmer." A corner of his mouth lifted. "Boyland liked the ladies, even as a minor. Before the war, he got a tutor 'with child.' The family kept it hush-hush, provided the girl with a cottage and a small allowance. The boy had many issues, kept getting in trouble with the law—vandalism, truancy, escalating violence. Once the boy turned fourteen, he was enlisted into 'The Guiding Light Project.' Floyd Kent is Boyland's son. The truth was revealed after Boyland's death, five years ago. The will outed him."

What a soap opera. "What connects Floyd to Rosemary?"

"His mother was a piano teacher. He worked part-time as a grocery delivery boy. He was in and out of the Green's Apartment, and Rosemary visited his home every week. Rosemary even drew a picture of *them* on his bicycle. Floyd's mother, Emily Knapp, vouched he'd been in bed with the flu on the night of the murder."

Knapp. The name rang a bell. "So, you're down to one suspect?"

"No. We're back to three."

"Why is Jane's ex-husband a suspect? What kind of trouble did he get into as a youth?"

"Drinking underage. Break and enter. Statutory rape."

"What!"

"He was seventeen and Jane was thirteen. They did more than just hold hands."

I couldn't picture high-class Jane as a bad girl.

"Disturbing, I know. The whole Jerry Lee Lewis pretext. But Jane wrapped her father around her little finger. She insisted that Boyland allow James into 'The Guiding Light Project' to keep him out of juvenile detention. She was sent off to some private boarding school in Penetanguishene for a year or so, then had a tutor. The story goes that she went on a hunger strike, and the lovebirds were legally married when she turned fifteen. James lived on his own until Jane received her diploma." His mouth tightened. "If my little girl wanted to marry, I would have done more than turn him in, I'd have turned him inside out. Now, James and Jane had a good, long run—fifty years. But James is an alcoholic. He has had several DUIs. He lives in the Boyland cottage, on the outskirts of Bliss River, rarely goes anywhere. His family wants nothing to do with him. Apparently, the feeling is mutual."

"Wait. Did Boyland know Rosemary or Fayette? What about James?"

"Small town, remember? During the war, there were few dollars available for upkeep. Boyland was so committed to beautifying Bliss River that he bought up property. By '57, he owned half of the town, including the bakery, hardware store, several shops, a restaurant, and all the apartments above them. Fayette and Rosemary were his tenants." Mac paused. "He put James to work, to test him, I think. James, the son of a plumber, became Boyland's superintendent. The boy lived in a rent-free studio across the hall from Rosemary and her mother."

I didn't know what to do with all the information. The pieces fit too easily into place. "So, Floyd is his son and James is his son-in-law. But what is Len to Boyland? Just a protégée?"

"Henry—Len's father—and Kingsley were old war buddies. The story goes Warriner saved Boyland's life in the Battle of Normandy. They remained best buds until Warriner suffered a fatal heart attack in '85." Mac added, "Len used to call him Uncle Kingsley."

Degrees of separation are so small. I thought of all the people who I saw on a regular basis, those feeble social bridges that stretch between us and the strangers we see every day. Proximity makes for easy marks, and routine lends a false sense of security. Like the road we travel every day and take for granted until one fateful night a SUV plows right into us.

Kingsley Boyland had marked the place where Rosemary's light had been snuffed out. Her murder had scarred him, condemned him to a private hell. Jane's portrait was both his Rosetta stone and a storyboard. He'd never accepted his role as an accessory after the fact. And what of Mig Daybutch? An innocent youth wrongfully condemned? Another life destroyed? Boyland's guilt must have been excruciating.

Mac waited, let me sort things out, but nothing added up.

"I'm not buying any of it," I said. "Loyalty is one thing, but how could Boyland live with himself? What if the killer had struck again?"

"But the killer didn't, and that one fact has always baffled the authorities. Predators of this kind tend to go serial. You know what I think? I think one of those boys confessed to Boyland, and he used the admission as a way to castrate the killer. He kept him close, watched every move, and became his fulltime warden."

"Mac, you know these men."

"You asking if I like one of them for this?" His brow furrowed. "Floyd Kent has always had issues. He even abused animals as a kid. The parsonage is his old stomping ground. His next ex-to-be claims he likes to get rough. He must get some help from a blue pill, considering his age." He held up a hand. "Again, this is privileged information. Obviously."

A thought came to me. "Kent! I believe Kent is one of the characters in Lear! The name may even be Irish, which would also connect him to the Celtic knot! Mac, I know Floyd was illegitimate, but was his mother religious, devout in some way?"

His eyes widened. "She married Reverend Thomas Knapp. Their engagement was the talk of the town. She won over naysayers by dressing for her role, dutifully playing the church organ, and giving piano lessons. The Knapps were missed when they accepted the charge of the Anglican Church one town over." Mac stood up. "What made you ask about religion?"

I told him about the apples in the birch tree, the serpent in Bliss River's garden.

"Floyd has faced his share of contempt. Maybe Rosemary represented what he couldn't stand in himself— the fifty's rank of love child. His stepfather tried his best to repair the damage done. His mother was tough on him, pushed him to live an exemplary life. The mural is pointing us toward *him*. It's all there. Len must have put it together too." His gaze met mine. "I need to find them. Fast."

10

I RETURNED TO THE parsonage a little after four, disappointed the one day of sunshine had been a fluke.
The patrol car was missing. *Boy or girl,* I wondered. I
envisioned Johnston peeling down the street. Another
officer had probably been dispatched and would show
up soon enough.

Afternoon sunlight streamed into the parlour, and
the hazmat suit helped to keep me warm. The left parlour was chilly. Even though their heating vents were not
sealed off, all the other rooms were cool, too, due to the
hit-and-miss furnace.

Again, I felt as if I wasn't alone. A more-than-an-old-
house sound had me cringing. Something had moved on
the second floor. A week earlier, I would have said I'd
allowed the whole ghoulish-Gothic vibe of the assign-
ment to get to me, but Lilith had been right; this wasn't
a run-of-the-mill art restoration.

Nervously, I walked upstairs, peeked into the rooms,
and stood stock-still, listening.

Nothing. My hand lifted to open the attic door just as a mouse skittered down the hall. I yelped and laughed at myself. The next trip into town, I'd buy a humane trap and some stinky cheese. Lilith would approve, tell me to feed them a nice Munster and a smidgen of pâté.

It was close to five. After I'd taken more photos, I worked on my reports. The nausea hit me an hour later. Raising my arms felt impossible, as though the force of gravity had tripled. Parker had been sick! Some flu bug must be going around town. A nap might put me right, help me to fight off the overwhelming fatigue. Frustrated, I collapsed onto the cot. I didn't bother to remove my slippers. I noticed the phone in my hand. I let it slide to the floor, feeling stupidly lazy, as feeble as a newborn.

The world disappeared. Someone called out to me. My reoccurring nightmare. I expected a bloody hand to clasp my arm, but it was Rosemary who came out of the darkness. Her curls gleamed—soft coils of light—and her eyes were wide with fear. She ran toward me, pink sweater winging behind her. "Wake up!" She screamed. "You must wake up!"

Somehow I managed to open my eyes. The room spiraled, tilted, and I tried to move, but my body felt so impossibly heavy. Had I been poisoned? I reached down for my phone, fell out of bed, and cursed as I hit the hard floorboards. Weakly, I pushed the three digits.

"Nine-one-one, what's your emergency?"

"Can't . .wake up . . ."

"Where are you? Can you give me an address?"

"Felicity Street." Each breath was agony. "St. George's . . . parsonage . . ."

"Are you in pain? Are you hurt?"

"Dizzy." I tried to stand. "Falling . . . sick . . ."

"Ma'am, you need to get outside right now! Help's on the way. But get out!"

I managed to crawl a few feet before I collapsed again. I struggled to lift my head. Everything blurred, spun like a merry-go-round. The sound of sirens. Too late. "Tell Mom . . ."

"Stay with me! We're almost there!"

I heard something shatter. Mac screamed my name. The sound of running feet. He barreled toward me, scooped me into his arms and rushed us outside. His hold was unbreakable. I could let go, give in. When I did, everything rippled, and the darkness stole me away.

જ⁓ન

He hovered over me as the first responders took their readings. Bile rose in my throat, and I almost vomited.

"You're going to be alright." His jaw tightened. "It's carbon monoxide poisoning. What were you thinking? Why did you heat the place with the oven?"

I tried to shake my head but couldn't. There was an oxygen mask on my face. I looked into his eyes, desperate to convey, *Someone tried to kill me.*

"You didn't turn on the oven, did you? You wouldn't."

I inhaled the oxygen and nodded. I knew I needed to lower the toxic levels. I also knew I may have suffered permanent brain damage. The thought had me gasping.

He leaned close to me and squeezed my hand. "Slow, deep breaths. You're safe now.

We'll get you to the hospital. I'll follow the ambulance."

My head began to clear. By the time we reached the ER, I was no longer scared. I was furious. One, I should have recognized the classic symptoms of CO poisoning.

Two, I was ready to hunt down Floyd Kent myself and kick him in the groin until he blacked out. *Suck on your own tail pipe, Psycho!*

I hate hospitals. I do not hate doctors, not entirely. Many of them do their job well. The doctor who treated me was firm but patient and knew how to put me at ease.

"You'll need oxygen for several hours," she informed me. "Your blood will be tested. If the CO level is too high, you'll be airlifted to a hospital with a hyperbaric chamber. Otherwise, we can treat you here. One step at a time, okay?"

A seasoned nurse came in to take my blood. She brought me a warm blanket and told me colour had returned to my face and that I was "doing wonderful." After the blood test, I just lay there, breathing, and tried not to hyperventilate. The curtained enclosure was typical of any ER. Its pea-green fabric was too thin to blanket a young boy's never-ending whimpers. Someone down the hall sobbed. Someone closer asked questions but wasn't getting answers.

Thankfully, the mask prevented me from smelling a thing, but the unnatural lighting hurt my eyes. The pillow had flatlined, no life left in it, and those glaring high beams were itching to expose all things private, As said, I hate, hate, hate hospitals.

Somehow, I fell asleep despite the dryness in my throat and the awkwardness of the mask. I awoke feeling disoriented but better.

The doctor arrived, chart in hand. She sat down on the wheeled stool and rolled it closer. "Good news. Though you experienced an acute poisoning, you fall below a carboxyhaemoglobin level of twenty percent. We do need to continue to monitor you, but the treatment we've started should be able to bring down the CO levels quickly. If you'd been in that room any longer—" Her frown disappeared as she added, "Just a few more hours here. We also need to run a few tests, including an EEG. I know this is stressful, but remember, it could have been a great deal worse."

I'd been given time to think. About Mac. I was attracted to him, but a romantic involvement would be a mistake. I went where my work took me and couldn't tie myself down to one place for too long. Besides, if we squeezed our joint baggage into the same room, there'd be no space left for us to so much as rub noses.

He still wore his wedding ring. What more did I need to know?

The nurse took my blood again. Six hours had done the trick; I could take off the oxygen mask. The doctor asked me a series of questions, and I must have aced the test because she beamed at me, said I'd soon be free to go. It was five AM. Had the parsonage been aired out? Was it safe to return? The longer I stayed in the ER, the more spooked I became.

CO poisoning is serious, I knew. But a part of me wanted to make a run for it, streak out of the hospital in my backless puce gown. The slight buffer of the oxygen mask was gone.

Memories were hitting me like pieces of shrapnel. I kept staring at the curtain, willing it to open.

Mac appeared out of nowhere, and I told myself he was just doing his job, following up. "You have a choice." He rubbed his neck. "Stay with Lilith, her irritated husband, and her teens, or use my guest room. Grace's bus arrives this morning. She would love to keep you company. After you rest."

"No, thank you. I can take care of myself just fine."

"If you argue, Beth will find you a bed on one of the wards."

"Beth?"

"Dr. Wishart. My cousin. And your doctor."

"How freaking small is this town!"

"Not as small as it was a week ago. We've been in contact with Floyd and James, and we're searching for Len." His voice lowered. "We botched up. Our detachment deals mostly with petty crimes and dealer take-downs, search and rescue, assault and battery. It's made me, and my constables, too comfortable. It's not safe for you here. We should reconsider—"

"Oh no, you don't. I *will* clean every square inch of that painting," I said. "And why didn't he destroy it? He had the opportunity. What haven't we seen yet, Mac?" My throat hurt. "In the sixty years since the murder, no other girls have gone missing?"

"Yeah, we've had our share of teen runaways. Two years ago, a young girl was abducted, a custody battle gone bad, and the girl was quickly reunited with her father."

I considered asking him if the nearby towns had unsolved murder cases. Sudbury was an hour's drive from Bliss River. The city would have been a prime hunting ground, but even though Toronto was a much longer trek, any suspect could have travelled those extra miles, lived out his sick fantasies, and returned home. A field trip. The thought made me queasier.

The doctor arrived, greeted us, and said, "So, Mac, you'll be watching over our patient?"

"Yay for nepotism," I grumbled.

"Gee, something tells me she can't wait to get out of here." She turned toward me. "You must take it easy

for a few days. You can't exert yourself. Should you feel
dizzy, I want you to return to the hospital immediately." She made eye contact. "It takes a month to see
if your system has suffered any permanent damage.
So far, everything looks good . . . But if you experience any muscle tremors, memory loss, or even if you
aren't quite feeling yourself, come see me or make
an appointment with your family doctor as soon as
possible."

I thanked her, and they left the room so I could
change. It took willpower to stop myself from dashing
out the door, to keep my steps slow and even. The sunrise nearly overwhelmed me. I stared at it until my eyes
misted. How close I'd come to death. Again.

Once we were in his truck, he sat there quietly for
a minute, then said, "A friend of mine came back from
Kabul with PTSD. Your reaction to the attack is normal.
Your reaction to the hospital isn't." His voice gentled.
"I'm a great listener."

The accident is not something I discuss. Even after
all these years, it still hurts too much. I took him back
to Boxing Day, 1994. My mother had been sick. She'd
been unable to make the trip to my grandparent's farm.
So, off we'd gone without her. I told Mac how she'd
blown kisses from the window. We'd had a lovely time
at the farm, stayed longer than we should have, and left
around ten in our rusty station wagon.

I'd been thirteen and had called shotgun. Maeve—
eleven—was annoyed. She sat behind me, huffing. Tess
was nine. She sat behind my father. Charlotte, almost
two, sat in her car seat between Maeve and Tess.

I babbled to Mac about the weather conditions, the
falling snow, the black ice.

Charlotte giggled, playing with a toy. Maeve kept pressing her feet into my back. I turned in the chair, yelled at her, called her a jerk. Dad cursed, and he never cursed. I spun back around, watched as a speeding SUV on the other side of the highway hit another, sending it out of control. Everything happened in seconds. The black Bronco came at us like a bullet. It tore into the driver's side, full force, and spun us out. The car behind us crashed into the back passenger area. Our car rolled into the ditch and flipped over and over, landing on its wheels.

There was so much blood.

I found the words to tell Mac Tess and Maeve died on impact. Little Charlotte screamed in pain or panic— I couldn't tell which. Dad had slumped over the steering wheel, his mangled face turned toward me. His left eye was missing, but he was alive. I looked back again. Charlotte seemed to be okay. Dad needed me more.

I managed to undo his seat belt. My door was open. I dragged him over the seats but tried to be gentle as I pulled him out of the car and onto the ground. I cradled his head. He told me I was such a brave girl. Blood pooled in my lap. And he was gone.

I couldn't get to Charlotte. The car wouldn't let me. Its front seats had been crushed together, and the roof was flattened. I half-climbed through the back window, tried and tried and tried to move Maeve's body out of the way, but I still couldn't reach Charlotte and she screamed, "Nory! Want Nory!" The screams got quieter, turned into garbled words, then gurgles. There had been an awful silence, broken by the wail of a fire truck. By the time the first responders arrived, it was too late. I was the only one alive.

The driver that hit us did not survive. The driver of the other car did not remain at the scene of the accident. He'd gotten out of the vehicle, holding his hands to his head. I'd pleaded with him to help, hysterically screaming at him, collapsing as he'd driven away. The police explained to my mother the SUVs had been street racing. The person responsible for the accident had never been found. He'd gotten away with murder.

Murder. Silence followed the word, a stillness that held words left unsaid. Mac's eyes were bright, and the empathy within them left me undone.

"Your father was right," he said. "You're stronger than you'll ever know."

"No. No, I'm not."

He slid the key into the ignition. "Let's get you home."

Once again, we drove past that roadside cross. Someone had changed the wreath. Fresh pink ribbons flailed in the breeze. I knew how long they would take to fade and unravel, and I knew another and another floral arrangement would take its place. Some loving mourner would return each season, climb down the ravine, wade through garbage, and tend to the aging marker.

Just like my mother had tended to the one for her husband and children.

Just like I would tend to Rosemary. Come hell or high water.

CHAPTER

11

I T SMELLED LIKE a bakery. I opened my eyes and stretched. Although the mattress was comfy, the sheets were fusty. Mac had apologized for the state of the room, explaining it hadn't been used for quite some time. I'd reassured him it was fine, but now I understood why he'd looked so hangdog earlier; dozens of totes in various sizes were stacked in each corner. Most bore labels of "Thrift Store" and "Shelter." At some point, he'd started to sort through his wife's clothing and personal belongings but hadn't been able to finish the task.

I swallowed hard. Things are never just things. A tiny pair of white patent leather shoes can shatter an Easter morning. I'd once come across several lily-of-the-valley clippings Maeve had carefully pressed between the pages of a dictionary. They'd hit me like grenades.

Mac had stopped by the parsonage while I slept. He'd piled some of my clothing on a chair that was positioned beside the bed. A pillowcase contained my socks, bras, and underwear. I flushed at the intimacy, then picked out comfort wear: black yoga pants and a soft lilac tee-shirt. Feeling like an interloper, I left the sad, cluttered room. I discovered the washroom had been modernized, and it was both clean and spacious.

Someone—Mac?—had even installed one of those luxurious rain showerheads. I stood under its spray for a long, long time, allowing the hot water to loosen the knots in my neck and return my equilibrium. When I finally opened the door, steam followed me into the hall. My stomach mewled as I made my way down the floating stairs.

Mac lived in a mid-sized house. Family photos brightened the stairway, so I took my time descending and allowed each picture to tell me its story. There were photos of them at the beach, riding horses, picking apples. There were school and Christmas portraits. His wife had possessed a natural allure, and her wide smile spoke of her love for life. Every frame displayed her unabashed fulfillment. My heart ached for Mac, for his daughter, and for the woman who had loved them both.

I passed a '70s-style sunken living room and heard pop music. Mac struck me as a blues man . . . or maybe a classic rock devotee. Discreetly, I peered into the funky orange kitchen, surprised to recognize the young woman who danced by the sink. During one of my university liaison lectures, she'd asked whether restoration could be construed as an act of vandalism. She'd questioned if the best of intentions had ever destroyed a painting's integrity.

"Hi." Her cheeks pinkened. "Did I wake you?"

"No. But your muffins did."

She smiled. "We have lemonade, juice, and carbonated water, which Dad totally hates.

I'm assuming he bought the Perrier for you?"

"He knew I'd need my fix."

Her eyebrows rose. She took a bottle out of the fridge and placed it on the oval white table. I asked her about what she thought of York. She filled me in on her courses, her professors, her dorm mate, and her heated views on the cost of a higher education.

I ate two muffins, leaned back in my chair, and said, "I'm going to need the recipe."

"Sure! Hey, Dad said if we didn't keep you busy you'll try to escape. FYI, Constable Andrews is outside. I know from experience, he's a stool pigeon." Her expression grew serious. "I can't believe somebody tried to kill you."

I didn't quite believe it myself. "Did your father tell you what happened?"

"He thinks while you were out, someone lined the oven, turned it on, and opened it." She gathered our dishes and took them to the sink. "Then he turned it off, closed it up, and waited for you to return to the parsonage. They think he hid in the attic. Once you'd gone to bed, he went back downstairs and repeated the process. The kitchen doors were closed, but the office door had been left wide open."

It sounded so implausible and idiotic . . . or insane. I could have returned earlier, caught him in the act, or woken up. Had he meant to frighten me off? If so, he'd be disappointed.

Grace stood by the table. "If it's okay with you, I'm going to work out."

I assured her I was fine. "Do you know if your dad found my phone?"

"Yup. And your laptop and purse. They're all in the living room."

"Perfect. I'll make some calls, then check my mail. Would that be considered staying out of trouble?" A waggle of my brows elicited a snort. "I can't stand daytime television, so I might forage through your bookcase, find something to read."

"*Mi casa es tu casa.*"

I planted myself in a nest of pillows. The gas fireplace gave off a pleasant warmth. My laptop had been placed on the coffee table. I fished my phone out of my purse, turned it on, and sat there, chewing my lip as I wondered how forthcoming I should be.

As usual, my mother picked up her phone after two rings. "Annora?"

"You sound croupy."

"It's just a cold, but I phoned in sick. Tomorrow, the kids will go on and on about the cooler-than-me sub." She chuckled. "Like I don't already feel old enough."

Across the room, tiny flames danced behind glass. "I love you, Mom."

"What's happened!"

"Ouch. Seems I need to say those three words more often."

"Honey, it wasn't what you said, but how you said it. Where are you? Bogotá, again?"

"No, no. I'm in Bliss River. Four hours northwest of you." I played with the silky fringe on one pillow as I told her what I could, explaining the need for confidentiality. I don't exactly lie to my mother, but sometimes half-truths are easier on both of us. "Now, don't freak out, but last night, I went to the hospital because of carbon monoxide—"

"How bad is it?"

Good thing we weren't face to face. "I'm fine now. The cause is under investigation. Something about a gas range."

"What aren't you telling me?"

I'd put a knot in the fringe. "The building's been made safe, and I'll be returning to work in a day or two. I'm staying with new friends while I recoup."

I tried to change the subject, but she interrogated me until I told her—verbatim—what the doctor had said. I veered the conversation toward her upcoming cruise. We talked about the ship's ports of call and how excited she was to visit Giverny and walk through Monet's gardens. We chatted for over an hour, bantered for a bit, but as we said our goodbyes, I could tell she was worried. She was always worried about me. Even when I was home.

I opened my laptop, grateful Mac had enabled a guest network. I replied to emails, including a charming one from a teen working on an art essay. He quizzed me about conservation. The tension left me as I shared the particulars of my career, happy to help the young man who thought conservation was "amazing."

Next, I called Lilith. She couldn't talk long as she had a full house. She asked how I was, but she sounded flustered, almost resentful. Was she anxious about the museum or was something else bothering her? I didn't ask. We made some small talk, and I assured her I'd be able to finish cleaning the mural. After the conversation, I felt fidgety and didn't quite know what to do with myself. The brush-off had stunned me. *Hey, Sorority Sister, sorry if an attempt on my life delayed the grand opening. Is there some way I can make it up to you?*

Grace popped her head into the living room. Her forehead had a slight sheen. "I'm going to take a shower. Everything okay?"

I gave her a thumbs-up, shut my laptop, and approached the bookshelves. My fingers walked the spines of dozens of paperbacks. Readers lived here. Someone enjoyed thrillers and psychological suspense. A literary aficionado had collected a decade of award-winning fiction. Classics cozied up to contemporary poets. I pulled out a meaty anthology of short stories and scanned through the table of contents, finding several intriguing tales written by notable authors.

Feeling lazier than I had in close to a year, I curled into the sectional and opened the cover. Grace flopped onto the cushions across from me, clutching a textbook on Italian Renaissance art. I couldn't remember the last time I'd experienced the simple pleasure of reading *with* someone. Our legs lined up like baguettes on a baker's shelf. I half-heartedly read a story about a woman who'd left her husband and two young sons in order to restore her freedom. I couldn't relate. Did that make me a nonfeminist, an independent thinker, or a romantic?

I had a good life, filled with friends, adventure, work, and purpose, but sitting across from Grace, knowing Mac would soon join us, made me realize I'd still be satisfied with my life had my choices been different. Surely, feminism and family could coexist under the same roof. Evidently, Kit MacGowan had found a balance. I very much doubted she'd longed to abandon the thankless tasks associated with being a mother and a loving helpmate.

I nestled into the cushions, let the book drop against my chest, and closed my eyes. The quiet soothed.

Nothing so much as creaked. I only heard Grace slowly turning pages. My mother had once bought me a cat in an attempt to put some life back into our soundless home. Its purr became a comforting white noise. Mac's house needed a cat.

I woke by degrees, feeling lost. The Wonderland feeling grew stronger when I discovered Grace using chalk pastels to sketch me.

"No fair," I groaned. "I'm no Venus."

"But you have good bones."

I snorted. "Right. And even better laugh lines."

"How did you get that scar by your collarbone?"

"It's a long story."

An eyebrow lifted, but she accepted my reply, didn't press me. So, I stayed still, shut my eyes, and let her finish my portrait.

"Done." She held up the sketchbook and turned it toward me. "Whaddya think?"

She'd managed to capture the aftereffects of a near-death experience. The dark circles under my eyes and sallow complexion were bang on. Yup. I looked like total crap.

"This is good. I mean "Mary Stephenson Cassatt" good."

Her face lit up. "You think so?"

"You've applied the chalk deftly, haven't glamorized your subject, and kept it real."

"For my tenth birthday, my parents gave me a book about her. I've thumbed through the pages so often the spine is loose."

"Books are meant to be loved to pieces, I think, though I know several book conservators who would chew me to bits for saying so."

One topic led to another. Grace's intelligence and passion for argument filled the rest of the afternoon. She ordered a pizza and let me know that although she was a vegetarian, Mac loved his traditional slices. "I wish Dad were here too," she said.

We scrolled through the television guide and decided on the old classic *Laura*. Grace hadn't seen it. I let her know it was one of the top mystery films of all time. We lost ourselves in the story as dusk faded away.

I'd slipped into another woman's pair of shoes. They were wonderful shoes, doeskin soft, and still somewhat warm, but they weren't mine. Though she'd passed away, Kit's essence clung to her home, and yet her presence was in no way hostile or unwelcoming. Any awkwardness I felt stemmed from my attraction to Mac. I sensed that he felt a connection too, but I wouldn't rush him through the grieving process. Once, others had tried to rush me through mine. The end results had been detrimental and long-lasting.

Mac came home toward the end of the flick. Grace put a finger to her lips, shushing him. He glanced between the movie and the pizza. He grabbed two slices from the box, sat on a nearby chair, and ate. On the small screen, drama played out in a black-and-white living room as the detective hunted for the truth, trying to stay on track while dealing with a romantic distraction. I was no femme fatale, but I saw certain similarities between the movie and my experiences over the past few days.

I turned my head and saw Mac's expression. His face held mixed emotions, showed a sorrowful indecisiveness and more than a hint of guilt. How many times he and Kit had sat on this very sofa, nestling, talking about their day . . .

The sudden scream of a siren had us turning toward the window and jumping to our feet. Another and another and another fire truck chased after the first. Mac rushed toward the phone, picking it up as it rang. His face tensed and he barked a few words into the receiver. In less than a minute he was making a dash for the door.

"Stay here."

"Dad!" Grace called after him. "Where's the fire?"

"The old mill!"

He hopped into his truck and drove away, leaving the door open behind him.

Grace and I walked outside and stood on the stoop. We'd sidled closer together, and I felt her slight quiver. Far off, on a hillside, an odd orange glow seared the skyline, and even from a distance, I smelled the smoke's indescribable noxious quality. Others had also left their houses. Under streetlamps, townspeople started to congregate, and several pointed toward the historical site. I reached out a hand, thinking it had begun to snow. I was wrong. It was ash.

I wrapped an arm around Grace's shoulders, and she leaned into me.

"What's happening?" Her voice quavered. "This isn't the Bliss River I know. This can't be my hometown."

12

THE FIRE BURNED throughout the night. By morning, all that remained was smoking rubble. Mac returned, saying next to nothing as he dragged himself up the stairs. I prepared the turkey and slipped it into the oven. Grace put a Tofurkey into a crockpot and asked if I wanted to go to church for the Thanksgiving service. I was up for hymns and a comforting message, something placating. I changed into my black slacks and an ivory angora sweater and actually spent some time on my hair. Grace met me at the door, wearing a quilted navy jacket, a white tee, and jeans.

Mac was still sleeping, so we left as quietly as we could. Inside, delicious aromas wafted from the kitchen, but outside the air smelled rankly of smoke. A lingering haze hid the sun, and the neighbourhood remained ominously hushed.

Grace said nothing as she unlocked the car, but I could see she was upset.

I touched her arm, and a half-smile replaced her frown.

I knew the ride would be short, but I dislike being in the passenger seat. I need to feel in control. Though Grace proved to be a cautious driver who braked for every suicidal squirrel that darted across the road, I still couldn't relax. The streets were eerily empty. Finally, I spotted someone, a woman, vigorously sweeping a front porch, ensuring everything was just so. I thought about my mom, hoping she'd be spending the day with Aunt Cheryl.

The town had several churches, so I hadn't assumed I'd been invited to St. George's. She pulled up in front of the parsonage, and I groaned. Yellow police tape criss-crossed the door, and each window seemed darker and far more disturbing than a week ago. We stepped out of the vehicle as the church bell sounded, clangs carried by a gentle wind, each peel falsely optimistic.

Parishioners filled the church. Some chatted or checked the bulletins while others dozed. I'd always found sanctuaries to be ideal spots for contemplation. I was no longer certain about God. Blind faith had died with my sisters. Still, serendipitous occurrences like a child surviving a mudslide gave me hope that there could be such things as guardian angels. I just wished they were more dependable.

Grace and I squeezed into a pew a few rows from the back, and I noticed several people were openly gawking at us. Lilith caught sight of me at the same time I caught sight of her. She waved, and I waved back. John turned his head. I was glad to see Kate and Parker were there with their parents.

The sight of familiar faces in no way surprised me, though I'd have never taken Jane Boyland Powell for a choir member. She didn't seem like someone who enjoyed sharing the spotlight. Perhaps I was being too critical of her. She stood in the second row, looking suitably humble in a simple blue robe.

To the left of us, Constable Johnston cradled his newborn son, oblivious to the world around him. His wife's head rested on his shoulder. I shifted, as if the seat was making me uncomfortable, and continued to scan the rows as covertly as I could.

My jaw nearly dropped as I made eye contact with the mysterious Mr. Thousand Words. He'd chosen the pew closest to the door and hadn't removed his coat. I averted my gaze; in doing so, I caught sight of Mig Daybutch. He was talking to a woman I assumed was his wife. She lightly tapped his cheek, and he made a silly face. He noticed me and winked, and I snorted.

Grace mouthed, "What?," and I shrugged.

The young minister seemed spunky, and his sermon was on point. He spoke of the mill, its closure, and its slow fall to ruin. He commended the volunteer firefighters on their bravery and service. He mentioned the parsonage, and several heads swiveled my way but quickly turned back toward the pulpit. The minister cautioned that Bliss River was a community at a crossroads, plagued by a long unsolved crime. He entreated "the guilty one" to resist any further evil impulses, to come forward and confess his sins. Finally, he asked us to pray with him for justice and peace. I bowed my head, totally impressed.

When the offering plate was passed to me, I slipped in two tens and continued to sing "For the Beauty of the Earth." Many of the parishioners were seniors, and some were old enough to have known Rosemary. Perhaps a few had been her friends. Others may have snubbed or tormented her. I wondered if they'd thought they could redeem themselves for their past taunts, all those nasty acts. And what of her killer? Was he a worshipper too? The church was so close to the spot where he'd taken her life.

The service felt short. As was the custom, we stood in line to shake the minister's hand. He was reed thin, tall, and far from priestly looking with his nose ring and man bun. However, his sympathetic gaze held mine as if he wanted to say something more, but he couldn't. I decided to drop by the church the next day.

As soon as she was back in the car, Grace switched on the radio and hummed along to a hit rap song. Perhaps, the service had restored her faith in her community. My thoughts were darker and kept circling back to evil impulses. I looked out the passenger window, feigning an interest in the picket fences we passed. In no time, we returned to her home.

Mac was still in bed, so Grace and I worked side by side in the kitchen. She made an apple pie while I washed, peeled, and diced vegetables. It felt so bizarrely domestic to me.

Around four, Mac joined us with an apologetic grin, and I thought about the week ahead of me. My time in Bliss River would be impossible to forget. I couldn't wait until my work at the parsonage was completed, but another part of me . . .

I was glad we would eat at the kitchen table. Formal dining rooms often stifle conversations, I've found. As we served ourselves from pots and roasting pans, I said, "Your home is lovely. I like the timbered ceiling and all the skylights."

"We took out the last of the shag carpeting ten years ago, but the rest of the '70s features grew on us. Guess I should get around to redoing the kitchen."

"I'll believe it when I see it," Grace chided.

We sat down, and I took a bite of mashed potatoes, savouring the creaminess. "I haven't had a traditional Thanksgiving dinner in three years."

"Three years?" Mac blinked.

"I enjoy working abroad, and each country observes different holidays. Last Thanksgiving, I was in Prague, where they don't have a thanksgiving. They do, however, celebrate the creation of Czechoslovakia—Independent Czechoslovak State Day.'"

Grace asked, "Were there fireworks?"

"The Czechs take the holiday seriously. No fireworks. There were exhibits at the castle. The museum was closed to the public for . . . renovations. I'd forgotten! Talk about déjà vu," I said. "Anyway, I continued to work on Joseph Šíma's *Return of Ulysses*. Later, I trekked back to the bed and breakfast where I stayed. My hosts reheated schnitzel, and then we drank far too much slivovice."

"Slivovice?" Grace helped herself to more stuffing. "Is that a brand of beer?"

"Actually, it's a plum brandy that smells like jam but packs a wallop. We'd ended up getting tipsy and discussing Kafka until the wee hours."

"Ooh." Grace grinned. "Love Kafka."

"To quote Raymond Chandler, 'Scarcely anything in literature is worth a damn except what is written between the lines.'"

"Dad likes to pretend he's Phillip Marlow."

Mac opened his mouth.

Grace cut him off. "No Bogart impressions, please."

The MacGowans did their best to make me feel relaxed, and I appreciated their efforts. But, in a way,

I'd already returned to the parsonage. Which area was I supposed to focus on next? I couldn't remember. The sky? The water? The trees and hills over her left shoulder?

"Annora?"

I turned toward Grace. "I'm sorry. I drifted away, didn't I?"

She nodded. "More wine?"

"No, thank you. I need to get up early. I'm going back to work tomorrow." I sent Mac a challenging look. "But I won't overdo it."

He studied me, shaking his head. "Fine. But I'll be checking in with you."

"He's serious. Dad has a habit of showing up at the dorm, claiming he was just 'in the neighbourhood.' As if he hadn't driven five hours to get to my door." She reached out and grabbed his hand. "It's kinda sweet in that old-school way."

"Old-school, huh?" He dipped his free hand in his glass of water and flicked his fingers at her. "Ooh, burn! This Dad's got finesse. Hashtag 'cool pop.'"

"You are *such* a dork."

Mac volunteered to clean up and told us to go do whatever somewhere else. Grace asked if I liked horseshoes. It had been years since I'd played, but I was game. She lent me a jacket, and we headed outside. The backyard was large for a modern build. The garden needed some attention, but the grass had recently been mowed. It was good to play, move, be silly, and toss horseshoes as the sun sank lower and lower. Grace threw two ringers. I was happy when one of my shoes almost touched the stake. Hues of violet and apricot began to colour the sky as we went back inside.

Mac had set up some board games in the living room. Soft jazz streamed from a stereo as we arranged our Scrabble tiles, spelled out words like "mazier," "enamor," and "tzar."

"'Aliquot'? C'mon, you made it up. Cheater." Mac reached for the dictionary. "'Aliquot: an integer that is an exact divisor of some quantity.' Egghead, what's your IQ, anyway?"

"It fluctuates."

"Bull-uh-bologna."

"Dad, I'm eighteen. You don't need to censure yourself. I use the word too."

"Potty mouth." He gave her the stink eye.

She laughed. "When it's warranted."

The banter was soothing. Sometimes, it hurt to be around fathers, and I envied women who still had that precious connection. Grieving had been put to rest, but I knew I'd been robbed of countless tender moments and one, just one, adult daughter–father conversation. Dad had been a wonderful man. Like Mac. I pictured them side by side. Yes, they would have liked each other. The thought irritated me. I needed to stop expanding on what was a professional relationship. Geez. I'd only known the guy for a week.

I asked to sit out the next game, so Grace and Mac took out a chessboard and forgot I was even in the room. Grace won, and soon after, I excused myself.

❧

The next morning was a mad rush. The three of us got ready and were out the door before eight o'clock. They dropped me off at the parsonage. Grace hopped out of the car to give me a bear hug. I returned it, feeling oddly shy and uncertain. I've never liked goodbyes. I'd said too many. Still, I watched the car drive away, touched by the carefree kiss Grace blew me.

Clumsily, I skirted around Constable Andrews' cruiser and flew up the parsonage steps.

Wood had replaced a small window panel. I struggled to unlock the door, needing to jiggle the key repeatedly, as if the old house didn't want me to return. After many attempts, it slowly swung open. I noticed the broken glass had been swept away. My footsteps sounded unnaturally loud as I headed toward the study. There, I found a bouquet of flowers waiting, a bountiful arrangement of sunflowers, lilies, and chrysanthemums. The card read, "Good to have you back. From the OPP Bliss River Detachment."

I left the study and made my way to the kitchen. Never one to be outdone, Lilith had placed an even larger bouquet of crimson roses in the kitchen. I walked the few feet to the butler's closet–turned-office, hesitating in the doorway. It was like the attempt on my life had never happened. The room was immaculate and smelled mildly of lemon disinfectant. Someone had remade the cot with clean white sheets. Even the desk had been straightened, and I chuckled. Someone had placed Bliss River postcards by the library books. Beside the fanned stack, a pencil cup held an array of pens from the tourist office, including one topped with a googly-eyed "Blissy the Happy Beaver." The gesture was classic Lilith, the one with a sense of humour and a love for pranks. I'd thought her long gone.

I picked up a postcard—a pretty one of the river— and considered sending out a few, penning something like, *Hey, I had a near-death experience while helping to*

solve a homicide. Oh, and the locals have it out for me.
Glad you're not here.

Instead, I once again organized my desk before heading back to the mural.

Rosemary's eyes followed me, almost beseechingly. Soon, I was on the scaffolding, dabbing at the surface of the mural. I began to focus on the river. The muddied surface's hues changed from murky grey to a dozen shades of blue and green. Blood trickled into the water, trailing down the river like a thin, red vein. The reflected Christmas lights wavered in the shallows. I half expected my swab to reveal something menacing in the depths, but after several hours, all I'd revealed was Boyland's imagery. I stepped off the scaffolding, frustrated.

The knock at the door made me jump. "Break time," Mac said, carrying a bag.

He filled me in on his morning. He'd had to contend with numerous wolf sighting reports and one vandalism charge. I let him know my morning had been disappointing.

His lips twitched. "I met up with Barb Martin."

"And!"

"Hold on." He began to clear away our garbage. "You were right. Again. Yes, she had some old photos, and yes, there was a necklace. Rosemary wore it often. According to Barb, it was a large, heart-shaped locket. She'd often ask Rosemary to open it, but Rosemary kept its contents secret." Mac paused. "Would you like to see the photos?"

"I think so." A week ago, my answer would have been more decisive. A week ago, I hadn't felt motherly about a girl I'd never met, could never meet. "Yes. I'd like to see them."

Mac handed me the black-and-white snapshots. Rosemary's bright hair appeared a drab grey, but the lack of colour had no effect on her curls. Barb, on the other hand, once had possessed waist-long blonde tresses as straight as railroad tracks. The photos had captured stereotypical girls' play of the era, dolls and tea sets. There was a total of five square photos.

I used a magnifying glass, and there it was: the heart locket. It was egg-sized and embossed with a rose. I saw a running theme. My gaze moved from the jewelry to the smile above it. She looked at peace with her place in the world, as if there was nothing to fear and nothing could hurt her. Young Barb's eyelashes had once been as long as wild grass.

Rosemary wore a different outfit in all five photographs; it seemed each picture had been taken on a different day. One picture showed spring flowers in the background while another showed late summer blooms, but I noticed Rosemary wore the necklace in all five pictures.

"Fayette never once mentioned the locket?"

"No. And like you, I'm wondering why."

"Mac? Do you think you'll catch the killer?"

He took a deep breath. "If we're right, he's alive. And he's scared. He *will* slip up."

After he left, I studied the mural, deciding to work on the skyline.

I wasn't surprised Boyland had used the sunset to halo Rosemary. The mural was a shrine. I continued to reveal the ethereal shades that hovered over her and exposed blots on the horizon. The splotches were crows, seven of them.

Curious, I opened my laptop, typed into Google "crows + superstition" and had my answer. Seven crows is the devil himself.

13

ROSEMARY'S AURA OUTSHONE the stars. Seeing me, her eyes brightened. I tried to get to her, but the path was slippery. Her small hands raised, and I thought she was going to beckon to me. Instead, she unclasped her necklace and wrapped the thin, gold chain around one finger, letting the locket dangle. It swung like a pendulum, winking in the moonlight as I sank deeper and deeper into loamy soil. The repetitive trilling of a whippoor-will reminded me of an alarm. Its endless fretting almost hid another noise, a squelching sound that put my heart in my throat. Someone was coming. Rosemary and I turned toward the footsteps. She shook her head and raised a finger to her mouth. Terrified, I froze. Reeds parted and a hand grabbed hold of me.

Rosemary screamed as I tried to twist free.

"Miss Garde? What are you doing out here?"

Where was I? "Constable Johnston?"

He looked worried, and I didn't blame him. I stood a hair's breadth from the river. My damp nightgown clung to me, and my feet were caked in muck. Grey had begun to tint the sky, which meant it was predawn.

It had been twenty years since I'd walked in my sleep.

Though I knew she'd been part of a dream, I couldn't stop staring at the spot where I'd seen Rosemary. She couldn't have been there, and yet her scream still rang in my ears. The mud and the moon were real enough, but no whip-poor-will warbled.

Johnston placed his hand under my elbow as if I were feeble. Though the gallantry irritated me, I let him escort me back to the parsonage and assist me up the steps.

"My little brother used to play video games in his sleep."

He was trying to be kind, so I asked, "How's the baby?"

"Declan's always hungry. He keeps Amy up all night, but it barely fazes her."

I felt stupidly vulnerable. "Well, goodnight and thank you."

Once inside, I locked the door. I thought about my mother, about what I'd put her through. For two years, she'd tried to keep me safe. The somnambulism had been debilitating for both of us. My condition had led to her long bout with insomnia and an occasional panic attack. I wasn't alarmed that my sleep disorder had reappeared. Most likely, exhaustion, stress, and the details of this case had caused a single reoccurrence. At least, I hoped it was a single reoccurrence.

I tramped upstairs to wash the mud off my feet, leaving a trail of footprints behind me. The dirty floor could wait. A walk would help shake off my anxiety. I dressed in jeans and a hoodie, then set off for the beach. The sun hadn't yet risen. A raccoon waddled across the street as if it wasn't the least bit intimidated by my presence, as if it owned each yard.

With their manicured lawns and same-same-sameness, the suburbs are my idea of purgatory. Still, Bliss River was beautiful, a lakeside village surrounded by wilderness, and the old cottages I walked past had a certain charm. Sandy walkways rambled toward such rough-and-tumble front porches. I dug my hands into my pockets and kept my pace slow and even. The sound of waves grew ever louder. There is something uplifting about a great body of water. It's as if all that vastness, its breadth, reduces problems to their proper size.

I found a bench and sat down. The sunrise was worth the wait. Sunsets on Lake Huron were legendary, attracting both professional and amateur photographers, but the way morning broke over those waters took my breath away. It was as though Night was bashful and Day had made it blush. Seagulls scolded me as I strolled along the shoreline. I returned to the parsonage, level-headed yet tired, so I set my alarm and took a nap. When I awoke, I was ready to get down to business.

By noon, I'd completed the skyline. I'd finished cleaning three quarters of the painting.

All that was left was its top left quadrant. I studied the trees, the glade, almost falling off the scaffolding as something boomed. The beep of a jalopy horn made me jump. I kept forgetting about that crotchety old Ford.

As it sputtered away, what I heard next had me running for the front door and tearing it open. A fire truck. I held my breath, hoping I was wrong. I wasn't. Another and then another fire truck joined the first.

Constable Andrews motioned for me to go back inside. It all felt so chillingly familiar. I searched the sky over the rooftops. This time, I couldn't find smoke, saw no evidence of a fire. People again gathered on the sidewalk, turning in circles and squinting at the horizon. I considered joining them, but I knew it would put Andrews in a tough position—either to guard me or the mural. Instead, I turned on the radio, and sure enough, the regular programing had been interrupted by breaking news. Local firefighters were battling two blazes. An abandoned cottage was engulfed by flames on the east side of town while an old sugar shack on the west side was burning out of control, and it had spread to the woodlands that surrounded one ward. The fire was threatening nearby farms.

They were calling in reinforcements from other municipalities, from as far away as Sudbury. Fire rangers were already on the scene. Residents were warned to stay off the highway and to stay tuned in, as an evacuation might be necessary. Across the room, Rosemary studied me. It was so damned frustrating. There was nothing I could do.

Feeling resigned, I gathered my supplies and packed them up. I secured all my chemicals, placed the kits by the door, and did the same with my clothing, wondering if I was being overly cautious. I wasn't.

The DJ didn't hide her concern as she warned, "The fire on Lakeshore Road has been put out, but the fire on rural road thirty-three is continuing to spread. The residents on Mill Road and Spring Road have been evacuated. Please, be prepared to leave in the eventuality this fire is not contained in the next hour. Your cooperation is needed. Remain calm."

I finished packing the rest of my belongings. Twice I picked up the phone, wanting to call Mac, just to hear his voice. I also wondered how Lilith was and if she needed my help. I'd become less of her friend over the last week, though my intention had been to reconnect with her. Our worlds were so far apart. We'd been nothing alike as young women either, but we'd still *liked* each other. The new tension between us was caused by outside influences.

I called her, unsure of what I'd say.

"Hello? Is someone there?" She spoke before I'd heard one ring.

"It's Annora."

"Hon? I was about to phone you. I heard you sigh, but I hadn't even entered the number. Uncanny, right?"

"Are you okay?"

"I can't believe this is happening. The fire's just a few kilometres up the road from us. Four farmhouses have been lost." Her voice shook. "This has to be arson. Somebody is putting lives at risk, endangering the whole town. My head's spinning."

"I could come over. Help you pack up."

I heard her take a long, deep breath. "I appreciate that, but we've loaded up all we can take. You should head out too. Nory, you've already done so much, and I haven't come close to thanking you enough. I regret getting you involved in this mess. I'm so sorry. I should have called sooner. I should have—"

"Rosemary deserves justice. And I'm holding off on leaving for a bit longer."

"I'm supposed to be leading by example, putting on the brave face, but I'm scared too. Some mayor I am, right?"

"Hey? You've got this." I agreed to call her if I needed to leave.

I gazed out the window. The lady across the street was chucking boxes into the back of her truck. Dozens of cars drove by, many of them filled with children. Parents must have picked up their kids from school. It was a pandemonium of panic. The people of Bliss River stood to lose everything. As frustrated as I felt, this was not my home.

I decided to load up my Jeep, just in case. I started down the path with my haul, but Constable Johnston met me halfway and asked me to put my bags down.

"I'm sure you're stronger than you look—no offense," he said. "But you're on light duty, and Mac will ream me out if I let you carry all that alone."

"You should be with your family."

"Amy and Declan are on their way to her mom's place in Huntsville."

As we loaded up the car, I noticed the young reverend hosing down the roof of his church with a garden hose. It was such a futile thing to do, so faith driven and irrepressibly stalwart that I felt a kind of odd appreciation for his actions. Without knowing what to say, I crossed the church's front lawn. Though it had rained, the brown grass crunched beneath my feet.

His smile was sad. "So, you're on your way, then?"

"If I'm told I have to go, I'll go."

He continued to water the roof as if it were a flower bed, as if it were an everyday occurrence. "St. George's is older than the town, built on sacrifices and the generosity of parishioners." His shoulders slumped. "It's my charge, but I can't protect it from an inferno."

"I was in Funchal, the largest city on Madeira, when fire hit the island. The blaze wiped out woodlands, homes, livelihoods. Three hundred people were hospitalized."

A flock of blackbirds darkened the sky, and we winced at their frantic cries.

I waited until they'd flown off before continuing. "The fire was quite a distance from the Sacred Art Museum, where I was, but the smoke, those horrible plumes, were visible for miles." I glanced at the church's gothic windows. "Three thousand hectares burned. Thousands lost their homes, and there was nothing they could do. Eventually, the fire was brought under control." I cleared my throat. "Not far from here, many dedicated people are trying to put out another fire, save other homes, save lives. But buildings can be replaced. Lives cannot."

"Right." He straightened his shoulders and put down the hose. Water trickled toward the sidewalk. "Ms. Garde, how do you feel about prayer?"

"Dubious at best. Guess it can't hurt, though."

He chortled. "My name's Sawyer. How about you and I join the neighbours?"

"I'm the outsider poking into the past. I think many just wish I'd go home."

"'Be among men and things, and among troubles, and difficulties, and obstacles.'"

"Jesus?"

"Not quite. Henry Drummond."

Across the street, a face popped out from of a second-floor window. A woman yelled, "The fire's out! It's over!"

Old and young began to embrace each other, and I turned, intending to head back to the parsonage, but Sawyer would have none of it. He looped his elbow around mine and said, "And why would you want to miss out on the celebration? Why not join in? It can't hurt, right?"

Constable Johnston lost his hat as he jogged over. "Looks like you're staying!"

I was relieved, but I also knew three fires in less than two days meant there were more to come. The neighbours returned to their homes. They were excited, giving triumphant whoops. I said nothing as I walked back to the church with Sawyer. He, too, was quiet.

"I wanted to give you something. I mean, I wanted to give you something to keep in the parsonage for the remainder of your stay." He asked, "Will you come inside for a moment?"

We walked to his small but serviceable office. I admired the rich wood floors and the tall bookcases. Sawyer's collection of snow globes—of all things—filled three shelves. I'd ask him about them some other day. He fished through his desk's contents.

"Now, where did I . . . aha! Here it is." He slowly removed an old, leather lectern bible from the bottom drawer. Its leather cover gleamed, despite its age. He reverently placed the book on a felt square. "Since the murder, people have reported seeing a ghost peering through the parsonage windows or wading in the river." His hands dove into the drawer again, and he pulled out an ornate wood cross.

"You don't actually believe the parsonage is haunted, do you?"

"One night I thought . . . I don't know what I saw. But it wasn't of this world." He placed the cross beside the bible. "Once, these were housed in the parsonage. Would you do me a favour and keep these items in your quarters for the remainder of your stay? Humour me?"

I thanked him and carried the sacred antiquities back to their original home. Out of respect, I placed the bible on the small desk, though it crowded the workspace. I took a landscape print off the wall and carefully placed it in the kitchen pantry. Then, I hung up the cross. It was beautifully crafted, like wooden lace. How many hours had it taken to complete? How many fingers before mine had lightly traced its Celtic pattern?

At five, I realized that I needed to go shopping again. I was weighing my options when Mac's truck pulled up. His day must have been grueling, one crisis following another.

His jaw clenched. There was no preamble. "We're under siege," he growled. "If we don't find this lunatic soon, someone just lighting a barbeque will end up getting bushwhacked." He raked his hands through his hair. "You hungry? Wanna grab a bite to eat?"

I tried to ignore the fluttery feeling in my chest. "Should I change?"

"Why? Oh. Um, Bonnie's Fish and Chips is very casual. Would you prefer—"

"Sounds perfect." I grabbed my purse.

Bonnie's was a cheery little place, flamboyantly decorated in Black Watch tartan and lace.

Locals packed the eatery, but our timing was ideal. The tucked-in-the-corner table had just been cleared. We seated ourselves. A nearby exit door kept the table isolated and lent us more privacy. The place had a unique laissez-faire approach to service. Instead of a regular menu, there was a tick-off-your-selection menu pad. Amused, I checked off my choices. A server brought over a jug of water and some dinner rolls.

Mac leaned forward and lowered his voice. "We'll be instating an emergency curfew law, effective tomorrow." He frowned. "Still, today's fires were started in broad daylight."

"It's official? The fires are suspicious?"

"Arson has been confirmed. Both places were firebombed."

"Could there be more than one culprit?"

He rubbed his forehead. "Possible. In fact, if it were homes or businesses being targeted, this could even look like a terrorist attack. But—so far—the arsonist has selected vacant buildings. I'm not convinced he or she meant for more than a shack to burn."

"Any idea of the motive?"

"My gut's saying it was a diversion."

"Then I'd better finish what I started."

After dinner, we took a short walk along the pier. A cabin cruiser docked, and Mac called out a greeting to the skipper. They exchanged friendly waves and a bit of good-natured ribbing about fishing and trophies as we headed back to the truck. I tried to decompress as we drove to the parsonage.

Twilight in autumn makes me restless. Shorter days feel unnatural. I was already wound up, already edgy, so when I heard the fire truck, I gasped. It rounded a corner and sped down the road, heading in the opposite direction.

"You've got to be kidding me!" Mac did a three-point turn and gave chase.

We pulled down a side street I recognized and parked the car. I threw open the door and stumbled over the curb, dazed by the scene unfolding before me.

Flames had engulfed the Boyland carriage house.

Firefighters blasted their hoses at the outbuilding and nearby estate. Even from a distance, the waves of heat could be felt. The roof rippled and a window exploded, causing the crowd to gasp.

Mac turned to me and muttered, "This day just got a helluva lot longer."

14

JANE STOOD IN her neighbour's yard amongst a troop of supporters. Lilith was glued to her side as if the older woman might collapse, but Jane appeared composed. I wondered if she was in shock. Her clenched fists suggested otherwise. Jane looked ready to take on the arsonist herself.

High flames hissed, reaching out to lay claim to her beloved family estate. Another window exploded, Lilith shrieked, and the throng shrank back from the inferno. But Jane raised her chin and straightened the collar of her housecoat. My mother would have called her "plucky."

Another ladder truck arrived. An exhausted crew pushed them closer to the breaking point. Yet, somehow, they manned up, hitting the fire with every reserve of energy they had left. It was awe-inspiring to watch them dig in their heels, work together side by side, and refuse to waver as the fire fought back, surging and hazing the asphalt under their feet.

Mac handed me the keys to his truck and encouraged me to go back to the parsonage. It would, perhaps, have been the wiser decision. Instead, I greeted Sawyer when he pulled up in his rusty Fiat. His face paled as he grasped the magnitude of the fire and the imminent risk to the heritage house. We stood by the car and spoke briefly. Despite his youth and inexperience, Sawyer exuded a type of calm that defied explanation. He strode through the crowd, spoke to Jane, and then curved an arm around her thin shoulders. We all watched as the firefighters put their backs into extinguishing the massive blaze.

When the flames diminished, the locals gave a wary cheer. Distress and disbelief remained etched on their faces. The residents of Bliss River understood an enemy lived amongst them, a nemesis eager to set anything ablaze. First, nobody said a word, but soon small pools of conversations began to erupt here and there. I heard the gradual change in tones. Fury replaced fear. People congregated and did not return to their homes, though the police advised them to do so. Three constables attempted to soothe the angry throng.

Mac was on the phone. His expression was hard to read, but I sensed the situation had worsened, if that was possible.

He ended the call and headed toward me, but before he'd walked more than a few steps, Jane called out, "Everyone, can I have your attention?"

Almost immediately, the crowd quieted. "Friends, please go home. Tomorrow, I will be offering a ten-thousand-dollar reward for any information that leads to the arrest of this criminal who starts these fires and risks our lives."

People murmured excitedly, and nobody moved.

Jane pressed on. "Thank you for being here *for* me, for being here *with* me. I'll never forget your kindnesses, but, please, please, do what our police are asking and let them do their jobs. We need to help them best by returning to our homes."

Her words struck a chord. Dozens filed past her, respectfully, and several seniors paused to pat her hand, offering a few words of support. Within fifteen minutes, the crowd had dispersed, though intermittent sparks flared, and firefighters continued to hose down a few stubborn embers.

I waved goodbye to Sawyer and climbed into Mac's truck. He quickly joined me. The fire was almost out, but he looked like he was about to step into the ring.

"What's happened now?" I asked.

"They've found a body."

"What!" My mouth went dry as I stared at the coach house. "Here? Could it be Len?"

"Human remains were discovered at the Lakeshore fire. The cottage was thought to be vacant." He hesitated. "The victim had a pacemaker. Len doesn't. But Floyd does. Did."

"Wait a minute. The main suspect is dead?" My voice sounded shrill, even to me.

"Could it have been an accident, could he have—"

"He was shot in the back of the head."

I struggled with the news, could barely grasp it. "I can't see Len as the murderer."

"He's missing. Why? James was questioned, and he was cooperative. Neither legally owns a gun, and we have no evidence to link either of them to the murder. Yet . . ."

"I think I'd better get back to the parsonage." The urgency of the situation grew with each passing hour. "The past is catching up to Rosemary's killer, and he knows it."

"The post-mortem should be completed by mid-morning. I've scheduled a press conference. Jane's been forewarned." He frowned. "Someone torched her property; her half-brother's dead, and her best friend is nowhere to be found. How much more can she take?"

"You'd be surprised how tough women are."

He started the truck. "Yeah, I've seen that grit up close."

We didn't speak as he drove. He pulled up to the parsonage. I gazed at the building through the car window, burdened by an even greater sense of responsibility than I'd felt before. It was late. A pot of coffee could help me pull off another all-nighter.

Mac sized me up. "Tomorrow, we hit this. Tomorrow."

There was my signal to step out of the vehicle, but I didn't want to say goodnight, walk past Rosemary, not quite yet. "Did you sense it would get this violent?"

"Hell, no."

"He's not going to turn himself in, is he?"

He rubbed his neck. "No, I don't think this will end well."

I didn't want to think about Mac's duties. Small town or not, his job came with risks. Still, my father had been a teacher, and his vocation hadn't kept him out of harm's way.

As we walked toward the parsonage, the rookie constable gave Mac an exaggerated thumbs-up, and I pretended not to see him flip Andrews the bird. I also ignored the slight flush working up from his collar. His face practically glowed. Did he find me attractive? Scott MacGowan was far too interesting. He stood close to me, close enough I could have kissed him. And I so wanted to kiss him.

He tucked one of my curls behind an ear. "We've got to do something about those eyes."

He lowered his voice. "I'm supposed to be concentrating on the case. You're incredibly distracting, Egghead."

"So," I said, "we'll always have Paris?"

"I want to get to know you better. I can't stop imagining us together. Paris would be a mind-blowing, non-stop ride. Unforgettable." I lost the ability to speak, nodded, and headed inside. I stood there for another five minutes after he'd left, waiting for my pulse to slow and for me to stop picturing French kisses and fireworks and those warm hands of his, roving.

❧

I was too late. There was blood in my mouth and blood in my eyes. Everything bled—the sky, the ground, the water. Rosemary watched me with crimson eyes. The top of her head was grotesquely concave, and the ends of her hair dripped red, red, red. I tried to take a step forward, but she grabbed my hand and tugged me back toward the parsonage. As gently as I could, I towed her in the opposite direction, toward the riverside. She shook her head and sent pulpy droplets flying. I inhaled gore as I wiped her face, again and again. Her brow wouldn't come clean, no matter how hard I tried. Trustingly, she laid her cheek on my palm, and her young life leaked out between my fingers.

She lifted her head, and her face began to flatten as she backed away. She turned from me, looked over her left shoulder, and started to sing, "Rock-a-bye . . . in the tree . . . the tree . . .

Her lips closed, shaped themselves into an enigmatic smile that had become familiar.

Though she did not speak, I could still hear her. She glided away from me, and the splatter lifted off her, pulsed overhead, like a gruesome version of Van Gogh's stars, as if the carnage had a life all of its own. Skin brightened and the white of her eyes returned as she floated back, back, back onto the mural. She blinked repeatedly and froze into position. I took one step and almost fell off the scaffolding.

My gut twisted as I woke up. Somehow I'd made my way through the dark kitchen, past the barrier, and into the dim front parlour. The room was not quite pitch-black, thanks to un-curtained windows and the glow cast by streetlamps. Still, even awake, it would be difficult to maneuver around the intersecting extension cords. How I'd stepped onto the narrow wood plank without ending up with my face planted on the floor was a mystery.

Night camouflaged the mural. I turned on the lights and glared at the clock. Five AM.

I'd never get back to sleep. Instead, I took a two-minute shower, made a strong pot of coffee, and returned to the scaffolding. *Which tree, Rosemary?* There were several I hadn't yet touched.

I chose an oak and began at its roots. I revealed a small rabbit. It sat on its haunches with raised ears, as if it heard an approaching threat. Next, I lavished attention on the base of the tree, wondering what else I'd find there. A swab exposed an odd, yellow shape. I kept dabbing. As more of it was revealed, I realized it was a boot. A child's rubber boot.

The turtle pace was nerve-wracking. Hours passed as I cleaned the boots, the knees above them, a torso. Out of nowhere, a tiny face peeked-out from behind the weathered oak.

Someone had witnessed the murder. A girl with a contorted face and waist-length, platinum-blond hair. I was sure I recognized the girl, but I hoped I was wrong.

It was mid-morning, so Mac was in the midst of a media circus. I decided to postpone the call. Wearily, I shuffled to the study and plopped onto the window seat. The doc had been right about it taking time to feel like my old self.

Sun streamed through the window, and the repetitive rustling sound of a neighbour raking leaves was oddly lulling. My head fell back against the cushion. Maybe a short rest was warranted.

The smell of dark roast brewed to perfection woke me. Wait . . . I hadn't . . . I opened my eyes. Mac had squatted down beside me. His expression was a sensual mix of humour and concern. He held out a large cup, invitingly.

I reached for it. "Thank you," I said before taking a slow, appreciative sip.

"I knocked, and you didn't so much as budge." He stood and looked at me quizzically.

"Couldn't sleep."

"About last night, I shouldn't have—"

"Oh no, you don't, MacGowan. No takey-backsies," I teased, faking a confidence I did not feel. *"Non, je ne regrette rein."*

He laughed, and the room got very warm. "So what's up?"

"Nothing."

He leaned against the wall. He kept standing there, waiting, as if we weren't in a rush to find a killer, as if some homicidal firebug wasn't humming his next torch song.

Shyly, gracelessly, I told him about my sleepwalking. I told him about my exploits as a young adult. Like the time I'd been found circling the top level of a parking tower, and the time I awoke on my bicycle. He asked me about preventative measures. It was humiliating, in a way. I can fine-tune an engine, take down a pickpocket, drywall, even scuba dive. But sleepwalking was a weakness, another obstacle neither Mac nor I needed during this investigation.

I ran out of words, feeling ridiculous, and a part of me wanted to hide.

He walked toward me and offered me his hand. We stood face to face. I hadn't expected him to pull me into a tight, comforting hug. His chin rested on the top of my head. He pulled me even closer and said, "Confession: I talk in my sleep."

Unconvinced, I tilted my head back, checking to see if he was serious.

"Yes, ma'am. I do not lie. I've been known to sweet talk, baby talk, and back talk. Once I wake up, I can't remember a word I've said." He chuckled. "Back in Police College, my roomies used to record me mouthing off offense codes in my sleep."

It was difficult to extract myself from his arms. Our cuddle felt so good, so right, but if I didn't put space between us, I would glue myself to him. I backed up, yet I couldn't seem to break eye contact.

"Sunglasses." He groaned. "We'll get you a pair of ugly, dark ones. Huge granny horned rims the colour of pea soup."

"Okay, mister. Enough of that." I picked up his favourite toy—the head-mounted magnifier. I handed it to him and said, "Rosemary wasn't alone."

One moment he was Mac, the tease, and the next, he was Mac, the cop. He grabbed the magnifier. "Show me," he said. "Where?"

I had a hard time keeping up with him. Since we'd only be in the room a few minutes and I'd already cleaned away so much of the mould, neither of us had suited up, but we had put on our masks. We approached the mural, and I pointed to the tree.

He zoomed in on the girl, studied her for several minutes, and cursed.

We left the room and headed back to the study.

"Is it her?" I asked.

"Don't know. But yeah, it could be Barb Martin."

"If she'd seen anything, wouldn't she have said something after all these years?"

His expression was hard to read. "I'll question her, but I'm not going to grill the woman.

I've known that sweet lady my whole life. Hell, she was my Scout leader."

"Bet you got all your badges."

"Watch it."

"I'd pay big bucks for a picture of little-rascal you in a cub's uniform."

His eyes glinted with a smile. "Go on. Keep it up."

Gulp. I let my gaze skitter away. "I missed the news conference."

"The pacemaker's serial number matched the one in Floyd's medical records. If only there was as simple a way to ID the killer."

"This murder might have nothing to do with the past and everything to do with the present. You mentioned exes."

"Possible. But not probable. Dead men don't pay alimony. He made it known the academy would be the sole beneficiary of his entire estate—his art, property, and all his holdings and investments go to the school. He may have been a sadistic ass, but his death will benefit the town. The bequest will provide scholarships and help hundreds of young artists." Mac pulled up his jacket's zipper and put on his hat. "We should both get back to work."

"Thanks for the coffee."

"I feel like an enabler."

"I'll cut back to my four cups a day once this job is complete."

"Then, it'll be back to the bubbly water?"

I laughed. "It's French, you know."

"Ah, yes, that explains a lot. *Au revoir, chérie.*" He turned, opened the door, and started to whistle "La Marseillaise." He continued to whistle the tune as he sauntered down the path.

I glanced at the chair where I'd napped, where he'd crouched beside me as I slept. The thought of him watching over me made me quiver in the most wonderful way. I thought about what could have happened if I'd kept teasing him. I remembered how well our bodies fit. If only I could forget I'd be leaving Bliss River in another week.

15

I'D MADE SOME progress with the tree. Its right side had been cleansed from its root to its top branch. I'd focused on the second girl. Additional cleansing revealed the oddity of her clothing. I couldn't tell if she was dressed in an oversized coat or a badly hand-knit sweater. White? Symbolic or realistic? The sleeves were long, as if the girl wore a hand-me-down. The look of horror on her miniaturized face was the stuff of nightmares and would give Edvard Munch's *The Scream* a run for its money.

Hunger annoys me. It interrupts my work and forces me to change gears. I checked the weather and put on an additional layer. I'd just opened the door, when the phone rang. I read the number and sighed. "Can I call you back?"

"Not until you tell me why my mom-dar is going off the charts."

I weighed my options. If I told her too much, I'd be on the phone for hours, but If I kept her in the dark, and she heard the news elsewhere, she'd obsess and worry herself to death. "Here's the short version. An arsonist is setting fires, but I'll be finished with my work here in a few days and—"

"And!"

And I'm attracted to the cop in charge of the case. "The authorities are all over this. The parsonage is under police protection. I'm safe, okay?"

"Mm-hmm. I'm beginning to wonder about the long version."

"Mom, I need to cut this short. I skipped lunch."

I heard a pen clicking. Something she did when she felt confused or overwhelmed. "I know you can take care of yourself. I'm just a worrywart." She sniffled. "Honey? You're a resilient, capable powerhouse, and I'm proud of you."

My eyes teared. "As soon as this is all over, I'll come for a visit. Promise."

Before something else delayed me, I scooted out the door but paused long enough to wave to Constable Patel. The street was quiet. As I drove, I noted the reduced traffic. People were not venturing far. I passed several seniors sitting on their front porches, watching and waiting. They sensed a face-off approaching, felt its inevitability.

Take-out seemed the best option, so I parked at the Lucky Dragon Palace. I placed an outrageously large order, so there'd be leftovers for days. I let the cashier know I'd return in twenty minutes. Across the street from the restaurant, there was a village green. A flock of geese jam-packed its small pond. I recognized the man whittling on one of the benches. He did not look happy. His Scottish terrier, however, wagged its tail enthusiastically as I neared them. I sat down beside Mig Daybutch. The dog licked my hand, and I petted its head, smiling as it flopped down at my feet with a snort.

Mig kept carving, his movements agitated. "Same crime. Same mistakes."

"Mistakes?"

"Barb Martin. So help me, if I hear she was harassed—""

"She isn't a suspect." *Had I said too much?*

"Cops know that some kids are plain evil." He turned to me. "But Barb Martin was a caring, gentle girl, and she would not protect the butcher who killed our friend." His voice broke. "For over twenty years, that woman helped keep me sane and fought for my release. I know her story, and she knows mine. Whatever her secrets are, they will not identify the killer." His knife slipped and he nicked a knuckle. "And I want that monster to suffer."

His words sent a chill down my spine. "The police—"

"The police see what they want to see."

I hesitated, then asked, "What do you make of Inspector MacGowan?"

"Mac?" The frown lifted. "He's a good man. His father's son."

"How do you think he'd treat Barb?"

"He's a good judge of character." He gave me a knowing look. "Ah. I see your point. He'll treat her with kid gloves."

I glanced at the penknife in his hand. "What are you making?"

"Dunno. The wood hasn't told me yet what it wants to be. It will."

I wished him a good day, gave the dog one more pat, and returned to the restaurant. I lugged two bags of food to the Jeep. Within minutes, I stood on the porch, ferreting though my purse for the parsonage key.

When the door swung open, I jumped.

Mac eyed the bags. "Get any General Tao chicken?"

"Funny. I took you for a steak guy."

"Sure, I like a good porterhouse." He relieved me of the heftier of the two bags. "But I love spice—tandoori, wasabi, five-alarm chili. You?"

As we walked toward the kitchen, I boasted, "Won a jalapeño eating contest, once."

"Did it involve tequila shots?"

"Maaaay-be."

We opened the take-out boxes and served ourselves. Mac had been decorating again.

Two bar stools had been added to the kitchen. I arched an eyebrow at him.

"Barb wasn't a witness, but she found Rosemary before my grandfather did." He cleared his throat. "You already know the horror she faced. She ran home and told her parents. They forced her to keep it a secret, feeling since she didn't witness the murder, her testimony wasn't needed. Finding her friend that way was . . ."

"Traumatizing."

Mac poked at his food. "Rosemary asked Barb to meet her behind the parsonage at nine. Barb said she would but didn't. She changed her mind again and snuck out around eleven." The words were softly spoken. "She believes if she'd arrived earlier, Rosemary would still be alive."

"She's carried that guilt with her all these years?"

"It hasn't incapacitated her. But she's never forgiven herself."

"Doesn't she realize what she was up against?" I felt for the woman, identified with her. "He'd have had a second victim."

"Like you said, those scars haven't faded. I doubt they ever will."

A riot of crows was a welcome interruption. I asked him about Grace.

He grinned. "She likes you. Keeps grilling me in texts. I haven't had . . . I mean, I haven't dated since—"

I gave him an out. "Mmm, you were right about this chicken."

Between bites, I told him about my three-month stay in Hong Kong, courtesy of an art conservation exchange program. The awkward moment disappeared as I blathered on about my ten-by-fifteen "spacious" apartment, Fujian opera, blown-sugar candies, the Po Lin Monastery and my costly introduction to mah-jong. I gazed down at his left hand and stopped babbling. Mac no longer wore his wedding ring. The implication wasn't lost on me. Reeling from the observation, I took a long sip of water.

Together, we tidied the kitchen. I opened the fridge to put away the leftovers, and my heart did a little jig. Mac had picked me up more Perrier, goat's cheese, and a few other things. I thanked him for his thoughtfulness, and he thanked me for the entertainment. It was best to keep our relationship professional, and sex was out of the question. I repeated this to myself as if it were a mantra. He opened the door and we stepped onto the porch.

A woman frantically crisscrossed the street. "Lucy!" She screamed. "Lucy, where are you? Lucy!"

Mac rushed down the steps. He and the woman met up in front of his squad car. The woman's hands kept moving. She pointed down the street, raked her fingers through her hair, and finally covered her face. Her body shook, and Mac wrapped an arm around her quaking shoulders. My hand flew to my mouth. Without hearing a word, I knew what was being said.

A child was missing.

ॐॐ

Lucy Quesnel, nine, had not returned from Bliss River Elementary. The school was half a kilometre from the Quesnel's bungalow. Doug, her father, dropped her off most mornings, but she'd been walking herself home since September. She was proud of her new independence, and she did not dawdle. Though she'd only been missing an hour, her mother, Tess, was adamant something was wrong. Lucy had missed her piano lessons, and she'd been looking forward to them all week. Those travelling the roads and highways were to keep a lookout for a girl matching her description. I gazed at her picture, and my blood froze. Lucy had strawberry-blond hair and fair skin. Mac issued an Amber Alert.

Lucy Quesnel was last seen wearing a pink ruffled jacket with hood, jeans, a shirt with a pony pattern, and bumblebee rain boots.

Residents were asked to look high and low, to check boathouses and garden sheds.

Parents were encouraged to question their children, and a search party was organized. The sun would set in a few hours.

Constable Johnston and I headed behind the parsonage.

"We moved here two years ago," he said. "We thought Bliss River would be a great place to raise a family." His expression turned stony. "The Quesnels moved here from Toronto this past summer. They probably thought the same thing."

Once we reached the water's edge, I turned left and he turned right. We began to comb through the tall reeds. I hadn't walked very far when I tripped over something, something half-submerged in the muck. It was a boot, a yellow-and-black-striped boot. Johnston came running. I don't recall screaming, and I don't know if I yelled a name. I'd been holding onto the impossible hope the boot was old, that it had been lost weeks ago, but the name written in black marker obliterated all doubt. It belonged to Lucy.

The sun sank as both the OPP marine unit and volunteers took to the river. The owner of the hardware store donated every pair of fishing waders he had in stock. Dozens arrived wearing their own. Those of us with high rubber boots slogged out as far as we could. A hundred more used walking sticks to probe the wetlands. The temperature dropped, and there was a forty percent probability of snow. Each breath became a small, white ghost. My feet became numb, even though I'd been given thermal socks. Several times, I slipped and caught myself; the riverbed sludge made the search all the more difficult.

A vigil was held by those unable to physically help with the search. Behind the church, a dozen people gathered with Sawyer in a tight circle. They held hands and prayed, stood with the help of canes and walkers. Some sat in wheelchairs. The woman's auxiliary had managed to put together a warm-up station. Barb Martin offered hot drinks and soup to those who were chilled. Though I'd been in Bliss River for a short time, I recognized

several people—the librarian, Mig Daybutch, constables, and firefighters. I was staggered when Jane rushed
toward me.

She thanked me for my help and said I'd "obviously
been raised right."

A bonfire was lit. Searchers periodically warmed
themselves, whispering sadly to each other. The
Quesnels haunted the banks, turned their backs to the
murky shallows, and called to their daughter over and
over. Their desperate pleas became more and more panicked. Lilith walked *with* them, called *with* them. John
was one of the links in the human chain spanning the
waterway.

Mac steered a boat downstream to check each bend.
The sun was sinking fast. Someone shouted, "They've
found her! She's okay! She's okay!"

Everyone burst out with a thankful hooray. Relief
brought tears to my eyes, but I saw the pattern: a situation endangered the town, residents gathered, and the
threat was eventually defeated. Patterns are unreliable.
I understand the erratic nature of the "butterfly effect."
Bliss River was not immune to further devastation.
Though fires had been put out and one child had been
found, tragedy would strike again. How long before the
townsfolk realized they hadn't yet won the war, that it
was still underway?

They added more wood to the bonfire. A flask was
passed around, and nobody questioned its contents.
Some linked elbows. Several couples kissed. Sawyer
bounded down the hill with a guitar. He settled onto
a log and began to strum a popular tune. I should have
left those good people to their persevering cheerfulness.
Instead, I joined them, making a conscious effort to echo

the joyful exchanges. Mig stood nearby. His expression told me I hadn't fooled him. He knew that this search may be over, but I was still on the hunt, trying to find someone.

My cell rang. I moved away from the victory celebration, dashed to a quieter spot under a maple, and checked the number. "How's Lucy? "

"She has mild hypothermia, but she'll be fine."

"What happened?"

"The classroom salamander died, so she decided to replace it. When her boots got stuck in the mud, she was afraid she'd get grounded and miss her best friend's Halloween party. She hid out in said best friend's tree house." Though he was sharing good news—great news—something about his tone sent a chill down my spine. "Her parents smothered her in kisses and haven't let her go since she was found. Lucky girl. Not all of us are that lucky."

The bonfire sent tiny sparks toward the stars. "Where are you?"

He didn't answer and I thought we'd been disconnected.

"Mac?"

"I'm at the morgue."

I almost dropped the phone.

"First, we found Lucy," he wearily said, "then we found Len."

I MASKED MY SHOCK, waving to the other searchers as I trudged toward the parsonage. He told me the cause of death couldn't be determined without an autopsy. The icy water had slowed decomposition, but abrasions covered the body. They'd found Len under the Olmstead Bridge. Had someone tossed him over the railing, or had he taken his own life?

Mac's voice warmed. "Thanks for helping with the search."

Not yet eight o'clock, and I was a bundle of nervous energy. I'd just reached the parlour, when the lights flickered, then went out. I moved toward the window and peered outside.

Though I craned my neck, I couldn't see a single light.

Constable Johnston knocked on the door. "Someone hit an electric pole. It's affected a few blocks. Could take a while for the power to be restored. Thought I'd better let you know."

I thanked him and relocked the door. The hall's emergency backup light helped me search through my purse for a penlight. After finding it, I made my way to the kitchen, where I'd stored the emergency supplies. I lit two votive candles and carried them to the office. One, I placed on the window ledge; the other, I set on the desk.

Thankfully, my laptop was fully charged. Book-keeping and documentation would have been a practical way to pass the time. Instead, I checked out the local tourism site, found the event calendar page, and scanned it. Both movies at the cinema were not to my taste. A book launch would have been right up my alley, but I'd missed it by an hour.

I whooped out loud when I found an art opening. The one suspect who was still alive was unveiling new work. James Powell's solo exhibition, *Unforgettable*, was being held the next town over from nine to eleven. The write-up indicated James's artistic vision had undergone a radical change, promising that "his fresh perspective would astound former critics with its provocative vul-nerability, and unapologetic rawness."

I rummaged through my bags and found my make-up bag, a wrinkle-free black dress, and a pair of kitten heels. How cliché to walk up the stairs of an old, creepy house carrying a candlestick. Cue the long shadows, the flickering flame, the shaky hand reaching for the Newell cap. The parsonage was no Thornfield Hall, and I'd make a god-awful Jane Eyre. What was so appealing about the Byronic, deceptive Mr. Rochester anyway? My sardonic bark did more than break the silence; it issued a challenge.

I reached the landing, froze, and sniffed the air. For a moment, I thought I detected a faint trace of perfume.

I looked down at the dress folded over my arm, realizing what I was smelling was fabric softener, nothing more. "There I go," I said. "Imagining things, again." Something feather-light, barely discernible, grazed the middle of my back. As soon as I shuddered, the sensation disappeared. Then, one of the bedroom doors slowly screeched open. It shifted almost indecisively, opening and closing, opening and closing, waving like a flag in a gentle breeze.

I scurried into the washroom and locked the door.

Fifteen minutes later, I forced myself to walk, not run, down the stairs. The low chignon looked better messy, I told myself, and the choice of a dab of lip-gloss had nothing to do with my trembling hands or dry mouth.

I shook off the atmosphere as I finished getting ready. My Indonesian batik scarf provided all the accessorizing I needed. I threw on my coat and locked the door. The air had gone from chilly to sub-zero, and I began to wish I'd worn my lined leggings and my thickest sweater, the turtleneck one. I waggled my fingers at Constable Johnston as I bolted past his patrol car. I groaned as I sat down on the biting leather, and it took multiple attempts to start my car. So much for a clean getaway.

The GPS said I'd reach my destination shortly after nine. It felt good to hit the open road, to free myself from Bliss River for a few hours. My fingers drummed on the steering wheel to Neil Young's "Helpless," feeling more a babe in the woods when I read a sign that warned, "Do Not Feed the Bears." Evergreens reached toward an almost full moon, as if they longed to shelter it deep within their branches.

A lynx and her four kittens appeared in the beam of my headlights. I braked just in time. She stared me down as her young scurried into the forest before following them. The wilderness drew closer as I slowly shouldered the next bend. My father would have loved this section of highway, and the thought put a lump in my throat.

I passed the village sign, a gas station, and two antique shops. St. Brigid's Art Centre was located in a former community hall, so it was bigger than I'd expected, large enough to also house an art school. The event was popular. Three times I circled the parking lot before finding a spot. I grabbed my purse, straightened my hem, and dashed to the door.

I hung my jacket in the cloakroom, then followed the low buzz of voices. In a large multipurpose room, people milled about in small groups, mingling as they sipped beverages from plastic cups. Most wore denim. Seemed I'd overdressed. Though my neckline did not plunge and everything above my knees was amply covered, my formfitting sheath stood out.

Ah, well. I worked it.

The space had too many windows for traditional hangings. The paintings were displayed on easels, lessening the distance between art and viewer, to intensify the one-to-one experience. Even from a distance, I was floored by the intimacy of the work. I wandered toward a large canvas, taken by both its composition and palette. The subject—in her twenties, I guessed—was no stranger. There was Jane, wading into Lake Huron, as large as life. Her expression was a blend of playfulness and vulnerability. Droplets put stars in her lashes and shimmered on sunburnt cheeks. I moved in closer, captivated.

"Holly Golightly, I presume?"

He was handsome for a septuagenarian. Although deeply lined, his face was neither puffy nor ruddy. He was of average height and weight, but his posture was unsteady, as if a strong wind would topple him. His speech was elegant. I'd never take him for an alcoholic or a hermit. I played it smooth, quipping, "I like her style, but pearls are overrated."

"Especially when cast before swine. Do you think my work should be preserved for prosperity, Ms. Garde?"

So, he knew who I was. "Eventually. But I'll be retired, by then."

"Ha. Jane was right. She said you were whip-smart."

"She's here, then?"

He gestured toward the back of the room, where a photographer was keeping Jane busy. She'd been positioned alongside another painting and had replicated her own pose. His smile was lenient, mild but warm. "My ex thrives on the limelight. Meanwhile, I'd rather be home."

"It is cacophonic, isn't it? I can barely hear myself think."

"I don't mind the bloody noise. It's the people making it I'd rather avoid."

What to say. "Years ago, I visited a Jesuit retreat. Silence is underrated."

"No, silence comes at a great cost." He abruptly turned and wandered away, right past someone I hadn't expected to see. Mac. His eyes widened, and I watched his expression shift from surprise to delight, to exasperation. He looked good in casual wear, way too good. We walked toward each other, meeting up in front of another portrait.

I resisted the impulse to flirt and faced the painting instead.

He whispered, "What to do with you."

"See all the witnesses? I'm not stupid."

"No. You're not." He sidled closer. "But how is this a good idea?"

I turned toward him. His eyes were not their usual warm pewter. They glinted dangerously. "Maybe we should talk about this later."

He crossed his arms. "Sure."

The portrait of Jane refused to be ignored. She sat on a chair, an infant suckling at her breast as she read a letter, bawling. The babe, however, looked content. The scene made me uncomfortable, as if I were a voyeur. "I wonder how Jane really feels about this exhibit."

"She's always been a hard one to read."

Out of the corner of my eye, someone drew my attention, someone with a tattooed forearm and a camera bag. I nudged Mac's side.

"What is it?" Mac feigned interest in the painting.

"Mr. Thousand Words," I said as quietly as I could. "Is he local?"

"Never seen him before. Why?"

I looked around for a private place, spotting the double doors that led to the school. A doorstop kept one open. Mac understood my intent and nodded. We slowly made our way toward the back, lingering at a few portraits, blending in with the throng. I did my best to appear unaffected, tittering once as if Mac had told me a joke, then strolled through the doorway. I gestured at the corridor's display shelves and moved toward it. I picked up a bowl and studied its glazing. The pottery was, in fact, beautiful. At least my admiration wasn't an act.

"Well done, Egghead."

I grinned. "Marginally improved. Okay, so I've seen Mr. Thousand Words around town.

It's probably just a coincidence. But there's something about the way he scans a room. Like he's stalking someone."

"Stalking *you*? What the hell! And I'm only hearing about this now!"

"No, no. It doesn't feel as if he's following *me*. I think he's targeting the suspects."

"The person who killed Floyd is coldblooded, maybe even sociopathic."

"Okay. So, what next?"

"If Words is still here, I'll find out what he's driving, take down his plate number."

He sauntered back to the gallery as I nosed a display case, but curiosity got the better of me. I slipped my compact out of my purse and pretended to apply lipstick, using the mirror to watch Mac. He stood at the bar, ordered drinks, and waited for them to be made, leaning against the counter—nonchalantly—and scoping the room. Feeling like a snoop, I put away my make-up and studied a bizarre statuary of Saint Francis. A snake's fangs were latched to his right shoulder, and a snarling rat sat in his left upturned hand. The figurine reminded me of Floyd's twisted art. I turned away from it.

Mac returned with two bottles of beer and handed one to me.

I took a token sip.

"He's gone." Mac put down his bottle. "Who is this guy? If he's picking off murder suspects, what's his motive, and how's he connected to Rosemary? No way he's over sixty. He wasn't even alive when she was murdered."

"He could be a hitman."

"A gun for hire? In Bliss River?" His brow furrowed. "That would make him the arsonist too? Doesn't fit. And if you can identify his target for him, why would he want you out of the way? He'd want you to finish cleaning the painting."

"Will you put out an APB?"

"Not an official one. This is all hypothetical." he said. "These days, tattoo artists like to post photos of their work to their websites. Free advertising. First, I'll check to see if this guy's in our system. If not, I'll do some searching, see what I can find. In the meanwhile, avoid him." His mouth tightened. "Patrols will be on the lookout. But without any evidence . . ."

I set my bottle beside his. "I should get going."

He walked with me to the cloakroom and insisted on accompanying me to my car. I put my key into the ignition, but the car refused to start. Frustrated, I twisted the key repeatedly until he tapped on the window. I rolled it down, and he asked me to pop the hood. He got into his pickup, pulled up to the jeep, and took jumper cables out of his truck box. It took two boost attempts to start the car.

"Thank you," I mumbled, more than a tad embarrassed.

He was about to reply when a young man waved him over, shouting, "Yo, coach!"

Mac grinned and yelled back, "Gimme a minute! Be right there!" He ducked his head down toward the open window, so his face was closer to mine. "Mike just got his driver's license, and he and his dad have been working on that truck for a year. First time he's taken it for a spin, I'm guessing." He gave me a meaningful look. "Drive carefully. We'll talk tomorrow."

He casually swaggered toward a small group of men, and I enjoyed the sight of his long, easy stride. My cheeks warmed when I realized I was ogling him rather lustily. I left the parking lot, glanced at the fuel gauge, and swore. The tank was almost empty. I remembered passing a Petro Canada and found it, but only after I'd circled several dark side streets.

Running on fumes, I coasted into the station and prepaid at the pump, wondering if it was time to shop for a new vehicle, for something less likely to fall apart if I looked at it the wrong way. My mind elsewhere, I almost dropped the nozzle when Thousand Words strolled out of the station's store, sipping a coffee. Slowly, I turned my back to him and pretended to stargaze, posing as if I were in no hurry and had nothing to fear.

I willed the pump to stop and didn't once look over my shoulder. As soon as I heard the click, I removed and replaced the nozzle. Once I was back in my car, I turned the key, trembling with relief when the motor roared to life. Only then did I cast a sideways glance to the store-front. Word-man was plodding toward me.

B EFORE HE REACHED the Jeep, I took off toward the
exit. I peered into the rear-view mirror and saw him
toss his cup onto the ground as he sprinted toward a
Mercedes-Benz. Fighting the instinct to peel out, I
waited at the exit, forming a plan when I spotted an
eighteen-wheeler sailing down the highway. I continued
to idle there, knowing the Mercedes was right behind
me. I held my breath and hit the gas, making a sharp left
turn that narrowly missed the big rig.

The trucker blared his horn and kept blaring it as I
shifted gears, increasing my speed to pass a sputtering
minivan. I checked the mirror, again. The Mercedes'
high beams blinded me. The coupe wasn't glued to my
bumper, but it was trailing me. I needed to call for help.
My phone rang before I'd even reached for it.

I answered it, grateful for Bluetooth.

"I'm right behind him."

"Mac? I'm trying not to panic. Should I slow
down?"

"You're doing great—keep your speed. Go to the police station, pull into the lot, and then I want you to duck down and stay down. Understand?"

"Got it. So, nice night for a drive or what!"

"I won't let anything happen to you. I've already called in for reinforcements."

"Okay." I straightened in my seat. "Okay."

I sped by woods and farmland, rural exits, and private drives. When we reached Bliss River, I drove past the main exit and kept heading east. I was nearing the OPP station, and Words wasn't in any way deterred. He was still on my tail.

My heart raced as I barreled down the drive, steering the Jeep toward two squad cars. Both constables had positioned themselves behind their car doors and had their weapons drawn. I braked too hard, and the car did a doughnut. I got control of the car. As soon as it came to a full stop, I dove across the seat, squeezing my eyes shut as I heard the other car's tires squeal.

Mac yelled, "Put your hands up!"

What followed was a frightening stretch of silence. But there were no more shouts, and no shots were fired. Minutes felt like hours. At my wits end, I lifted my head, relieved to see the constables had holstered their weapons and were strolling into the station.

Mac crossed the lot and opened my door. "There's someone I'd like you to meet."

I accepted his hand and hopped out of the Jeep. The bitter wind had me pulling up my hood. We walked toward Words, who offered me a meek and apologetic smile.

Mac said, "Annora, this is Daniel Styles, Rosemary's half-brother."

I grappled with the information. "Why were you following me?"

"I've been meaning to contact you and the Inspector for days." Daniel shifted the strap of his laptop bag. "I saw you at the opening, but it didn't feel like the right time. So I left. When I recognized you at the gas station—geez, I didn't mean to scare you! I'm just trying to find answers too. I messed up—I should've handled this differently."

Mac shot him a look. "You think?"

"I read that news article and knew what it meant. Dad's in a home, and Mom passed away four years ago—Alzheimer's disease."

Mac said, "I'm sorry to hear of your loss. Could we finish this discussion inside?"

"Sure. I brought something I'd like to show both of you."

Daniel politely waited for me to walk ahead. I thought about the hardworking woman who'd been the target of the town's hate. Fayette had gone on to have another child, perhaps more than one. She'd found happiness, but she hadn't lived long enough to see justice for her daughter. How heartbreaking, how horribly unjust.

Once we reached Mac's office, he asked if anyone would like something to drink, then shut the door. He pulled his chair out from behind his desk. We sat down. Three constables strode past the window, talking amongst themselves. The florescent lighting buzzed. Daniel cleared his throat, and I shifted in my chair, wondering who'd be the first to speak.

Mac turned to Daniel. "The investigation is confidential. We are doing our best to identify your sister's killer. Once we've laid charges, you'll be the first to know."

"Look, I'm not here to pressure you." He slipped his bag off his shoulder and zipped it open. "I'm a photojournalist, so I tend to see the whole picture. There are always a dozen different angles to consider. Would you like to know more about Rosemary and my mom?"

"Anything you'd like to share with us would be appreciated," Mac said.

Daniel put the laptop onto the desk, searched through picture files, and started a slide show. It was hard to see pictures of Rosemary as a baby and toddler. There were photos of Fayette holding her sweet girl, and others of a gap-toothed Rosemary flying a kite, blowing out candles, tobogganing . . . then, a wedding photo of Fayette, in her thirties, posing with her new husband. Fayette, first pregnant and then cradling a girl with dark hair. Daniel fishing with his father. An older Fayette at an airport. She'd had a full life.

"My mother was the kind who went on field trips and overdid Christmas. She was very close to my older sister, Eileen. She loved us, but she refused to talk about Rosemary. We weren't allowed to ask questions or even mention her name. Mom struggled with depression. Some days, she didn't leave her room, and we'd hear her sobbing. Dad tried to be a buffer. But he felt helpless too." He paused. "All the dysfunction affected Eileen deeply, and she went on to become a child psychologist. Her specialty is trauma." The slideshow ended. "I wanted you to know that Rosemary still has family, and we want justice for her."

"You're here for your sister," I said. "Your mother would be proud."

"No. She'd be furious." Daniel closed his laptop and laid it on his lap. "I was told to keep clear of Bliss River. Mom said this town hides monsters, only protects its own."

Mac nodded, sent him a sympathetic look. "But nothing *stays* hidden."

"I want to see my sister's mural."

"No, you don't. It doesn't add anything to Rosemary's story. The mural doesn't show who she was or who she loved." Mac tapped Daniel's laptop. "But these pictures do."

Daniel lowered his chin, fought for composure. "Tell me you'll nail the bastard."

"Let us do our job." Mac paused. "Where you staying?"

"The Lilac Inn. I booked a room for a month."

"So, Margo's taking good care of you, then?"

"She reminds me of Mom—all those biscuits and houseplants."

"The best accommodations in town. So, we know where to find you." He leaned forward. "I'd like your contact information. And I'm asking you to keep a low profile. If you're planning to leave town, let us know. We're close to solving this case. You'll want to be here when we do, I'm guessing."

Daniel pulled a business card from his wallet and handed it to Mac.

We stood and the men shook hands. His eyes were so like Rosemary's, wide and green. I knew telling him this would not be kind. He hesitated as he turned to face me, and impulsively, I moved forward and gave him a brief, small hug.

"Thank you," he said huskily. "This is even more difficult than I'd thought it would be."

Once he'd left, Mac leaned back against the closed door. "Don't trust him."

I gawped.

"Yeah, he seems nice. But revenge makes for a strong motive." His tone softened. "Fayette had Alzheimer's disease. She may have relived her nightmare over and over, for years. Did she cry out for Rosemary but couldn't remember her son's name? How bad did it get?"

"Don't. Please, don't."

"I'm sorry. You've had a rough night."

The night didn't get any easier. The jeep refused to start. Mac pocketed my keys, said, "I'll give you a lift back and try again in the morning."

He had to clear off his passenger seat, looking shamefaced as he tossed fast-food bags into the back. The cab smelled of pine air freshener and stale fries, but his seat had a warmer, and within minutes my legs were no longer chilled. His radio was tuned to country, which shouldn't have surprised me but did. Patsy Cline sang about walking after midnight as we made our way down empty streets. Most townsfolk had been in bed for hours. We didn't speak, and I was grateful the ride was short.

The power hadn't been restored. I'd forgotten what it meant to live so far north. Mac parked his truck behind Constable Patel's cruiser. He retrieved a flashlight from behind his seat, entered the parsonage first and checked every room. Satisfied, he joined me at the entry where he'd asked me to wait. "It's freezing in here. Sure you don't want to use my guest room?"

"I'll be fine." I took the penlight from my purse and turned it on. Compared to the light cast by his long torch, my piddling beam barely cracked the darkness.

We said goodnight to each other. For a moment, I considered taking him up on his offer.

Instead, I locked the door behind him, already shivering. Though the renovation had taken aesthetics into consideration, I doubted any thought had been given to insulation.

I opened the blinds, and the gibbous moon cast ample light. Goosebumps covered me as I slipped out of my dress. The damp cold was a greedy leech; it latched itself to my skin and sucked away my warmth in seconds flat. Hurriedly, I layered fleece and woolens over yoga wear. By nestling deep under the blankets, I managed to restore some degree of comfort. Completely worn out, I shut my eyes and kept them closed. Even when I heard something that sounded like a nervous, prolonged whinny followed by rhythmic stomping. It wasn't a canter or a trot or a gallop. It sounded more like one hoof, wildly pawing the earth. Right below my window.

CHAPTER

18

THE SOUNDS I'D heard had ended almost as soon as they'd started, but getting to sleep had still been difficult. I convinced myself the pawing sound had been a low-hanging branch moved by the wind, and what had sounded like a whinny may have been a wild pig. I woke mid-morning, staggered upstairs, and washed my face with frigid water.

Breakfast had consisted of crackers, cheese, and grapes. Doggedly, I shuffled my way to the study. Rolling swabs and mixing solutions can become tedious. Rolling swabs and mixing solutions while shivering is mind-numbing. I got back into the hazmat suit, grateful for the added layer, but my hands were still cold. The thermostat in the parlour had dropped to fifteen degrees, and I tried to convince myself I wasn't miserable. It began to snow. Beyond the plastic shroud, snowflakes accumulated on the sills, and miniature drifts formed at their corners. Trees soon wore tufts of white. The world looked far too December for mid-October.

When the power came back on, I zipped to the kitchen to make coffee, but my contentment was short lived. The heating vents were not blowing air, cold or otherwise. Without the suit, I couldn't get warm, and I wasn't quite sure what to do.

I found the door to the cellar easily enough. The light switch worked, and the stairs had been replaced. The old stone walls had been recently mortared. There were no windows. Two naked lightbulbs painted odd shadows on an uneven concrete floor. Creepy came to mind. My teeth chattered as I bustled past a vintage Hoosier cabinet. Cobwebs draped shelves filled with mason jars. Mouse droppings covered its stained porcelain counter, and I wondered if the mouse had frozen to death.

Occasionally, my height is beneficial. Taller is not always better. Some would need to stoop in the space, but I didn't. I found the furnace. The antique beast gave me the cold shoulder while a brand-new, high-efficiency model pouted in a corner, waiting amongst parts. Mac's stop work order must have delayed its installation.

I tramped back up the stairs, frustrated. Hemming and hawing, I decided to phone Lilith. She didn't pick up, and her voicemail was full. Though I felt like a complete ninny, I rang Mac and explained the situation.

"Braved it out for as long as you could, didn't you?"

"No 'I told you so's'?"

"I'm on the way. After a pit stop or two."

I was engrossed with the chalky river when he showed up with three portable heaters. I waved from my side of the barrier, trying not to look too thrilled to see him.

He dumped the boxes in the hall, then moved closer to the plastic sheeting. "Took longer than I thought. Damn. It's like a meat locker in here."

"Mac, the cost of that heater alone, a hundred dollars, right?"

"Bah. Expenditures. Besides, I got it on sale."

I laughed. "One would have sufficed."

"It's a bad idea to have you lugging equipment around. Lilith called me this morning. She was polite but pushy. John must be driving her nuts." He gestured toward the boxes. "How about I take care of this?"

"Thank you. I'm used to doing things for myself, you know?"

"I have a hard time asking for help too." He hesitated. "Er, so, I tried to start your Jeep again. It was a no go. Was it alright that I had it towed to a local shop?"

"Yes, it was." I sighed. "I hope it's the battery and not the starter."

"If it comes to that, Billy will give you a good price."

He took the boxes into the study, and I continued to work. The left side of the mural was more infested than the right. Every inch took twice as long to clean. I stepped off the scaffolding and shoved it as close as I could to the fireplace. The thicker fungus required a different solution. I tested new mixes until I found one strong enough to get the job done. The work demanded my full attention.

"What is that?" Mac stood right beside me. The scaffolding leveled our heights, and if I turned my head, our masks would have touched.

I used the swab as a pointer. "This?"

"Yes. Can you clean it a bit more? Is it a twig or a cattail?"

"Hmm, I'll just . . ." I dipped and rolled. "These blooms are horrible!"

"Ah, hell. I think that's an arm."

It took another six swabs to clean the two-inch area. We stared at what I'd revealed: a girl drowning in the river, submerged to her chin, the whites of her eyes exaggerated. Her mouth gaped open, and one hand was raised.

I felt helpless. And angry. "Who is she? Why is she in this mural? Why?"

"I've no idea. There have been several drownings over the years. I'll have to go back, check our files. He's given us a few clues: young girl, bobbed red hair, freckles."

I left the parlour, shucked off my suit, and stormed to the back study. I plopped down on the window seat, watching the graceful fall of large snowflakes. A cardinal returned my stare.

Mac walked up to me and leaned against the wall. "I know, another child. Gets to me too."

Another child.

"Should we take a break? Step out for a bit?"

I blinked back tears.

"Does she remind you of one of your sisters?"

I swung my head toward him. "Maeve. She had freckles and hair just like that—titian. My dad called it Pippi-hair." The memory stung. "I'm sorry. I'll pull myself together . . ."

He sat down beside me, touched his forehead to mine. "Don't apologize."

Slowly, I tilted my head. Understanding lit his eyes, and something else. Longing. How had he become my safe place in only a week? I shifted my body and pressed my lips up to his. His arms wrapped around me, gently pulling me closer. He tasted like a cinnamon roll, sweet and deliciously piquant. It didn't feel like a first kiss. Though my heart pounded, though I already wanted more of him, the moment held no urgency or awkwardness. Our mouths moved with the deep intimacy of long-time lovers.

When we finally pulled away from each other, the surprise on his face must have mirrored mine. I touched his cheek, not quite ready for what came next. He caught my hand, turned it over, and pressed his mouth to my palm before weaving his fingers with mine.

I tried to smile. "Say something, for the love of Mike."

"Those eyes even translate. You're thinking too much. We'll make this work."

"It was a kiss, just one kiss, it's not like we—"

Mac swallowed my stroppy words, replaced them with something reassuring. He lifted his head, waiting for me to look at him. "This isn't good timing, and we need to slow down. I get it. But this connection between us, this chemistry, there's nothing *just* about it."

"It's all happening so quickly, but I do feel it too."

"We should give this a chance, Egghead, see where it goes."

I couldn't help but laugh. "I need to find you an equally endearing term."

"Ha. Okay, uh, Scott, could work for now. But never Scottie. Only my grandmother called me Scottie and got away with it." He stood up. "I should get going."

Normally, I'm not a shy person, and I'd made the first move. Yet as I walked him to the door, I became skittish and had no idea where to put my hands. He took one look at my face, snatched a brief, firm kiss, and left before I could even say 'Have a good day' or 'Honey, don't forget to pick up wine and condoms.'

On that note, I returned to the kitchen and made myself a pot of coffee. The heater made it far more comfortable. The model had several features, I noted. Auto timer this and dual heating that. He'd placed an oil-filled radiator with an adjustable thermostat in the office. The box touted that its operation would be silent, but the unit gave off intermittent crackles as the metal reacted to the heat. I couldn't care less. I moved the chair closer to it and held my hands up to the metal columns until each finger felt toasty.

The heater in the upstairs washroom could handle condensation. I turned the hot water tap, tested the temperature, and found it lusciously warm. I mulled over all things Mac . . . Scott . . . as I showered, but I refused to imagine us as a couple. Best to take it one day at a time.

Once back on the main floor, I decided to make an omelet so I'd be able to push on through till early evening. I poured myself a coffee and was busy chopping green onions when the phone rang. I dried my hands with a paper towel and answered it.

"Hi. It's Grace. Can we talk?"

"Absolutely. Can I put you on speaker phone, so I can keep making lunch?"

"I guess so."

"Is everything okay?" I cracked three eggs. "Professor Tight-Face getting to you?"

She sighed. "It's about Dad. I'm worried."

I stopped whisking. "He's okay. I saw him about an hour ago."

"I guessed as much. Look, I know he comes across as strong. But losing Mom? It wrecked him. I'm not sure if he could take a disappointment right now." Grace paused. "I spoke to him this morning, and when I asked about you, he went all dopey. It's obvious he's crushing on you. And I want to see him happy! I do! This isn't some 'girl missing her dead mom' thing. I don't want his heart to get broken."

I leaned against the counter. "I've no idea what's going to happen. To be honest, I'm a bit gun shy, but I'm . . . crushing on your dad too. Hurting him is the last thing I want to do. He's caring and funny and—and I don't know what else to say."

"I shouldn't have called."

"No! I'm glad you did! I understand. You're looking out for your father."

"He'd be cheesed off that I—"

"So, how about we keep this conversation between us?"

"I get why my dad likes you. I already like you too."

"Aww, the feeling is very mutual." My eyes misted. "Maybe—and this is just a suggestion—you and your dad could have a heart-to-heart. You should tell him how you feel."

We talked about a student art show in which her work would be featured, how nervous and excited she felt. Shortly after, we said our goodbyes, and I went back to making myself something to eat. The omelet hit the spot. I was about to do the dishes when I got another call.

It was the mechanic, letting me know that the starter was fine, but I needed a new battery. He said he'd do his best. "It'll be a day or two. "

I thanked him.

Finally, I returned to the parlour.

"Sorry for taking so long," I whispered to Rosemary.

The glare of snow changed the light in the room, brightening her smile.

I continued on with the monotony of cleaning the river, working on the thick coating of white. Over and over, I rolled the swabs across the small area of the mural, getting nowhere. Though the mould eventually lifted, all that lay beneath it were brilliant shades of blues and greens. I'd revealed dragonflies and placid ripples. My purpose wasn't to extract pretty things. My purpose was to find more clues, to press on until I'd exposed the entire mural.

As afternoon became evening and the sinking sun rouged the snow, my arms began to ache. When a muscle in my neck began to spasm, I decided I'd done enough for the day. The need to stop frustrated me. The river and its banks were finally fungus free. The job was nearing completion. It could be the remaining mould only hid trees and a skyline. What if the mural had no more clues to give?

I reheated leftovers, ate them at the counter, and kept toying with my phone. I decided to call Mac in the morning. My head felt heavy. And if I were to be honest with myself, my heart felt even heavier. I plopped onto the cot and had started to nod off when he called.

"Did you have a good day?" I turned so I faced the window.

"Kind of hoped you wouldn't ask. The coroner's report came back. Suspicious death.

Len drowned, but the head injury wasn't consistent with a fall. Forensics found blunt force trauma. The weapon was probably a hammer or a similar tool. We found blood splatter on the bridge. DNA—"

"A little less information, please."

"I'm sorry. Sometimes, I forget you're not a cop."

"Sweet talker."

He chuckled. "Find anything else today?"

I let him know I hadn't uncovered anything noteworthy, and kept my promise to Grace.

"Did some digging. Seven-year-old Beverly O'Dwyer drowned in 1954. She had bobbed red hair and freckles. The coroner ruled her death accidental, a summer tragedy. No witnesses. They concluded she'd tried to retrieve a favourite toy from the river, a doll with golden ringlets. She'd left home with it, but the doll was never found."

I bolted upright. "Why does the mural show Beverly drowning *without* her doll? Could the killer be suggesting something else happened? Had she tried to get away from him, or maybe he threw her in or—"

"Stop getting ahead of me. Keep to the plan. I'll handle the rest, okay?"

"About the plan. Two more days, I think, and the cleaning will be done. So far, we've been unbelievably lucky. Staining has been minimal, but we still haven't touched the top left corner of the mural and I'm concerned by the degree of mould there."

"It is what it is. You're doing an amazing job."

I settled back against the pillows. "But it's still not enough, is it?"

"Why are you so hard on yourself? My gut feeling is that you and I, we're going to solve this case. The answer could be right in front of us." His voice changed, became softer. "The mural has a purpose. I don't believe

in coincidences. The timing of the discovery, you being
friends with the mayor—everything had to line up perfectly, even your diligence, those hard-headed ways of
yours."

"Mac? You're not talking about fate, are you?"

"Did you know the town almost sold the property?
A developer was interested in erecting a six-unit condo.
They were going to demolish the parsonage."

"I'm still a sceptic. I believe in science."

"I believe in honky-tonk and Hockey Night in
Canada. I believe vacations are for kicking back, coffee is better with cream," he said. "And you. I definitely
believe in you."

Women my age shouldn't blush. "Reality check. I
can't cook. I keep a packed travel bag by my door. My
favourite things are opera, archives, and foreign films.
And I lose keys."

"That all you got?"

I took a deep breath. "I have survivor guilt and see
a counselor who works around my crazy schedule. You
still there?"

"I'm guessing honesty scared off some brainless, lowdown, bootlicking scumbag?"

I snorted. "Something like that."

"Real men don't run."

"Are you sure this isn't . . . too soon?"

"I want to talk to you about Kit, but not over the
phone. I will say I wasn't looking for someone, but this
feels right."

"Honky-tonk, huh?"

"Opera? Art flicks? And let me guess: ballet too?"

We laughed at ourselves and said our goodnights.

The cot seemed less a cot, and I knew if I lifted my hand to my face, I'd feel a smile there. The world stilled, and even the dark left me alone.

❧

"Cut it out," Maeve said.

I braced myself for the crash. Dad drove, but it wasn't night. He smiled, turned to me, and mouthed, "I love you."

All our lines were mixed up. I should have said, "Cut it out, jerk," and Maeve was supposed to say, "Make me, Doofus." Dad wasn't cursing. Where was the blood?

"Oh God, I'm so sorry!" I screamed. "I want you all back!"

Suddenly, we were out of the car, and Dad fished from a boulder. He waved to me from the other side of the river and blew me a kiss. Nearby, Tess chased butterflies and Charlotte—plump and perfect—toddled through clover. Mauve stood in front of me, so close I could have touched her. "I mean it. Cut it out," she said again. "You didn't do anything wrong."

"It was your turn to be in the front seat. You should have lived. I should have died."

"Stop it, just stop! You were a . . . good . . . sister . . ."

I didn't want to wake up. "Maeve, come back!"

❧

They were gone. I stood in the middle of the left parlour, barefoot, in a tee-shirt and flannel bottoms, trying to breathe, to come to grips. My cheeks were damp, and the cold floor punished my feet. I turned to leave the enclosure but heard something—a rustling of shrubs. I switched on the lights, and all quieted.

I walked toward the picture window and stared over a wide stripe of frost. Light struggled within the icy pattern like a firefly snared in a web, shimmering, almost pulsing. Something moved outside. My heart seized my throat and hammered in my ears.

In shock, I watched as something invisible began to slowly scratch at the ice. The sound rasped across the window, sounding off a faint hiss. I must still be asleep, held inside a new nightmare. A short, vertical line etched itself onto the white, forming a thin streak as dark as ink.

A half-circle quickly followed the first stroke. *P.* No, not "P."

The scraping continued, gouged out more frost. *R.*

The image transfixed me, froze me in place. "R" . . . for Rosemary? The scratching picked up speed, engraving a thin horseshoe.

U.

An "R" and a "U."

Are you?

Another letter blackened the ice with a notch of night: *N.*

RUN!

CHAPTER

19

WAKE UP! I told myself. I realized I was still asleep, but terrified, unable to even scream, I dashed toward the exit, but a low cackle had me spinning around just in time to see a large rock come crashing through the window. Shards flew toward me, scattering around my bare feet. In astonishment, still reeling, I registered what I saw flickering outside—a lighter! I gasped at the sudden blur of motion, the arched flight of a torch. I found my voice and cried out as someone hurled a flaming bottle through the jagged hole in the pane. It shattered on the floor, and a fireball shot toward the high ceiling.

In a flash, a blazing pool spread across the middle of the hardwood floor. There was no time for disbelief, no time to cower.

Trusting my instincts, I ran to the table, swiped my supplies away and flipped it on its side. I rammed it against the scaffolding, using it to block off the mural. Fear and determination had me hugging the walls, scrambling to the other side of the room.

The ventilation pulled the smoke outside, but the heat scorched my cheeks and stung my eyes, filling me with both fear and rage. With sweaty palms, I shoved the other table toward the room's center, putting my back into it. I roared back at the mounting inferno and grasped the table's edge, overturning it onto the flames.

It worked! The tabletop crushed the fire, temporarily restricted it, but those insatiable red tongues began to lick their way out from the underside. The thick, grey plastic seethed, bubbled, and started to blacken. I had minutes before the flare engulfed the entire room. I tore down the hall, threw open the front door and shouted "Nine-one-one! Fire!"

I sprinted back down the hall, ducked into the study, snatched a blanket, and burst into the parlour. I grabbed the jug of water, dampened the fabric, dropped to all fours, and scuttled toward the hearth, shrinking back from shifting flames. Desperately, I began to smother the fire with my bare hands, pressing the sodden material against it, again and again. The blaze fought back, hissed and crackled, a live and furious thing.

Johnston rushed into the room with a fire extinguisher. "Get out! Get out now!"

The sound of sirens grew louder and louder. I leapt to my feet, jumped on the scaffolding, and held up the steaming, wet blanket in an attempt to protect the mural.

Johnston pulled the pin, aimed the nozzle, and squeezed the levers. He swept the room with short, quick blasts. Flames sputtered as a cloud of chemicals filled the air, choked the room with noxious powder. The floor still smoldered in spots, but the fire had been put out. My heart pounded, and sweat scalded its way down my cheeks. I coughed violently and let go of the blanket, feeling dazed and helpless as Johnston dropped the extinguisher and swayed.

Mac burst into the room at the same time the fire truck showed up. He rushed toward me, and his eyes widened in shock. "What have you done to your hands!"

I looked down and shuddered. My palms looked like raw steaks. My right one had already started to blister. I hadn't even known they were burnt, hadn't felt a thing. But the pain set in and hit me hard. I staggered and slipped off the scaffolding.

Mac caught me and put his hand under my elbow. We hurried down the hall. I glanced back and noticed my bloody footprints on the floor. I must have stepped on broken glass.

Firefighters passed us as we walked out to the front door. A paramedic met us on the sidewalk. She helped me onto a stretcher, slipped an oxygen mask on my face, and took my pulse. My burns were covered in wet gauze, and bandages were quickly wrapped around my feet. As I was lifted into the back of the ambulance, I saw Constable Johnston step out onto the porch. He, too, was met by EMS. Mac jogged over to him, and they spoke briefly. He hurried back, hopped into the ambulance, and sat down beside me.

I struggled to sit up. "Johnston."

"Don't speak, please." The paramedic tucked a blanket around me. "Lie down."

"Pete's fine." Mac's hand reached for my shoulder, and he gave it a gentle squeeze. Relieved, I settled back, and the constriction in my chest eased.

We pulled into the hospital, and I was rolled into the ER. They rechecked my vital signs, asked me when

I'd last been given a tetanus shot, and gave me a booster. They also asked me about my pain level. I told them eight, but my palms throbbed as if I was still hammering the flames, as if I had scooped them up and carried them with me. The pain was a good sign, I knew. My nerves hadn't been damaged. Still, I writhed with pain. The paramedic parked the gurney in a hall across from a teen boy who gave me a sympathetic look, though his arm was in a splint. Not yet dawn, but nurses were preparing for the shift change. I tuned out their murmurs, chuckles, and small rants. I was worried and very, very angry.

A nurse practitioner told me I had first- and second-degree burns, cautioning, "Infection is the biggest concern." She said the cuts to my feet were superficial and wouldn't need stitches.

She popped two painkillers into my mouth while holding a glass for me as if I were a child. I sipped water through a straw, realizing what the injuries meant, how much independence I'd lost. It was difficult not to panic. Burns do not heal quickly, this much I knew, and everything I do requires a delicate touch. My hands are rarely still.

The nurse, Suyin, helped me sit in a chair and filled a small, white sink with water. She instructed me to submerge my hands, and the coolness lessened the heat radiating from my palms. Suyin put a warm blanket on my lap and touched my back gently, reassuringly. I thanked her several times. Once she'd left the room, I allowed one pain-filled moan to escape and immediately wished I had kept it to myself.

Mac looked ready to explode. "This bastard's going down."

"I hope he got sloppy, left some prints behind."

"Could you ID him?"

"No. It was too dark. I'm sorry, Mac."

"Stop apologizing! No, I changed my mind. Tell me you're sorry for fighting that fire. Your life is worth more than some piece of evidence, you hear me?"

At some point in his tirade, my mouth must have dropped open. I snapped it shut, took a deep breath, and tried to make him understand. "I had to do something! But if Johnston hadn't been there, I would have—"

"What? Let it burn? C'mon. I think you'd have kept beating at those flames until the roof collapsed. You don't know when to quit!" He paused. "Rosemary can't be saved. She's gone. You can't immortalize her."

I narrowed my eyes. "Says you."

Dr. Beth Wishart pushed open the curtain. "Bad timing?"

"No," I said.

"Yes," Mac grumbled.

The doctor put on her gloves and sighed.

She examined my hands and asked me a few questions. Then she got tough. "Should I even bother giving you instructions? You need to rest and drink plenty of water. It's important for you to take in more calories—you're going to need them. The dressings must be kept clean." She turned, scowled at Mac. "I don't care how right you are or how pigheaded she is; if you raise your voice one more time, I'll call security. Got it?"

"Got it," Mac said.

"Hey! I'm not pigheaded."

She ignored me and continued to write on my chart. "I'll be back."

After she left, Mac studied his feet as if he didn't know where to look or what to say.

"How badly does it hurt?"

"It's . . . manageable."

"I'll get you something to drink. Won't be long."

Without another word, he left. I bowed my head, wondering how many times Kit had said to him that her pain was "manageable"? He must have felt so helpless.

The nurse returned and gently cleaned my hands. I gulped at the large syringe and looked away as she drained my blisters. She placed something cool and damp on each palm. "These are hydrogel pads," she said. "They should help the healing process."

She was still wrapping gauze around my hands when both Mac and the doctor returned. I wondered if they'd had a conversation about me. They didn't seem to be in collusion.

The doctor said, "The left hand should heal in a week, but the right palm suffered a deeper burn—we won't be able to remove the bandages for another two weeks, at least. So, you'll need help with the dressings."

"She'll be staying at my place."

I couldn't stop myself from snapping, "Was that an invite or an order?"

His eyes widened. "I just figured—"

The doctor crooked an eyebrow. "I'll leave you two to hash this out." She turned to me. "He can be a bit caveman, but he means well."

Mac grunted. "Hey! I'm not a caveman."

Dr. Wishcart chuckled in the doorway. "No, you two are nothing alike. Not at all." She continued to softly laugh as she left the room.

Mac rocked back on his heels. "I am sorry if I came across as overbearing."

"I'm sorry, too. Guess we all have a breaking point." I waved my bandaged hands, wishing I could punch something. "How will I finish the commission, now?"

He stepped closer, crouched down beside me. "Partners, remember?"

"You were right. I was careless." A single tear escaped and slid down my cheek.

He cupped my face, and one of his fingers wiped the wetness away. "Egghead, you're scary brave is what you are. Not only did you save the mural, you also stopped the fire from spreading. I spoke with the fire marshal. His team has already started to collect evidence and check for structural damage, so the parsonage is off limits until the incident commander gives us the go-ahead." He added, "Although the floor is charred and we need to clean up the dried foam, it looks like they'll give us a thumbs up in a few days."

He covered me in his coat and wheeled me out to his truck. Great. I had no footwear and no clothing. Mac drove me back to his place and didn't insist on conversation. Gently, he carried me to his living room. He closed the curtains as I got comfortable on the sofa.

Two hours later, the doorbell woke me. I kept my eyes closed when I heard Lilith's voice. I didn't want to explain anything or be civil. Murmurs drifted down the hall, but the exchange was brief. Tranquility returned and I dozed. Throughout the day, I napped, drank water, and took more painkillers. Images kept replaying, troubling images of a warning scratched in ice and flames snaking toward me.

As evening approached, I propped myself up and examined my bandaged feet. They didn't hurt, but I'd also been resting for an entire day. I moved slowly, first sitting up, then carefully standing and tentatively taking a step. At a snail's pace, I walked to the fireplace and schlepped back. Not bad. The cuts weren't serious enough to keep me bedridden.

Mac appeared in the doorway. "Lilith brought you some things." He carried two shopping bags into the room and dropped them onto a chair. "She seemed pretty sure about your size and mentioned that nothing has zippers or buttons."

"She can be thoughtful."

"If you'd like, I can help sort them, stash 'em away." He sent me a shy sort of smile. "I, uh, cleaned the guest room. It's all ready."

In that moment, I knew he was saying more than what he was saying, but I wasn't sure if he'd truly thought things through, if he or I were ready to take the next step. He sat down on the sofa, leaned back into the cushions, and appeared to be in no hurry to move or for me to move either. We were still in the getting-to-know-you stage, but I was more than just physically attracted to him. Whatever I felt for him, it was stronger than lust. He sent me a knowing look, a lingering glance that suggested he'd read my mind.

I was the one who wasn't ready for a relationship. I absolutely wasn't ready. I kept telling myself this over and over, vehemently, even though I knew I was telling myself a lie.

CHAPTER

20

IRONICALLY, THE TEMPERATURES soared, breaking seasonal records, while things cooled between Mac and me. I was under police protection, but I think there was more to our romantic avoidance than "keeping it professional." When you've lost someone too soon, too suddenly, it can erect odd, emotional fences. My injuries, my vulnerability, had scared him. I tried to give him time and space, which was impossible since I relied on his help for the simplest tasks.

When my car was ready, he'd picked it up. I felt like a teen again. It had taken me three highly embarrassing tries to get my license. The accident had made me overly cautious. Two decades later, I still have to force myself to drive at the speed limit and not below it. It was both maddening and oddly satisfying to see my lemon parked in his driveway.

It took less than three days for me to develop a severe case of cabin fever. The burns presented dozens of problems. I had to figure out how to bathe and clothe myself, eat and drink, find a comfortable sleeping position, and cope with the diminished use of my hands.

Mac bought silicon oven mitts that kept my bandages dry when I showered. I air-dried my skin and caged my wild hair with a hairband. I also quickly learned to go braless. Baggy tops hid my curves, anyway. Meals were kept simple so I could feed myself. Unable to type, I downloaded a voice-to-text app. I still had to do hand exercises to prevent stiffness. Mac did his best to keep me sane; he went to the library and borrowed several old-style physical audiobooks and a few classic movies. I had enough to do, but I still felt like I was going stir crazy.

While Mac was at work, visitors dropped by with food or flowers. Mig Daybutch brought his chessboard, and we'd spent one afternoon in an epic battle. He'd won. Afterward, he'd reached into his bag and pulled out a wooden sculpture of a hawk. He placed it on the sofa and said, "This is for you."

It was incredibly well crafted. The bird's wings were outstretched, and the width of the piece was well over thirty centimetres. Two small eyehooks had been screwed into its back so if it were hung up, the bird would appear to be flying. I leaned down and brought my face closer to the wood, admiring its sharp, penetrating gaze. "How do I properly care for it?"

He tilted his head ever so slightly. "Dust it regularly and polish it with mineral oil every couple of months."

"Is it a totem?"

He nodded and gathered the chess pieces. "The hawk sees the whole picture, is not easily fooled. When it must, it will rise above and soar. But it is a bird of prey, powerful."

"I love this gift, Mig. My emotions are a complete mess, right now, so I'm doing my best not to blubber. Thank you."

"I blubber all the time. Glad you liked the gift. I should get going." He moved toward the hall, stopped, and pivoted on his heel so he could look me in the eyes. "I want the killer found, but your safety is more important. Don't take any more risks. Rise above, if you must."

Even before he'd left, Barb Martin arrived. Mig opened the door with a grin and deftly lifted the tin foil from the pan she carried. She slapped his hand but allowed him to nab a brownie. He took a huge bite, waggled his brows at me, and left.

Still at the doorway, Barb called out, "See you at bingo. You owe me two beers!"

"One!"

"Three!"

"Okay, okay, two," he hollered from his truck. "Meet you there!"

Quite at home, she bustled between the kitchen and the living room, carrying a loaded tray between the rooms. Once she'd gathered all that she needed, she eased herself onto a slipper chair and poured tea into the large travel mug Mac had given me. Its enormous handle made it easier for me to hold, and the stainless-steel straw kept me from spilling hot drinks down my shirts. She placed the mug on the coffee table.

"Thank you," I said. "You knew exactly what I needed."

"Carl worked at the foundry for thirty years. Back in the early '90s, he suffered a nasty, third-degree burn to his hands. He lost a pinkie and a ring finger but managed to keep both thumbs. It was so painful." She cleared her throat. "Then, Parkinson's went and stole him away from me. It's lonely here sometimes. I'd be lost without my friends and church and the senior's centre. They keep me above ground." Her frown disappeared. "Anyway, enough about me. I've been going through some boxes and found hidden treasure."

She went back to the hall and returned with a tote bag. From it, she carefully pulled out a vintage composition book. Her hand trembled a bit as she handed it to me. "Rosemary and I worked on our own silly versions of fairy tales. She was the illustrator, and I was the printer.

"She said my penmanship was better, but she was only being her sweet self. I gave most of our handmade storybooks to her mother, after . . . But this one I kept." Her eyes misted. "She could have become a great writer or artist or a vet. She had so much potential."

The notebook's marbled cover was in excellent condition. If my hands weren't bandaged, I'd have put on gloves. Even though Barb wanted me to read the story, I felt as if I were nosing through something deeply personal. I shifted on the sofa, bringing my knees closer to the coffee table. Surprisingly, the book in no way smelled musty. It smelled of—"Did you spray perfume on the pages?" I tried to keep worry from my voice.

"What? Oh. No, I didn't. I wrapped the book in several layers of brown paper and spritzed some pretty handkerchiefs with Yardley's English lavender. She loved that fragrance. I tucked the book and handkerchiefs into a leather satchel."

"By the fifties, Kraft paper was acid free. You did an excellent job archiving this."

"Thank you." She pulled a knitting project from the tote. "New grandbaby expected before Christmas. I wonder what you'll make of the story."

As her needles softly click-clacked, I studied the notebook's cover. There were the girls' names, side by side. Barb's penmanship was indeed lovely, with its symmetry and flawless loops. The story's title was "Hannah and Gretel." Carefully, so carefully, I turned to the first page of the notebook, using the tip of my thumb.

Once upon a time, there were two poor sisters. They had a good mother who worked very hard, and the mother rarely rested, so the girls formed a plan. They decided to gather wild berries and nuts to prepare a special meal for her. The next morning, they got up very early and wandered into the woods. Cleverly, they brought all their hair ribbons with them and tied them to trees so they could find their way back home. Hannah and Gretel travelled deeper and deeper into the forest and faced many dangers: they crossed a treacherous stream, ran from black bears, and hid from wicked nymphs who did naughty things and called them bad names.

Mean girls could be so hurtful. "These illustrations are richly detailed."

"She took those art classes with Len Warriner, and he taught her a lot. He was a gentle person, and he didn't deserve to die the way he did." The needle clicks grew louder. "Have you finished the story?"

"No. Not yet. It won't end horribly, will it?"

"Rosemary's stories always ended as they should."

I turned to the next page.

The sisters came across all sorts of animals—rabbits, fawns, a porcupine, hummingbirds, and a white owl that could not fly. Hannah and Gretel filled their basket not only with berries and nuts but also with wild vegetables and grains: asparagus, artichokes, leeks, sweet potatoes, and rice. Overjoyed, they danced in a sunny glade because they had found so much food. They were about to return home when a strange man approached them. Their hair ribbons were in his hand! At first, the sisters were terrified, thinking he meant them harm, but he explained he thought they had lost their ribbons and was only trying to be helpful.

"I'm sorry. Please, let me make it up to you," he said. "Come to my cottage."

I shuddered and glanced at Barb. "Just keep reading," she said.

The man seemed very nice. They followed him, wondering if he could be trusted. Soon, it became clear that he was no ordinary man; he was a wizard! He performed magic tricks for them. He pointed his finger, and the sunbeams danced. He waved his hand, and all of the shadows disappeared. They had a lovely party in his cottage. He served them buttermilk and biscuits and made them laugh, and he gave them a fancy cake to take home.

When the girls realized it was time to go, they told him they must leave. He looked so sad. Still, he was a good wizard. Using a wand and a spell, he took ordinary pebbles and turned them into glittering jewels that they could keep. Then he gave them acorns and asked them to put them into their basket too. The girls were puzzled but did as he asked.

Finally, he led them out of the forest and begged them to keep his powers a secret. He told them good girls with big hearts should always be rewarded. The girls returned to their mother with the food and jewels. When they showed her the things in the basket, they realized the acorns had magically turned into gold coins.

The mother cried tears of joy and exclaimed, "How lucky I am to have such darling daughters!" The girls replied, "We are the lucky ones to have such a loving mama!"

The girls kept the wizard's secret, and sometimes he would visit them to chase away shadows and make the light waltz in their tiny home.

The family lived happily ever after.

The End.

My mind whirled. "Mac needs to see this. Can I keep this book for a few days? "

"You'll return it?"

"I promise."

Barb's expression grew serious. "Wait, are you saying this could help find her killer?"

"I think that is highly improbable. Did she ever mention a mysterious man?"

"No! I did ask her, and she said he was made up." She looked crestfallen. "All these years and I never once thought of this little book as any sort of clue."

"And why would you? It's a dear memento, right?"

Her smile resurfaced but held a hint of sadness. Moments later, she packed away her knitting and left. I felt torn. Most likely, the storybook was just a creative outlet for a girl who had faced "many dangers." Did every private moment of Rosemary's life need to be dissected? No wonder Fayette had left Bliss River.

By the time Mac came home, I was in a right foul mood.

He walked into the living room, took one look at my face, and said, "Whoa."

"Barb brought me something today—"

His cell rang. "I'm still on the clock. Hopefully, this won't take long."

Whoever was on the other end of the conversation had his full attention. As he paced the room, his expression switched from impatient to contemplative. He froze in his tracks, slowly pivoted, and sent me a huge, almost conspiratorial grin. "Mig recommended her, did he? Let me see if she's up to it."

"Me?" I mouthed.

He covered the phone with his hand and asked, "You up for a field trip, Egghead?

"When do we leave?"

He chuckled and spoke to the caller. "She's onboard. About an hour. Yeah, yeah, nag, nag, coffee and butter tarts." He ended the call.

"Where are we going?" Even I heard the excitement in my voice. "At this point, you could invite me to hang out at the local junkyard, and I'd call shotgun."

"Figured as much. This is right up your alley, I think. Some idiot sprayed graffiti over ancient pictographs. We've opened an investigation with the Mississauga

First Nation police. The park isn't staffed. We don't have the resources to monitor the site."

"People can be such idiots," I fumed. They mourn the loss of the Notre Dame Cathedral, yet think nothing of destroying two-thousand-year-old sacred art." A thought came to me. "I know someone who specializes in rock art conservation treatment."

"Great!" Mac noticed the vintage composition book. "What's this?"

"I'll tell you on the way to the park. Is there somewhere secure to keep it? It has a lot of sentimental value to Barb, and it may even be evidence."

"Damn. I should look through this now. But we need to hit the road. As it is, we'll be getting home later than I'd like."

Lucky for me, Grace and I wore the same shoe size. Mac found her hiking boots in the back of his hallway closet. I looked down at the top of his head as he slipped them on my feet. It was an odd Cinderella moment that first irked me. I'm a grown woman, not a child, but when I noticed how the afternoon sunlight burnished his hair, I pictured running my hands through it.

His forehead hovered over one knee as he tied the laces. In my loose-fitting, grey jogging suit and slouchy wool socks, I felt anything but sexy. Still, *his* sex appeal had me resenting my bandaged hands. I bit back a sigh as he stood up.

Soon, we were heading down the highway to the Bliss River Provincial Park. As Mac navigated the twisting road, I told him about Rosemary and Barb's storybook, trying my best to remember the exact wording of the little tale. He listened intently, asking no questions, but his jaw clenched, and the glances he sent me were somber. Finally, I trailed off and spouted, "You look as if I just ran over your dog."

"Describe the wizard."

"He wore a hat and gown. No white beard. Oh, and he had big ears."

"Ah, hell. Could be Lawrence Wagner."

"Because he has big ears?"

His voice was gruff. "Larry is our former mayor." Mac pulled up to a roadside bistro. "He's also Barb Martin's older brother. He'd have been about twelve at the time of Rosemary's murder. And yes, he has big ears. He also loved magic, even then. By the time he was thirteen, he was performing at birthday parties. Card tricks and small illusions."

"Acorns to gold coins?"

"Exactly."

"Is he—I mean could he have—"

"For over fifty years, he's volunteered at the library, the museum, and the school. He's someone I've trusted with Grace, and it's a hard thing to earn my trust. Kit was a ward councillor, spent hundreds of hours with him alone. He's the male version of Barb—big-hearted, dependable, honest. Now I have to consider him a suspect?"

"But the wizard helps the sisters, even protects them, right?"

"The wizard insists on their silence."

"Young Larry probably let them in on his trade secrets, then made them promise not to out him when he performed. It may be that we've overreached."

He smiled. "See? You think like a cop."

I wasn't thinking like I cop. I was remembering what it was like to be a big sister. All those confidences siblings shared. Even though diaries were read without permission, or the occasional tattle-telling occurred, we had been fiercely loyal to each other. Did Barb and Larry share that kind of bond too? She obviously hadn't seen any resemblance between the wizard and Larry, or she'd have mentioned it, surely, with a kind of sibling pride.

The Good Witch of the North Bistro & Bakery looked old, but in no way run down. It was long but narrow, and its kelly-green paint showed no signs of wear or tear, as if the building had been recently spruced up, probably sometime before the beginning of tourist season. We walked through the glass doors, and my mouth watered at the aroma of freshly baked bread.

The waitress called out, "Grab a seat! You in a rush?"

"Aren't I always, Petra?"

Petra was tall, and her short-sleeved diner uniform showed off strong, sculpted arms.

She'd spiked her crayon-red hair, wore black lipstick, and the holes in her earlobes were the size of peach pits.

We sat down at a long counter butted up against the diner's windows, giving us view of forestry and The Oaks and Acorns Motel across the two-lane highway. The place looked two stars, at most. I imagined the reviews: walls too thin, not enough towels, dirty sheets.

Mac recommended the chili because it was thick and perfectly spoon-able. Petra brought us a jug of ice water and a basket of warm, sliced bread; she took our order, and her urbanite vibe made me feel at home. Mac asked for a box of tarts, and she said they were already bagged and waiting at the counter. The diner had won first place in Ontario's Best Butter Tart Festival and Contest three years in a row. "Careful," she playfully warned me, "they're addictive."

The chili was hot and seasoned just right. Though the bandages were like gauzy mitts, making it difficult to clasp about anything, I'd found a way to hold cutlery. The Big Bopper was singing about Chantilly lace when I noticed the bright yellow Mini Cooper parked at the motel. I glanced at its custom license plate and almost choked.

Lilith emerged from one of the rooms. She flipped her hair over her shoulder and slowly sauntered to her car. I don't think she noticed me staring at her like she had two heads. A minute later, a beefy man strutted out the same door. I recognized him. He'd confronted me during my lunch with Lilith—the raging knuckle-dragger who'd asked me to hurry up and get on with my job. What was his name . . . Matt—no. Mark. Mark the Snark, who worked for John.

Mac remained suspiciously quiet. He squirmed and avoided making eye contact.

"You knew! You knew and didn't tell me!"

CHAPTER

21

RECOGNIZING I SOUNDED childish, I pushed my bowl away and watched a fox scuttle across the road. It dashed through cattails, never once looking back. As it disappeared into the boreal forest, an older couple entered the diner and chose a small table. The man pulled a chair out for the woman, and she thanked him. They seemed to be devoted to each other . . . seemed to be. I couldn't stop myself from sighing.

Mac leaned sideways and rested his arm on the back of my chair. "Look, I don't bother with local gossip. Lilith is a good mayor, and that's all that matters to me."

"It just took me by surprise." I lowered my voice. "She's never once indicated her marriage was anything but happy. I've kept it real with her. Meanwhile, she's living a lie."

"If she knows you so well, she'd also know how you'd feel about her choices."

"I dislike pretense."

"People make mistakes. There's no such thing as a living saint."

"I would wager a million you never cheated on Kit."

"No. I didn't. But a year before we had Grace, she left me for another man. We were young and fought non-stop about my job. She moved in with a nice, safe accountant for a few months. When she figured out she still loved me, I forgave her, and we started over."

"Oh, Mac!"

"I had a brother. Noah. At nineteen, he got high, went boating, and drowned. Happened while I was at the academy. We'd fought about his addiction, weren't speaking to each other. I'd do anything to take back those last words I said to him. Instead, I visit his grave and coach teens, give them something more to do than drugs or getting sloshed."

My eyes began to mist.

"I didn't mean to make it worse. What I'm saying is to let it be for a day. Lilith is still your friend. John reminds me a lot of Noah. We deal with a lot of substance abuse in the North." He stood up. "I'm not sure what happened to their marriage. All I know is what Lilith's done for Bliss River. Because of her, the arena's been repaired, kids have a drop-in center, and then there's the new museum. All her doing."

I nodded. Mac paid for our late lunch. We left with butter tarts, a box of coffee, and all the fixings. He turned on the radio, and I stared out the passenger window, fascinated by the landscape. The wilderness slowly became denser, and I saw less and less sky. The music filled the uncomfortable silence. One particular song soothed—"Nature Boy," a jazz standard that strangely blended with the scenery and my melancholic mood.

The asphalt highway became a dirt road as we travelled very far very far . . . and the further we went, the narrower the road became. If I reached out, I'd be able to touch the papery bark of silver birches.

Mac navigated the road carefully, keeping his speed below thirty kilometres an hour, but when we rounded a bend, he slowed down to a mere crawl. He turned to look down a hidden drive on his left, and I caught sight of a silver SUV parked under a massive sugar maple.

He lowered the radio's volume. "We just passed the Boyland's country retreat. Jane has been generously allowing her ex to live in her father's sprawling cottage. The building is falling apart, but the property is worth over a million."

"James Powell does not seem a roughing-it kind of guy."

"Havencrag is a four-thousand-square-foot cottage that has five bedrooms, three balconies, an indoor pool, and an art studio. Jane used to host Scout sleepovers way back, and I remember the great room was big enough to fly a kite. The place may need major repairs, but trust me—James has been pampered. And he wouldn't take incarceration very well."

I looked down at my hands. "We haven't discussed the mural—"

"We will. But not today."

"Not so long ago, you grumbled about me wasting time by filling out a report. Now, you're fine with a two-week delay. You bewilder me sometimes. Two murders, a firebug, new suspects popping out of the woodwork, your lab rat partner is incapacitated, and yet you're totally calm, not anywhere near blowing a fuse like I am."

"Two attempts on your life and you think I'm calm? I'm a time bomb. I should send you on your way and show up at your doorstep as soon as I can. But it's not like you can drive." His expression darkened. "Am I ready to blow? I'm ready to rip this town wide open."

Like a madwoman, I'd waved a red flag at the bull. "There's no guarantee that if I return home, I won't be followed. This person is demented. What does he think I know or can prove? My instincts say that I'm safer with you."

"If I thought otherwise, you'd already be home." He took a corner a little too sharply, then slowed down and sent me an apologetic look. "We're so close. We just need the last pieces to fall into place."

"I could call in a few favours from some colleagues. We're talking two days of work, and the commission would be finished."

He drummed his fingers on the steering wheel. "Let me think about it."

We turned right and drove down an unpaved road. He pulled into a small clearing, parking his truck beside two OPP vehicles and a truck that had seen better days. "It's a bit of a hike. About a kilometre or so."

I grabbed my messenger bag by using a pincer-type grasp and slung it over my shoulder. "I'm guessing there's no cell service in the park?"

Mac wiggled a can of bug spray. "It's hit or miss."

"I'm hoping to send some pictures to Jean Paul." I turned and lifted my hair so he could spray the back of my neck. "I don't want to get anyone's hopes up, but he may be able to remove the graffiti without destroying the pictographs."

Mac retrieved the goodies bag from the back seat and carefully tucked it into a large backpack before we headed into the woods.

Civilization disappeared. Towering pines filtered the afternoon light, glazing the interior with a soft, green haze. Though the trail was well cleared, I needed to watch out for rocks and roots, puddles and felled trees. Our footsteps resounded as we trekked over dried leaves and pine combs. The rustle of branches seemed to shush us as we moved further into the forest.

We hadn't gone far at all when we came upon a glade that had been used for a bush party. Crushed beer cans and broken wine bottles littered the forest floor. Someone had lit a bonfire. Large rocks circled a blackened stump. Even from several feet away, I could smell the stench of piss, making it easy to guess how the fire had been put out. Mac grumbled something.

Sickened, I stepped over a used condom, thinking even the wilderness kept its share of secrets . . . *wicked nymphs who did naughty things* . . . What naughty things had Rosemary seen?

I stumbled over a long-dead squirrel, pulsing with parasites. Something sleek and brown darted past me, tore through the brush.

We soldiered on, and the trail turned, running parallel to a wide stream; light bounced off cascading water and restored peacefulness to our surroundings. Chipmunks peeked at me from ferns, and I paused to appreciate several purple finches resting on a leafless elm, pink feathers looking like cherry blossoms, as if it were spring, not autumn. The serene feeling stayed with me until Mac abruptly dropped down into a squat. I walked up behind him and peered over his shoulder, looking down at the huge track in the earth. It was larger than his hand.

"Black bear," he said, "A hefty male from the looks of it. He's bulking up for hibernation, eating non-stop. Stay close to me. Just in case." He pointed to a pile of scat swarming with flies. "It's fresh. So, our friend passed by here yesterday sometime. But there's a chance he might return."

I nodded, and once again I thought of Rosemary, of two girls wandering the woods, alone and vulnerable . . . *they crossed a treacherous stream, ran from black bears . . .*

The trail and the stream began to run downhill. The path became steeper—more perilous—the further we walked. Mac warned me to watch my step, to slow down. We descended into the canyon, and I heard waves slapping against rock.

The bluffs rose out of nowhere, and I stopped for a moment as I took in the astounding view of rock, water, and sky. Far below me, a moose swam toward the bay's shore. At first, all I could see was its massive head. Then, it found its footing, lumbered through the waves, and stepped onto land, shaking the water from its body.

We kept hiking until we reached flatter terrain. About a hundred metres down the trail, two uniformed officers and a man in a tan, fringed leather jacket stood in a small huddle. They heard our approach and turned toward us.

One of the officers waved and called out, "Yo, Mac! Tell me you brought coffee."

Mac yelled back, "Nice to see you too, Lindsey!"

Our laughter echoed, agitating grey jays and sending them squawking toward distant trees. Soon, we'd joined the small group and introductions were made. Detective Constable Lindsey Brown served with the Bliss River OPP detachment, and Constable Mike Petahtegoose had been recently appointed to the Mississauga First Nations Police. They both offered me welcoming smiles as Mac put down his backpack and unloaded the refreshments. The officers helped him.

"This is Chief Eric Wemigwans." Mac handed him a paper cup. "Black, right?"

"I'm off sugar." His eyes sparkled with humour. "Now, where are those tarts?"

It was a short break for Chief Wemigwans and me. The constables had completed their report and documented the vandalism, so they kicked back, gabbing about sports and holiday plans with Mac. The caffeine and syrupy deliciousness were exactly what I needed. I added my garbage to the bag Mac had brought.

Awkwardly, I told him one of my shoelaces needed tightening.

He crouched down and fixed them as Chief Wemigwans said, "The water's calm today, so we can step out onto the ledge."

I nodded, looking forward to the next leg of the hike. The chief and I moved down the trail as the others stayed behind. We headed toward a crevice that looked as if the cliff had been parted like a curtain. We stepped into the gap, and it swallowed us. Moss and lichen softened the high stony walls. Carefully, we descended the staircase hewn in the rock. It was all so otherworldly that I stopped to admire the sky, startlingly bright against the cold, dark granite.

Chief Wemigwans said, "This place re-energizes the whole being. Nature is a pure force—it supports us but only if we respect it in return."

I understood what he meant, and the feeling of being connected to the space grew as we reached the bottom. The lake stretched colossally into the distance, a massive body of water that pulsed with gentle swells and white-caps. How small we are, mere droplets.

"I brought a camera," I said. "Can we take some pictures?"

His voice deepened. "Please do. The message needs to get out there that our heritage is being erased."

"Um. I was wondering if you could take the pictures."

He glanced at my hands. "Ah, yes. We appreciate your help."

"There should be stronger penalties for defacing the art," I said.

"Indigenous culture is still undervalued in Canada. If this were Newfoundland's Viking settlement of L'Anse aux Meadows, what would the punishment be for spraying graffiti on those walls?" He raised his chin. "What you're about to see is what remains of my ancestor's vision quests. We still come here to find ourselves, to receive direction and experience visions. Sadly, the paintings are disappearing. The sun, the wind, the rain—all these things have caused many paintings to fade from existence." He frowned. "A mixture of animal fat and powdered hematite can only withstand so much, and people ignore the signs."

"They touch the paintings?"

"I can understand the temptation: the want to literally trace the history of this site. They mean no harm. What they fail to grasp is the oil on their hands is like paint thinner."

I winced. "If I can get Jean Paul onto this project, maybe local newspapers and blogs will run the story. It might educate people who know no better."

"Hope is always a good thing." He reached into his pocket and took out a small plastic bag. "We will sprinkle tobacco on the water and ask for permission to view the pictographs. This shows our respect to the Lake spirits and requests safe passage. Several people have fallen off the ledge." His eyes crinkled. "But that won't be happening to us today."

Luckily, the long, uneven rock ledge was dry. After offering our gifts, we started to make our way across the granite shelf; Chief Wemigwans protectively kept his hand on my elbow, and together we shuffled along the overlapping, stone slabs. I almost tripped, but the chief tightened his grip. Slightly out of breath and completely out of my element, I was relieved when we finally reached the cliff's face.

The pictographs were more opaque than I'd expected. I studied the red ochre sketches of canoes, turtles, and fish. A snake with legs—a human serpent—held me spellbound. Each image freeze-framed life: eagles soaring, a horse galloping, a bear wandering, figures holding baskets. My feelings of connectivity intensified as I imagined someone standing exactly where I was standing, a thousand years ago, painting figures for reasons we could only guess. And there, overshadowing the indigenous art were stupid yellow emojis, hearts and peace signs, and happy smiling faces. The irony of the symbolism had me huffing with anger.

The chief snapped dozens of pictures from different angles, ensuring he'd captured both the untouched pictographs and the ones covered in graffiti. Waves lapped at the ledge just a foot from where we stood, and the water became choppier. The damp rock became slick. Fifteen minutes later, we shambled back to the outlook. The chancy Wi-Fi service was cooperating, so I quickly sent Jean Paul the photos as Chief Wemigwans patiently waited.

"He's somewhere in Colorado," I explained, "so I'm not expecting him to—"

My phone rang, and Jean Paul excitedly told me he'd love to get involved in the restoration. He asked whom he should speak to, and I handed my cell to the chief. "It's for you."

While they talked, I took in more of the breathtaking scenery, noting that the sun was beginning to sink. We'd need to leave soon, or we'd be hiking in the dark. Still, I wanted to linger, to forget about murder and the mural for a while longer. Five members of the Group of Seven had been as captivated as I was by the power of this rugged landscape. There, right there, was the place that had inspired a dozen Canadian masterpieces. I wished I had a sketchbook and several hours to fully embrace that majestic vista.

Chief Wemigwans approached me with a wide grin and returned my phone. "No promises were made, but your friend believes the overall damage can be reduced," he shared. "He should be able to visit with us in a week or so. Restoration will need to wait until spring, of course. Still, this is better news than we expected."

I hesitated. "Will the restoration be provincially funded?"

"We'll make a pitch, though an elder has offered financial assistance. Mig Daybutch. You're surprised?"

The lines on his face deepened, "The province paid him eight million for the hell he suffered. Mig is generous with everyone but himself. He lives modestly."

I nodded, wondering how a boy wrongfully imprisoned had not only survived his long incarceration but had become a caring, generous man. How easy it would be to hate.

We walked back up the stone steps and returned to the spot where we'd left the others.

Mac was alone. He explained that the constables had already left. The three of us hiked back to the clearing as quickly as we could. Shyly, I excused myself and made use of the outhouse. The chief thanked me once again, and we said our good-byes.

Twilight was fading. The last trace of red disappeared from the sky as we climbed into Mac's truck. Soon, we were travelling down a dark, bumpy road, and my earlier peace of mind vanished. We were in the middle of nowhere, and I don't like country roads at night.

I relaxed as the road widened, and I realized we were approaching Havenscrag. The highway was just a bit further up the road. I gazed at the moon's mystic halo, and the tension slowly began to ease from my body, but I jerked forward in my seat as Mac slammed on the brakes. The seat belt strained painfully against my hips and shoulders.

"Don't look!" Mac yelled.

But I did.

Less than six feet from the truck stood a large, grey wolf, fully illuminated by the beams of the headlights. I stared at it, horrified, because it stared back without dropping what it carried in its mouth. A leg. It was carrying a bloody human leg.

22

THE WOLF'S EYES reflected the yellowish green light. I was shocked by the animal's fearlessness; instead of retreating, its ears flattened defensively, and it took several menacing steps toward the truck. I couldn't take my eyes off the leg. The ankle was clamped between the wolf's fangs. The foot had been gnawed, as had the calf, and the knee was missing. I gagged at the sight of the grotesque stump, the flap of skin, the pulpy mangle of muscle and tendons.

"Look at me!"

I turned my head and focused on him.

"It's run off." His gaze locked on mine. "I'm going to call for backup. They should be here in just a few minutes. I want you to wait for them here."

As he pulled over, I gawped at the empty road. "It killed somebody!"

"Wolves are opportunistic. Most likely, it found the body." He raised a hand and pushed a curl behind my ear. "Stay in the truck. Honk the horn if you see anything strange."

Anything strange! Like more wolves with other body parts?

He called the station, and I half-heard the codes he rattled off. Rationality slowly returned as he un-holstered his weapon, grabbed his flashlight, and moved to open the door.

"Shouldn't you wait for the others?"

I sounded as frightened as I felt.

"Wolves hunt in packs, and I need to act fast before the entire cadaver is——"

"Got it! I'll stay in the truck, safe, while you face off with the predators, alone."

"Comes with the badge, Egghead."

"Have you considered another vocation?"

"Have you?" He opened the door. "Help's on the way. Now, stay put."

I nodded and bit my lip, hating that I'd been slotted into the helpless female role.

He closed the door and walked around the back of the truck. I watched him disappear down the driveway. Awkwardly, I opened my messenger bag and found my phone. I turned on its flashlight mode and continued to rifle through the bag's contents, giving myself something to do. I found my trusty Swiss Army knife and managed to pry out one of the largest knives. It was a flimsy weapon, but at least I felt armed. I glanced at my phone. Mac had only been gone two minutes, but it felt like two hours. I jumped when lights appeared between the trees, somewhere much further down the drive.

Then I heard the shots. Three of them. I threw the door open and hit the ground running, knife in hand, phone stupidly left behind in the truck. The gravel drive was covered with wet leaves, and I slipped. Without thinking, I raised my arms and used my hands to cushion my fall. I lay there, sprawled on the sodden ground. I searched for the knife on my hands and knees, found it, and pushed myself to my feet. My hands should have stung, but I felt nothing.

When I rounded a bend in the drive, a sensor light flicked on, and then another and another as I continued to run. The lights allowed me to increase my speed, but I still couldn't see Mac. My heart felt ready to explode out of my chest. *Where was he?*

The drive cut through dense woodlands. Something crashed through the bush, racing past me toward the road. The pack had been chased off. I sprinted down the long, winding curve until I reached the end of the drive. What I saw brought me to a full stop. Mac had been right. The wolves had been busy.

"Freeze! This is the police. Drop your weapon!" Mac stood in front of the ghastly scene, and I realized that I was partially hidden by shadows.

"Don't shoot! It's me!" Unsteadily I walked toward him.

"Annora, turn around, right now!"

Too late. I had already seen what remained of James Powell. Sensor lights had become stage lights. The horrifying image burned itself into my brain, and even from a distance, the reek of death overwhelmed me. Powell's body dangled from the upper balcony of Havencrag. His dark robe hung open, revealing boxer shorts and a bloated torso. More than one leg was missing. His other foot was gone too. Powell must have knotted the hell out of the rope, because the pack had been unable to pull him down, though they must have tried. The corpse had been shredded from the thighs down. A hand had also been devoured, and I guessed ravens had feasted on his face. I saw the empty eye sockets. I saw the lipless mouth, the exposed dentures.

My stomach rolled, and I fought for control, but Mac knew it was a lost battle. He helped me lean forward, rubbing my back and crooning comforting words. I was still dry heaving when I heard the sirens.

Within minutes, six constables had arrived at the scene, and Mac began to bark orders.

"Annora, Constable Johnston will take you back to my place and stay with you, okay?

This is going to take a while. Most likely, we'll be here all night."

I'd lost the ability to speak and felt oddly numb, but I managed to nod.

I can't remember getting into the squad car or the hour that followed, but I recall curling into a ball on his couch, shivering. Johnston covered me with a quilt and made me an herbal tea. The aroma of clove and orange helped to ease my queasiness, and I held the mug to my face and breathed in the fragrance, erasing the stench-memory of rotting flesh. He sat down on a chair and chatted to me non-stop about his baby boy, meeting his wife, the town, and his work. The normalcy of his prattle had a calming effect.

"Last year, I was asked to go check on Old Man Wilson, a wild character who lived alone in a small trailer just west of town. He'd been dead for quite some time. He had cats . . ." Revulsion crept into his voice. "I lost my lunch, and I had training. So don't feel embarrassed for being human." He cleared his throat. "I'm sure Mac could say this better than I did."

"I think you said it quite well. Thank you."

The hours slowly passed. I dozed but was too restless
to actually sleep. Around midnight, I gave up, changed
my muddied clothes, ate a few crackers, and realized my
phone was still in Mac's truck. I knew I shouldn't call
him anyway, but I wished I could.

The audiobook I'd begun was a thriller, and my
night didn't need any more excitement. I'd reached
my suspense limit. Pete picked up the TV remote and
scrolled through the late-night movie choices. We both
snorted at the selections—*Halloween, The Shining, Car-
rie*. He sensibly picked a Roy Rogers marathon that
lulled us into a stupor. Sometime after four, I nodded
off. Sunlight woke me up, and I felt ridiculously happy
to find Mac fast asleep in his favourite chair, still in uniform. There were shadows under his eyes, and his jaw
was covered in stubble. I tucked a blanket around him
and tried to forget the reason he was home so late. I gave
in to temptation and kissed his forehead.

"Night, Grams," he mumbled.

I wasn't sure if I should kiss him again or poke him
extra hard. I did neither.

Feeling better and a bit hungry, I headed to the
kitchen and toasted two frozen waffles. I ate them plain
while staring out the window. Mac had said the local
housewives in the fifties used tranquilizers to cope with
drudgery, emptiness, and sexual frustration. Suddenly,
I could relate to them. I already felt like I was losing
my mind, like everything was spinning out of control. I
allowed myself a five-minute pity party. What I needed
was a little fresh air, so I retrieved my jacket and boots
from the front hall closet, then tiptoed out the back
door, leaving my jacket unzipped.

It was one of those perfect fall days. A garden rake rested against the wooden fence. Decisively, I decided to do a bit of yard work and went to search out leaf bags in the shed. They were easy to find, but I soon discovered that not only was it difficult to rake wearing bandages, but the activity also made my palms ache. Frustrated, I tossed the rake aside and marched toward the swing. I plopped on the seat and began to rock. Squirrels leapt between branches, complaining about my presence. I didn't hear the door slide open.

"Wanna talk?" Mac stood on his deck with his hands behind his back.

I kept swinging.

"You look thirsty." He revealed a bottle of Perrier, holding it out like it was Dom Pérignon. "How about I join you and give you the lowdown?"

"Fine. But no gory details."

Mac twisted off the cap, took a straw from his shirt pocket, and inserted it into the bottle. Then he joined me on the swing and handed me the bottle.

I took a long sip.

"I'm worried about you," he said. "What you experienced was traumatic. There's a reason first responders suffer from PTSD."

"My therapist would agree. So would my support group."

Mac studied my face.

"Yes, I've been triggered, but I'll get over it! Powell wasn't even likeable," I blurted. "Great. Now I feel even worse."

"Why? You're right. His friends gave up on him. Even family stopped visiting. Booze sharpened his tongue, and I'm fairly sure the coroner's report will show a staggeringly high blood alcohol level." His expression gentled. "Who he was has little to do with it. Your reaction to seeing his body in that state was normal."

I glanced at the squirrels, trying to un-remember.

"He hid his depression surprisingly well." His brows lowered. "Jane is in shock and their kids are angry. Nobody saw this coming. Nobody."

"Then, it was a suicide?"

"We found a note beside an empty bottle of vintage Wiser's Whisky."

"What did it say?"

"It wasn't a straightforward confession. He wrote, 'My death should put an end to this. I have no right to ask for forgiveness. I can only say how genuinely sorry I am. Finally, we can all rest.'"

"He acknowledged his guilt."

"No. He acknowledged he *feels* guilty." He leaned back into the seat and crossed his arms. "If he's the killer, it provides closure for everyone. A disturbed boy commits a violent crime that he regrets. Decades pass, he drinks out of remorse and self-loathing, kills himself, and the town goes back to being sleepy and secretive."

"But wasn't that your premise all along?"

"James may have been a mean drunkard, but he's never raised a hand against anyone. He disliked confrontation and avoided it at all costs. If he was willing to hang himself, why kill his two best friends *first*? It doesn't add up."

"Murder-suicides happen every day, don't they? And you said he wouldn't be able to handle the realities of prison life. Perhaps Len told Floyd what he'd seen in the mural, and they confronted James and gave him an ultimatum. He arranged meetups and killed them, but then guilt ate him alive."

"And James hid out in the parsonage and turned on the oven? He was the arsonist too?"

I sat there, essentially left speechless. I thought about the crazed cackle I'd heard just before the firebomb had been tossed into the parsonage. I thought about James's low, quiet voice and his discernible frailness. I'd only met him once and had spoken to him for a brief time. Even so, it was hard to imagine him hiding in bushes or in an attic. He'd genuinely seemed broken.

I had a difficult time picturing him as a homicidal maniac who torched mills. He'd been antisocial and a tad antagonistic. Could he also have been a psychopath? His portraitures were brutally honest but were not sadistic or maniacal.

Mac waited, watching me with an intense expression that had become familiar.

"We need to finish cleaning the mural!" I said.

"I know. But what can we do?"

"Okay. I'm gross right now. Rank. I'm going to take a shower, and then we may be able to figure something out. Like I said, I know people who can take care of this."

He laughed. "You sounded a bit like Don Vito Corleone there."

"Ha. Well, I could pull in some favours. The problem will be timing—availability on such short notice. Conservators tend to require advance notice."

❧

I emerged from the washroom feeling like a wet string mop. My hair was a matted mess, and I wore yet another

pale grey jogging suit. I'd never felt frumpier. The shower
had helped clear more than my mind, but my bandages
were filthy, damp, and tattered. Lost in thought, I made
my way back downstairs and found Mac spreading first-
aid supplies out on the kitchen table. He'd become a pro
at changing my dressings. After he'd cut away the dirty
gauze, he sent me a look filled with reproach, and it so
reminded me of my mother's stink eye that I laughed.

One eyebrow lifted. "How is this funny?"

"I'm waiting for you to tell me I'm grounded."

"Pointless. Besides, you see the doc in a few days,
and she'll lecture you plenty."

I lowered my head, and my hair fell over my eyes.
Futilely, I blew at it. "I may ask you to take me to a hair
salon soon so they can lop a foot off this nest."

"Tell me you're joking."

"What? It's a bunch of knots and split ends. It'll
grow back."

He slipped the elastic tubular netting over my bandaged hands, checked his work, and peeled off the ster-
ile gloves. Quickly, he cleared the table by returning
everything to a large plastic container he handily kept
on the back counter. Mac moseyed back and stood quietly behind me, then lifted my damp hair off the nape
of my neck. "I've been told I can work magic." His voice
deepened. "I'd love to brush your hair, Egghead. Will
you let me?"

Mistake or a memory in the making, I wasn't sure
which but said, "It'll take a while."

"Be right back."

Mac left the room, and I realized I was in trouble.
He'd already scrambled my brain and set my pulse racing. Minutes later, he returned with a brush and held up

a small bottle of Moroccan argan oil. "I bought this for you today," he said. He opened the bottle and poured a generous amount onto his palms. It smelled earthy, exotic, seductive. When he began to rub the oil into my hair and to gently massage my scalp, I melted.

He picked up the brush and started at my ends, slowly working from the bottom up.

Those big, warm hands sensually tamed my curls. I lost track of time, closing my eyes as heat coursed between us. His long fingers lingered against one of my ear lobes, trailed lightly across my shoulders, brushed against my temples. Again and again, he ran the brush through my hair, long after it was soft and pliant, and I didn't stop him. I sensed if I tilted my head back, his mouth would lower to mine and that kiss would lead us upstairs.

"You know how you keep saying that I'd make a great cop?"

"Mm-hmm."

"I think you'd make an excellent art conservator."

"Oh, really." His low, erotic chuckle curled my toes.

"I mean, you have such a light touch . . ." A thought flew into my head. I jumped to my feet and grabbed his forearm. "Mac? I'm gonna make you an offer you can't refuse!"

H E STARED AT me like I was crazy.

"It will work."

"No. It won't. I can't even keep my truck clean."

"I'll be right beside you the entire time, guiding you through the procedures step by step," I coaxed. "We'll take it nice and slow. Art conservation 101."

"What if I do something wrong?"

"Don't you think it's worth a try?"

He pursed his lips and narrowed his eyes. We stood there, face to face, and I refused to budge. Finally, he conceded. "There's that orneriness I admire. Sometimes."

"So, is it time for us to pack?"

"Not exactly. First, I'll head over to the parsonage with a few supplies and check our status. Though the building was deemed safe, it'll need some groundwork before we start working on the mural. Could take a few hours. Hard to say. While—"

"I'm coming too."

"Why?" He took one look at my expression, then raised his hands in surrender. "Never mind. If I leave you here, most likely you'll overdo it again."

Perseverance is a strength, I reasoned, but I kept the thought to myself.

Mac grabbed his toolbox and tossed it into the back of his truck, along with more bedding, a blow-up mattress, water bottles, two bags of food, and a box filled with cleaning supplies. We stopped at the hardware store, where we purchased more plastic sheeting, several tarps, and six rolls of duct tape. Though I'd been impatient at the shop, as we drove down Felicity Street, I tried to hide my nervousness behind small talk, and I stopped speaking the minute the parsonage came into view. I couldn't believe that Mac hadn't prepared me.

I gasped.

Mac swiveled his head. "Dammit. I should have—"

"Yes. You should have."

The building was surrounded by a six-foot-high fence, and lofty floodlights had been erected in each corner of the yard, making it look like a penitentiary. All of the lower windows were boarded up as if the home were still abandoned. The temperature had dropped again to seasonal norms, so Mac had cranked the heat in the truck; regardless, the decrepit scene chilled me clear to the bone. My bravado vanished, and I pressed my back into the seat. What fresh snags waited behind the steel barricade? How many more complications could we handle?

I thought about Lilith and John and the museum's grand opening. From what I could see, the centennial celebrations would be held elsewhere. Though I'd been told the fire damage had been localized to the back parlours, I also knew smoke was invasive. There was no way the renovations could be completed in time.

Mac took off his sunglasses and placed them on the dash. "Sure you want to do this?"

I nodded and unbuckled my seat belt, keeping my apprehension to myself.

We unloaded the truck, placing all of our supplies inside the barrier so Mac could lock it securely behind us. Then—despite his protests—I helped carry bags up to the porch. Once we'd moved everything onto the porch, we opened the front door.

Stepping into the frigid vestibule was like entering a crypt. I wondered if Mac also felt the stifling desolation of the place. What had once seemed merely dreary had become more oppressive and as formidable as an armament. Victorians would have said the very air was saturated with melancholia. All I knew was that I had to force myself to shuffle forward and disturb the strange, sad stillness. Unquestionably, the loss of natural light exaggerated the bleakness, as did memories of the arson attack. My chest tightened at the thought of the scarred room, my recent battle zone. I managed to grab a bag of food so I could put off facing Rosemary for just a little while longer.

"I'm going upstairs to open a few windows," Mac said. "Be right back."

The pot lights had been left on, so the hall wasn't completely dark. Soot coated the walls and ceiling. I could smell smoke, and the taupe paint had greyed, but as I headed toward the kitchen, I breathed a sigh of relief. From what I could see, the damage had, in fact, been contained to the back parlour and hall. The room was freezing, so I left my jacket on and fumbled with the heater until it began to glow. I managed to unpack a bag, but I dropped a small jar of strawberry jam, which shattered the silence and brought Mac running down the stairs.

"You okay?" He glanced at the floor. "Ah. I got this."

"I'm sorry about the mess. I can't wait for these stupid bandages to be removed!"

"I know how frustrated you are. One more week. Would you like to—"

"I'll check on the mural." My words came out in a telling rush.

He frowned. "Wait." After rummaging through a bag, he found a respirator mask and helped me put it on. "Avoid the center of the room. And please, try not to freak out when you see how badly—"

I left the room before he could finish.

"Walk, don't run!" He shouted.

But I didn't slow down.

へ∽

It was worse than I'd feared. Powder from the fire extinguisher dusted the pitted, charred floor, and black specks clung to the walls like thousands of tiny spiders. All the plastic sheeting had melted, and odd, crispy strands hung from the scorched ceiling, here and there. Shaken, I staggered toward the mural; soot smothered every inch. Though the evidence had been documented and Mac had taken numerous pictures, I was still ready to scream. All my work, gone! If I could have, I would have punched a wall. Blood surged in my ears, and my vision clouded. There was nowhere to put my rage.

"Look at what he's done to you," I seethed. "I hope he rots in hell!"

Immediately, the toxic air lost its stench. I couldn't possibly be smelling lavender, but I was. I turned toward the boarded-up window, trying to find a reasonable explanation, realizing I could feel a draft. There were gaps in the boards on the window. I could see a crack in the pane. When I glanced back at the mural, my knees almost gave out.

The sooty film seemed to ripple, appeared to swell ever so slightly, almost imperceptibly. I stared at the wall in disbelief and didn't even have time to gasp. It was just an illusion, I knew, but I swore I saw Rosemary's lips turn downward. It all happened in less than a second.

Mac yelled something. I blinked, and just like that Rosemary was once again smiling, once again two-dimensional, a lifeless figure trapped under a layer of soot.

"Wow, talk about—Annora?"

I ripped off my mask, gasping, and sank to my knees. He was beside me in seconds. The way he scooped me up should have been comforting, not distressing. I put my arms around his neck as he grumbled about rest and more calories and hard-headed women. I considered telling him what I'd seen, but I knew if I did, he'd drive me straight to the hospital. It seemed a better choice to let him carry me to the office. He gently set me down on the cot and tucked the quilt around me. In a state himself, he held a wrist to my forehead, tsking. "No fever," he said, and left the room. He returned with a meal replacement shake, a straw already inserted into the bottle. He insisted I drink it.

I grimaced as I took several long sips.

"I'll check back on you in a bit." Mac turned off the light and shut the door.

I lay there, wondering if I'd lost my mind. I flipped onto my back, admittedly tired but unable to shut my eyes. Could the building really be haunted? What if all those stories weren't cautionary tales to keep children away from the river, and I hadn't been imagining things? The idea didn't frighten me. In fact, it felt like Rosemary wished she could protect me as much as I wanted to protect her. Still, a ghost?

Though I was no paranormal expert, I'd have to live in a cave not to know that billions of people believe in lost souls. As a young teen, I'd tried and tried to bring back the dead, and I'd once paid a so-called clairvoyant seventy-five dollars so she could contort her powdered face, moan dramatically, and tell me that Maeve was truly sorry for borrowing my jewelry without my permission. When I told the fake that I hadn't owned any jewelry as a child, she'd said that trinkets could be symbolic of something precious or personal. I told her it was cruel to lie to the bereaved, and I hoped karma paid her a visit. The memory put me in a foul mood.

Mac knocked on the door, and I let him know I'd be right out. I met him in the kitchen.

He was finishing putting away the food. "Well, well. You look refreshed."

"I feel great," I fibbed. "The rest did me good."

"We're all set up. I'll be bunkering down in the dining room. I cleaned the parlour the best I could and put up more plastic sheeting."

"I need to take stock of my supplies and show you a few things."

"Prepping we can do today. But we won't be touching the mural."

"But—"

His mouth tightened. "Tomorrow we'll get an early start and see how it goes, alright?"

"Fine." I took off my coat, hoping the other rooms had warmed up. "Prep work it is."

Smoke damage had left the study unusable, and I was glad I'd stored my extra supplies elsewhere. I asked Mac if we could bring the card table to the dining room so we could wash it down. We needed a workspace to prepare the solutions and roll the swabs, I explained. In less than an hour, we'd rearranged the room, shoving the blow-up mattress into a corner and adding a small folding table we found in an upstairs room. I checked through my kits. Though I still had plenty of swabs and cotton, I worried we'd run out of surfactants.

Before we left, I made an excuse about needing to further assess the mural. Mac's brows raised, but he didn't follow me to the parlour. I hurried back to Rosemary and gently touched her arm, not caring what the soot would do to my bandages.

"I'll be back soon," I whispered. "I promise." I'd half-expected her to clasp my hand or whisper something in return, but nothing happened.

Mac called from the hall, "We should get going!"

I met him at the front door. Part of me desperately wanted to stay, and part of me couldn't wait to leave. Mac turned toward me, closed his eyes, and smiled. "Mmm. Are you wearing perfume? I know that scent . . . lavender, isn't it?"

CHAPTER

24

THOUGH WE'D STEPPED out onto the porch, I sensed I was being watched. I lifted my head and gazed past the fence, noting that about a dozen people stood across the street, staring at us, completely agape.

"Damn. I forgot about the ghost walk," Mac said.

"You're joking."

"I'm, ahem, *dead* serious."

I chose to ignore him. "Isn't that . . .?"

"Yes, it's Petra from the Good Witch Bistro. Every Halloween, she gives tours."

She wore a long, black cape and pale, wraithlike make-up. When she shouted out a greeting and waved enthusiastically, I gave a teeny wave back. The moment was surreal, as if I'd become a part of some TV prank show.

Mac tensed, then gently took my elbow and escorted me down the steps, which I begrudgingly allowed. As he opened and relocked the gate, he whispered to me, "Please, wait by the truck while I talk to him."

Him? I turned and found the source of his annoyance. Daniel Styles, Rosemary's half-brother, had signed up for the tour. He stood off to one side of the small troop. His camera was directed at us. He quickly lowered it when I glared at him, but his expression was more defiant than apologetic. Still, if I were in his place, what would I do? I wouldn't be sipping hot cocoa at some quaint inn, patiently waiting for the authorities to mete out an occasional update; I'd tap into the local buzz so I could learn as much as I could about the town, its residents. and its sordid past. I'd investigate my sister's murder.

I made my way to the pickup as Mac nonchalantly strolled across the street, as if he weren't in any way vexed, but Daniel wasn't buying it. Daniel-of-the-thousand-words folded his arms, widened his stance, and scowled. Mac gave him space, and the men quietly spoke for several minutes. Mac shook his head as Daniel pointed toward the parsonage repeatedly, and his gestures grew more agitated with each passing minute. My heart went out to him when his eyes closed in resignation. Feeling like a voyeur, I turned away from the emotional scene.

Absentmindedly, I gazed up at the second floor and sucked in my breath as a light flicked on in the empty building. The naked bulb grew brighter, then dimmed, softly strobing. I became mesmerized by the eerie rhythm, unable to look away. The light switched off as suddenly as it had switched on, and once again the window was dark. I jumped when Mac appeared and reached around me to open the passenger door.

"Sorry to keep you waiting." He gave me a strange look. "You okay?"

"No." I got into the cab, and he helped me with my seat belt.

"Want to talk about it?"

"No."

"Good. I'm not in the mood to talk either."

The day had been exhausting. Fury was slowly replacing acceptance. Since the car accident, I'd wanted so desperately to have proof of an afterlife. I'd watched for signs, but the only visitations I'd received had been through my dreams. I'd have given anything, absolutely anything, to see my father and sisters one more time, to know that they existed in some other dimension. Why had Rosemary been able to reach out to me, but they could not? My father had been a wonderful, kind, loving man. My sisters were just as sweet, just as innocent as Rosemary. Why wasn't I being haunted by them? Were they truly at peace? Had they forgotten me?

The ride was a bit of a blur. I cringed as Mac pulled into his driveway. Lilith sat on the porch, holding an enormous fruit basket.

Mac groaned. "You up for company?"

I glared at him.

He nodded. "Can you at least manage a smile? A little one?"

I narrowed my eyes.

"Ouch."

Lilith rose from the wicker chair as we approached the steps.

Perhaps it was because I was annoyed or it might have been because I was at the point of collapse, but whatever the reason, I tripped over my own feet, and I would have planted my face into the railing if it hadn't been for Mac's quick reflexes. His arm locked around my waist.

I stood there, swaying. When I finally steadied myself, he kept his arm around me. He gently touched my chin, his face close to mine. "Bedtime for you, Egghead."

"No arguments here."

He refused to let me go, holding me against his side as we walked up the few steps.

Lilith's gaze moved between the two of us quizzically, obviously detecting our less than subtle vibes. "You okay, Nory?"

"Mostly?"

Mac shepherded me to a chair, making me feel all the more stupidly fragile. His gaze softened, as if he'd read my mind. "You two chat. I'll make some calls."

Lilith handed him the basket.

"Kind of you," he said. "A bit much for two people, though, don't you think?"

"Our girl has a thing about peaches. She can eat three in a row."

"Good to know." He chuckled and disappeared into the house.

I fought a yawn, but it escaped. "You actually remember what fruit I like?"

"Roommates, right?" She shrugged. "I won't be long. Just dropped by to see how you are. By the way, we've found an alternate venue for the centennial celebration."

Gee, a murderer and/or arsonist is on the loose, people are scared to leave their homes, and the whole town is on red alert. Let's celebrate? "I'm surprised you don't postpone it."

Her chin lifted ever so slightly. "We need to get back on the horse. By we, I mean those who live in Bliss River—not you. As far as the parsonage goes, the damage is extensive. The museum is still a go. Eventually, we'll finish the job." Her gaze met mine directly. "I'm so sorry about all this. I wish I'd never contacted you. You should go home, hon. Call it a day."

"I'm glad I accepted this commission. And I'm staying."

"What? Why?"

"This case is close to being solved. We haven't completely given up—not yet."

I explained how Mac and I would work as a team. "I know he can do this with my help."

"My, my. You two have gotten quite chummy. And the way he looks at you . . ."

I cleared my throat. "Let it be." My palms were throbbing, and my emotions were just as tender. "Please? Drop it."

"You're the one who said "single by choice." Long distance relationships never work out. Why start something that will only end badly?"

I saw red. "So, how will things end between you and John? Does he suspect you're cheating on him? With his own employee?"

She shot up from her chair. "Don't you dare judge me!" Her eyes were full of hurt. "I won't apologize for being human or having needs. You know what? Screw you!"

She stormed away, and I wondered if I should call out, ask for forgiveness. Lilith had a point. I do expect too much from people. She peeled away in her Mini Cooper. I worried that at the speed she was going, she'd have an accident. Why hadn't I just kept my mouth shut? I sat there, lost in my thoughts, until Mac opened the door. He saw more than I wanted him to see. With a sigh, he pulled me to my feet, kissed the top of my head, and held me. We stood there in the dark for quite some time. He didn't quiz me, nor did he give me a pep talk.

Mac is, after all, a very smart man.

૭✦ⴄ

"I'm an idiot!" he bellowed.

"But you're getting it. Really, you are. You just need to use an even lighter touch."

"You actually like doing this for a living? Why?"

"Just wait. You'll see."

We'd been working on the mural for two hours. I was glad I wasn't alone. The parlour was a burned-out shell. Both air scrubbers had been reduced to misshapen lumps. Mac had scattered several tarps on the floor. The scene was like something out of an end-of-the-world movie, cue the radioactive fallout zombies clawing at the boarded-up windows. As an art conservator, I knew most things could be restored given enough time, resolve, and ability. Still, it was hard to imagine art ever again embellishing those blackened walls.

There wasn't much of the painting that I hadn't cleaned prior to the fire. The sky, some of the woods. Mac was slowly, very slowly, revealing the branches of one tree. I kept staring into Rosemary's eyes, trying to communicate to her spirit that we were doing our best. Mac's jaw was tight, and his movements were awkward. Still, we soldiered on. Every few minutes, I'd make another suggestion: roll the swab in this direction, lift your hand, check the surface, repeat. And so it went.

"What is that?" I finally asked. "See, right there? It's like the side of a box."

"A box in a tree? It's not a birdhouse. Oh, hell! It's a coffin!"

"I know you want to rush this, but you still need to use the same gentle pressure, the same slow movements. Okay?"

He slowly exhaled. "Got it."

The room became even chillier, and I sensed that somehow Rosemary was encouraging us. I could almost hear her sweet voice, pleading, *Please, please, give me peace.*

"Oh my God," I whispered. "There. It's a face. Is that the missing doll?"

We studied the emerging image.

Mac groaned and said, "No. It's a baby. A baby with blue lips. In a cradle."

"Rockabye baby . . ."

". . . in a treetop? What the—"

"Edmond Boyland!" we shouted at the same time.

"Boyland's infant son." Mac moved closer to the mural. "He died in his sleep. The actual cause of death was listed as hypoplastic left heart syndrome. I remembered because an uncle of mine was born with it too. The survival rate for newborns born with any kind of a congenital heart defect was pretty grim in the '40s and '50s." He rubbed his chin. "How does that creepy lullaby go again?"

I remembered my mother singing to me when I was sick, then singing it to all my sisters. "'When the wind blows, the cradle will rock. When the bough breaks, the cradle will fall. Down will come baby, cradle and all.' I don't know the rest."

I got my phone and googled the lyrics. Together, we read:

> Baby is drowsing, cozy and fair
> Mother sits near in her rocking chair
> Forward and back, the cradle she swings
> Though baby sleeps, he hears what she sings
> Rock-a-bye baby, do not you fear
> Never mind, baby, mother is near
> Wee little fingers, eyes are shut tight
> Now sound asleep—until morning light

I shakily turned toward the mural, sickened yet riveted. Edmond did not look like he had died naturally. His mouth was a small, black hole. This was no sleeping baby, and he would never hear his mother sing again. *'Mother is . . .'* I mentally peeled away the soot and focused on the composition, studying the branches, the way the tree oddly leaned to one side. "Oh, Mac! Mother is nearby! His mother. I think we're going to find Delphine!"

He insisted I down another protein drink but didn't eat anything himself. We pushed through the afternoon. Mac rolled his neck, grumbling under his breath. Then, we found her: poor heartbroken Delphine. Kingsley had painted her reverently. Though she hung from a noose, her features were relaxed, and she was luminous. As Mac removed more soot and the underlying mould, the effect increased until she practically blazed. A golden aura surrounded Delphine. Her countenance was pure, even holy, reminding me of a devotional card, the gilded illustration of some long-martyred saint.

"Do you need to stop?" I asked. "We could try for another six-inch square."

"Two more hours. You need more than a meal replacement. And to be honest, my muscles are aching. I have a new respect for your job."

"I've been told I have dancer arms. Whatever that means."

"Strong. Graceful. Sexy."

I blushed. "Ah. Well, then."

He laughed, and my toes curled. *"Be smart,"* Lilith had said. The devil on my shoulder told me not to listen. My mouth was dry, and I kept thinking about how his lips had felt on mine. The space between us warmed. I welcomed the distraction. The mission at hand was bleeding me emotionally dry. If I concentrated solely on the sorrow permeating the room, I would have fallen apart, become useless. Without his company, I would have been defenseless against the despair that shadowed corners, saturating each surface.

It took less than an hour for us to find the owl. It was perched on the lowest branch. It could not see the shocking sight of Boyland's dead wife and baby. Its head was turned toward Rosemary, and its snowy wings stretched out as if the bird believed it could still fly. But it was earthbound, an ethereal and lost creature. Alone. And broken.

25

MAC TIDIED UP our workspace while I sat there, feeling useless. He ordered us a pizza before heading upstairs to take a shower. I wished I could at least make a salad.

I became slightly claustrophobic, hating how the boarded-up windows had drastically changed the room's atmosphere. Without the scenery or small glimpses of daily life, it felt as if we'd been locked in a wooden crate or nailed into a coffin. I needed fresh air, normalcy, freedom to move, and some natural light. I'd suggest an outing. A short walk along the beach might clear our heads. We could take in the sunset and find our second wind. Then, we could return to the mural and squeeze in a few more hours of work. I began to pace, shifting between the back door and sink, as restless as a caged cat. The overhead light flickered.

I froze in my tracks and whispered, "Rosemary?"

There was no response, not a single sound. I was about to call out to her again when I heard Mac walking down the hall. His phone rang; our pizza had arrived. The odd quiet vanished in a heartbeat, but I knew I hadn't imagined the moment.

Mac slid slices onto our paper plates. I wasn't sure if I could handle all the grease, deep crust, or tangy sauce. At first, my stomach clenched at the aroma, but my trepidation melted after one taste. Handling the slices was awkward. But was so worth the effort.

"We need to change those bandages," Mac said.

"Mm-hmm."

"Told you that you were hungry."

I eyed a fourth slice but decided three was my limit. "What do you make of the mural so far? It's quite the puzzle, isn't it?"

"Boyland was obviously one tormented man. It did surprise me to find Edmond and Delphine included in that twisted shrine. And what's with the damned owl? The thing keeps making odd appearances. In the mural. In Rosemary's fairy tale. In Jane's artwork."

"Jane indicated her father was fixated on that particular bird. Something about it being a ghost story, a tale needing to be told."

"He's sending us mixed messages." He tossed our paper plates into the garbage. "Like he can't make up his mind."

"Mac? Before we take care of my hands, let's go for a stroll. Please?"

"Sounds like a plan."

I grabbed my purse, heard the old jalopy backfire, and didn't so much as flinch. Funny how we adjust to our surroundings, become accustomed to things. We ended up driving to the beach, so we could spend the time walking along the shore instead of wandering down the town's back streets. The air was frigid, but there was no wind. I closed my eyes and faced the water, allowing the events of the day to fade into the background.

Mac sidled closer to me as gulls eyed us for food. Their angry squawks kept us company as we strolled along the water's edge. The stiffness in my neck eased as the sun dropped lower.

"Okay," I finally said. "Three murders and one suicide. It began with Rosemary, led to Len being attacked and tossed in the river, then Floyd getting shot in the back of the head. Finally, James hung himself."

"Let's not forget about the firebug."

I held up my hands. "Oh, I haven't forgotten."

My cheeks were numbing from the cold. A young man jogged past us at a steady pace. A black lab trotted happily beside him, a long piece of driftwood in its mouth. We watched as the figures disappeared around the bend. Puffs of smoke drifted from a few chimneys. I was grateful for the thick sweater I wore and the company that I kept. The tension between my shoulders eased, and I sighed.

"Peaceful, isn't it?"

"I see why you live here."

"Annora?" He put his arm around my shoulders. "In time, for the right reasons, I'd be willing to move."

I froze. "Really?"

"You look terrified. This isn't a proposal. I'm just putting it out there. Okay?"

"Okay." *Time to change the subject.* "Uh, do you still think Daniel is our arsonist?"

He removed his arm. "He has no priors, but his behavior is erratic."

A gull flew lower, skimmed the waves, and landed in a splash. It gave me a vicious, red-eyed glare. Another gull floated close to it, and the two screeched aggressively at each other. A thought came to me. "The Guiding Light Project. What if—what if Rosemary saw something that she shouldn't have. What if all three were involved, and decades later, when the mural was found, they started to argue amongst themselves? What if only one wanted to come clean? Maybe James had been stronger than he'd seemed, and he'd killed Floyd and Len before killing himself. Maybe James was the arsonist."

"Hmm . . . things *have* been quiet since his death. But you told me that Len seemed stunned by something in the mural. If he had been involved in Rosemary's murder, nothing in that portrait should have rattled him."

"You're right. And I swear his reaction was genuine. So perhaps there were two—not three—murderers. What if Len wasn't involved, but confronted Floyd? Then, James learns about Len's murder and hunts Floyd down. Unable to live with himself any longer, drunk and feeling like the authorities are about to close in, he hangs himself."

"That is one big stretch. But it's a possibility." He fished his keys out of his pocket. "What could Rosemary have witnessed?"

"Maybe the boys broke the rules of their probation. Maybe they were worried about being kicked out of the arts program and going to prison—"

"Whoa, that's a ton of 'maybes.' But it's also a motive." He shot me an appreciative look. "Damn."

"Glad I'm good for something."

"Hey-ho! You gotta stop bad-mouthing yourself."

"You sound like my mother."

"So she and I should get along fine, then?"

I laughed, unwilling to snuff the happy feeling rising within me. "Sure, if you survive the inquisition. She can get quite protective. A true mama bear." Though a warm amber glow lit the sky, it definitely felt like mid-October. I shivered.

"Time to get back," Mac said. "I'll make hot cocoa."

Grace called. I gave them privacy, so they could freely talk. I took a shower, standing under the hot spray for longer than I'd intended. The upper level of the parsonage was chilly except for the washroom. I wondered what we would have done if the fire had damaged the entire building's electrical system. As it was, we were pushing its limits with extension cords and power bars. I was beginning to wonder if we'd have been better off staying at Mac's and driving back and forth in order to complete the mural, despite distractions. I stuck my tongue out at my reflection. I looked like the before picture of a makeover.

I took my time walking down the stairs, as I was wearing slippers and the stairwell was dark. When I reached the kitchen, I stood in the doorway for a moment to appreciate the homey scene. Mac was pouring steaming milk into two mugs. He stirred both cups and then topped each with marshmallows. I couldn't remember any man doing this for me except my father. My resolve melted as he turned toward me and smiled. "Let's take care of those hands first."

I sat down on a stool and lay them, palms up, on the counter.

"Good," he said. "See? Improvement. How's the pain?"

"Less than yesterday."

He carefully dressed the burns, the ointment's pungent smell veiled by the spicy scent of his aftershave. He stood so close to me that I could feel the warmth of his body, and I wondered if he could feel the rising heat in mine. He finished the job and moved closer to me, grinned and lowered his face so that it was a mere inch from mine. "Annora?"

"What?"

"Can the cocoa wait?"

I nodded as I wrapped my arms around his neck. "Have something in mind?"

"Oh yeah, do I ever."

❧

Something woke me. I shifted on the blow-up mattress, turning my head. Mac was still asleep. I carefully sat up, grabbed my shabby nightshirt from the floor, and slipped it on. The portable heater clicked, and a dying fly sporadically buzzed in the corner, but I thought I'd heard something else. I inched off the mattress and stood up without disturbing Mac. We hadn't bothered to turn off the floor lamp, so I could see the hands on the old mantle clock. Three AM. I grabbed my phone off the table and walked toward the hall, pausing to listen. There was no wind, and the walls did not creak. No pipes banged, no dogs howled.

Then, I heard it behind me, behind the window, behind the wood boards, somewhere out back. Again. It sounded like small hooves pawing the ground.

I looked at Mac, wondering if I should wake him, wondering if he'd be able to hear it too. Would he think I was crazy when I told him about the ghosts? Would he brush it all off, brush *me* off? And if he did, could I blame him?

I quivered from more than the cold and remembered that the upper level's windows had not been boarded up. I turned on my phone's flashlight mode, dashed as quietly as I could up the stairs, and slipped into a smaller back bedroom. The stomping increased, became louder, more desperate. My eyes teared when I heard the whinny— long and anxious and heart-wrenching. I pressed my face against the frosty pane and scanned the illuminated yard. Nothing was there, and yet the frantic neighs and pounding continued.

I jumped when something touched my back, swallowing a scream. It was Mac. "Don't be scared," he whispered. "It's just me."

Suddenly: complete silence. I let out the breath I'd been holding. "I heard something out there," I whispered, nestling back into him, feeling like a coward.

He wrapped his arms around me. "When I was twelve, my buddies and I lied to our parents. We told them we'd been invited to a sleepover but camped out here so we could boast to classmates how we'd braved a night in a haunted house. We didn't see anything, but we heard something too. We all ran home before the sun came up. I crawled into bed and hid under the covers." He kissed the top of my head. "It's just trees thrashing in the wind, most likely. Or deer foraging nearby. Who knows?"

I shivered, and he pulled me closer.

"You're freezing." His lips shifted to my neck. "I know a good way to warm you up."

His way was very, very good, indeed.

*C*OFFEE. *MMM, DEFINITELY coffee.* I flipped on my side, yelping when my hip thumped the floor. The mattress had deflated. And I was not in the least surprised.

Mac squatted on his heels and passed me a large paper cup, his expression bemused. "Hello there. I went out and picked up breakfast."

"'Morning." I sat up, took a sip, and handed him back the cup. "Be right with you."

I wrapped myself in the top sheet. Mac held out his other hand. How could a simple touch set my heart racing? His smile grew as if he'd read my thoughts, as if he knew I was remembering that very hand doing marvelous things to my body. He helped me up, and I shuffled toward the door. Feigning confidence, I looked over my shoulder and winked.

"Enough." He laughed and clutched his chest. "I'm not twenty-four anymore."

Soon, we were seated on kitchen stools, munching away. I put half a blueberry muffin back into a bag, staring as Mac smothered his second chocolate croissant with butter and raspberry jam. "Methinks your eyes are bigger than your stomach."

He waggled his eyebrows. "You could help me work it off later."

"Not on that air mattress, I won't. I'm not twenty-four anymore either." I tossed my empty cup into the garbage. "Thank God."

"City slickers and their high maintenance."

"Whatever, Cow Poke."

We headed toward the back parlour, and all teasing ended. The smoke had cleared and though the walls were now charred, I knew that fire can further spread mould spores. As we had the day before, we wore ventilators and gloves. We approached the sooty mural, and I hid my gut feeling: this was an act of sheer futility.

Within the hour, Mac started to curse as he skinned an inch from the branch of one elm.

"It's okay," I said, hoping I sounded convincing. "It's a tree. Just a tree."

"Was it? How can we be sure? I'm a bull in a china shop!"

"Perhaps we should take a short break."

"I wish we could turn back the clock."

Go back in time . . . yes! "Mac, we can!"

"Egghead, we're usually on the same page, but I'm worn out."

A small seed of hope took root. "We both took photos. All we need to do is print them off and assemble a copy of the cleaned mural. It isn't ideal, but it's something, right?"

He draped his arm around my shoulders. "See? You're a cop at heart. And I feel like a rookie." He stepped off the charred scaffolding. "Okay, so we build ourselves a different kind of evidence board. I'll need to pick up a file from the station, fill out paperwork. Barb Martin said she'd love for you to drop by. Any time."

"I'd like to see her too," I said. "But I'll keep the visit short."

I called her, and she trilled, "Wonderful!"

It was barely nine AM when Mac pulled up to a strawberry box home set in the back half of a corner lot. He leaned across the seat and kissed me until I was breathless. I was nervous about making plans or trusting in the future. His forehead briefly touched mine, and I forced myself to smile. He helped me out of the truck, honked his horn, and drove off.

A fieldstone path led to a covered stoop. I admired her winter pansies and seasonal decorations. A sweet-faced scarecrow leaned against red bricks and costumed ceramic gnomes dotted her lawn. I quieted my thoughts, appreciating the pastoral scene. Nattering with agitation, a lone squirrel scampered up a tall maple as a cloud passed over the sun. I was warm, so I shrugged off my jacket and draped it over my arm. Across the street, laundry flapped on a line, reminding me of a Trisha Romance painting, the charms of a simpler life. Northeastern Ontario certainly had its appeal.

Barb opened her door and called out to me. I met her on the stoop, and she gave me a gentle hug. "My, my, you need some plumping up. And tea. Yes, you need a tea."

We entered her home, and I was immediately struck by its bright colour scheme. As she squeezed my jacket into her small hall closet, I slowly inhaled. It smelled like Barb had spent the morning baking . . . Was that gingerbread? . . . Or a spice cake?

Her tiny entry opened directly into a cozy parlour. I did my best not to blink at the wallpaper. It looked like a country quilt, as vivid as a Chagall lithograph, though a few patches had been muted by years of sunlight. Rag rugs dotted her parquet floor, and a velvet purple loveseat faced a stone fireplace that was flanked by two fuchsia slipper chairs. The clapboard ceiling had been painted teal. Unimpressed by my arrival, a sleek calico cat mewled, leapt off an old-style television, and moseyed toward the kitchen.

"I could give you the two-minute tour. I switched rooms, recently. Easier for me to sleep down here. Now, when my grandchildren visit, they have the upper level to themselves. I'm happy with my space, exactly as is. My daughter keeps telling me I live in a kaleidoscope, "that Boho gotta go." Do *you* think it too much?"

"I think your home is lively and cheerful." I sat down on the loveseat, settling back against a needlepointed cushion.

"Exactly! I dislike neutrals. And white? I've always loathed white, reminds me of maggots." She shuddered. "From the time I was a tot, I refused to wear it. I even dyed my wedding dress to match Carl's blue ruffled tux." Her eyes misted. "He said as long as I was happy, he was happy. I miss him so much. Some days, the heartache is too much to bear." Barb cleared her throat. "Excuse me for a moment, dear. I'll be right back."

She left the room. I heard cupboards and drawers being opened and shut, the clattering of dishes and utensils, typical kitchen sounds. She returned with a tray laden with a mismatched tea set and a platter of baked goods. "I hosted the heritage society's monthly meeting

yesterday. And now I'm stuck with far too many goodies. Please, eat, or I'll be snacking, again, at midnight."
She filled a plate with cookies, set it down on the coffee
table, and poured tea into a delicate cup for herself and
a mug with an overly wide handle for me.

"Jane is a member of the historical society, I believe.
How is she?"

"That poor woman." She clucked her tongue. "She
isn't sure if she should scatter Len's ashes or have them
interred. She thinks James should have some kind of ceremony, but her ex was a right nasty old bugger, burned
his bridges. Their children have refused to attend any
memorial service." Her mouth pursed. "One less worry
for her, Floyd willed his body to science. She is following
his wishes, gathering his work for a charity auction, even
though most locals dislike his art—too creepy. To be
honest, all three men were strange." Her hand trembled,
and hot tea sloshed onto her lap. "Serves me right for
speaking ill of the dead. Let's change the subject."

I asked her about her grandchildren. A skilled sto-
ryteller and obviously a doting grandmother, she spoke
about their ambitions, interests, and romances. When
others praise their loved one's achievements and share
milestones, I try to tune out my pain. My sisters had
been robbed of proms and parades, degrees, and engage-
ments, but life goes on, as it should. Barb had every right
to feel proud. I focused on her joy, but I was also edgy.
It was already mid-afternoon, and Mac and I still hadn't
worked on our evidence board.

Something Barb had said was needling me; I had
no idea what it was. If Mac and I could just study the
photographs . . . Barb was a lovely hostess, and I did not

want to be rude, but I was getting antsier by the min-ute and had to stop myself from repeatedly checking the time.

When we heard the knock, we both assumed it was Mac. I opened the door and gasped.

Daniel Styles looked as surprised to see me as I was to see him.

"You shouldn't be here," I said. "Weren't you told to lay low?"

He didn't answer me. Instead, he introduced himself to Barb.

Her forehead furrowed in consternation. "But—but I had no idea Rosemary had a brother! Nobody told me!" She cast me a sharp glance, then turned toward him. "Come inside."

We stepped back so that he could enter. Tension filled the small space, and Daniel pressed his back into the corner, keeping his hands folded in front of him as if he wanted to appear less threatening.

"May I speak to you, Mrs. Martin?"

"This is not a good idea," I interjected.

Barb again looked at me, obviously puzzled, but she nodded at Daniel.

"Please, ma'am, I need your help."

Her shoulders dropped as she stared at him.

"I know you've been asked about what happened. I believe you have my sister's best interests at heart, but maybe there's something you've kept to yourself?"

Barb wrapped her arms around herself. "It's a night I've tried hard to forget."

"I'm so sorry. I realize this is painful." Daniel's voice broke. "You're going to think I'm crazy, but last night, Rosemary spoke to me in a dream. She said, 'Tell her,

it's okay. She doesn't need to keep my secret any longer.'
Does this mean anything to you?"

Her hands flew to her mouth.

I shivered, unsure if Daniel had only been dreaming.

Barb turned toward me, stricken. "But I swear, it has
nothing to do with her murder. Nothing!"

She began to twist her wedding band. "Rosemary
knew Mrs. Knapp had left a spare key under a rock in
the front garden. She used it, so she could keep prac-
ticing piano. That night, she'd invited me to a private
rehearsal, but I was scared my parents would find out. I
almost didn't go, but I didn't want to hurt her feelings, so
I finally snuck out my window. When I got to the parsonage, the key was missing and the door wasn't locked, so I
thought she was still inside. I raced from room to room,
looking for her. I checked upstairs too. As I walked by
a window, I saw those lights, those strange lights. I ran
down the stairs and ran all the way to the river. That's
when I saw—when I saw—" She swiped away tears. "I
didn't want the town to know that Rosemary had been
trespassing. People can be so cruel. All those wagging
tongues. She wasn't doing anything wrong!"

I grappled with the information. "So, you never
planned to meet her by the river?"

She bit her lip and shook her head.

"Is there anything else you've kept a secret?" I asked.

"No! I swear!"

"I believe you." I sidled up to her. "We need to tell
Mac."

"I know."

Daniel was quiet for a moment. "The information
may not make a difference, but you're not the only one
who kept her secret. Neighbours must have heard her,

too, yet never said a word. Even after her murder. I think the community was . . . is . . . trying to protect her."

"A kindness given too late," Barb said. "She was an amazing, wonderful girl."

"I wish I could have known her." He gave her a shaky smile. "My mother found it too difficult to talk about her. I bet you have more stories to share."

They agreed to meet up again once the police had finished their investigation. We walked outside and watched Daniel drive away just as the truck pulled up. Mac leapt out and slammed the truck door. He stood on the road, hands on his hips, then turned toward us.

"Uh-oh," Barb said.

She took the words right out of my mouth.

Mac marched across the street and remained on the path, frowning. "Ready?"

"She needs her jacket," Barb said, and retrieved it in less than a minute.

"Thank you for having me." I gave her a hug, whispering in her ear, "I'll tell him."

She stood on her stoop, fretfully waving as if I were going off to war. The ride back felt much longer than it actually was, and I was grateful for the buffer of the radio. Still, it was impossible to ignore the tick in his jaw or the way he clenched the steering wheel.

Once we reached the parsonage, he grabbed a bag from the back seat and opened the gate. He didn't say a word until we'd reached the kitchen. He took a file from the bag and slapped it on the counter. "Did you arrange a meeting with Daniel? Didn't I make myself clear?"

"There was no time—"

"You should have called me!"

"They spoke for three minutes. Weren't you the one who asked me, 'What if you were Rosemary's relative?' Daniel *is* her relative, and he is desperate for closure."

His eyes narrowed. "This is not open for discussion."

"Fine. But I'm not apologizing."

"Are you always this frustrating?"

"Look who's talking."

He slowly exhaled. "If Daniel approaches you again, if you see him so much as drive by, if he contacts you in any way, you are to tell me. Pronto. You've survived CO poisoning and a firebombing. Let's not push our luck. My heart can't take much more."

He had a point. "I'm sorry for worrying you."

"Was that an apology?" He studied my face. "Forget I asked. Okay, so, how about we get going and start on our project. Should we use the study?"

"Upstairs, please. I'm fed up with boarded-up windows. There is plenty of daylight left."

"Okay. Sure. One of the bedrooms, it is."

We chose a smaller room. Its walls were primed, and the floor space was clear of debris. A mishmash of tools had been left on a small utility table, but we quickly cleared a spot for the file and tape. We hadn't even opened the file when his phone rang.

I sighed. "Seems like you're a wanted man."

He gave me a wicked grin. "Am I, now?"

"Behave. Hopefully, it is just another goat crisis."

He chuckled. "Rural policing has its moments." He answered the call, and his expression changed within seconds. "I'm on the way."

My heart started to race. "What's happened? Is anyone hurt?"

"There's a fire at Havencrag. Five-alarm. And Jane is missing."

Everyone knew the Boyland summerhouse was vacant. Local youths might see it as the next great place to crash. One forgotten candle would be all it would take . . . or the building could have been intentionally torched. Boyland could have painted another mural at Havenscrag! Jane could have discovered something and told someone. I hoped she was okay.

I kept these thoughts to myself, deciding to talk to Mac later, once he'd returned.

"I'm close to the end of my rope here." He raked his hands through his hair. "Promise you'll eat something— okay?—while I'm gone. I made sandwiches. And try to rest. It feels like I'm forgetting something. Is there anything else you need?"

You? "A phone call, so I don't imagine the worst."

I walked with him to the door, told him I'd eat and talk to my mother because I believed that was what I was going to do, but the silence wore on me, and I began to pace between the kitchen, office, and study, avoiding the parlour and the mural. I tried yoga. I ate half a ham-and-cheese sandwich and drank a bottle of Perrier.

Nothing worked. My brain refused to shut off. Thoughts kept circling: Mac and then Rosemary. *"The girls kept the wizard's secret."* The fires. Mac. *"I don't believe in coincidences."* The murders. Mac. Grace. *"I don't want to see his heart broken."* Barb. *"Some days, the heartache is too much to bear."* And something else that Barb had said. But what, *what?* Images, too, pricked at my brain: cracked mirrors, hungry wolves, a crimson river, Rosemary shifting in the mural.

I continued to move between the rooms, restless and frustrated. I thought about Rosemary playing the piano, about her preparing for her last recital, choosing her prettiest sweater. Perhaps she'd styled her hair, fought with her copper curls . . . Maybe she'd spritzed fragrance on her wrists. I took a deep breath and gasped. Her signature scent was overpowering. The providence of the moment hit me full force, and tears stung my eyes.

I whispered, "Hold on, sweet girl, just a little longer."

CHAPTER

27

I soaked my hands, so the bandages would be easier to remove. The heady fragrance had followed me to the kitchen, intensifying instead of waning, and the room grew quite cold. The pot light above me began to strobe, a small throb, and the bulb suddenly popped. I was not frightened by the notion of Rosemary trying to contact me. She had been a loving, gentle, old soul. What truly scared me was the thought that she might never find justice.

What had I overlooked? Mig's gift to me came to mind, his words suddenly prophetic: *"The hawk sees the whole picture, is not easily fooled."*

Carefully, I peeled away the bandages. The burns were not fully healed but were mending. At least, the skin no longer looked like raw meat, though it was pink and sensitive. I tentatively bent my fingers, exploring the odd, tight sensation. I slathered my hands in ointment and then slipped on a pair of plastic gloves. My palms were already tender. I took two extra-strength acetaminophen tablets, grabbed my phone, and went upstairs.

I began to tape the photos to the wall, overlapping them as much as I could, avoiding gaps. Instead of interrupting the process, I chose to assemble the entire reproduction before studying individual sections. I was mostly done when the phone rang. Though I didn't regret my decision to proceed without Mac, neither did I relish a lecture. Usually I'm honest, dislike deception, but I decided to keep mum about working on the evidence board without him. If I found a new clue or identified the killer, it would be worth the tongue lashings I'd receive. Besides, Mac was going to have to accept that I am unapologetically independent.

"How you doing? I meant to call you earlier," he said.

"Is the fire under control?"

"It spread to the outbuildings and the woods nearby. They've called in reinforcements." It was hard to hear him over the clamour of shouts and sirens. "We're blocking the roads, talking to the fire chief. They've brought in more equipment. It's gonna be a long night." He sounded resigned. "So, you staying out of trouble?"

"I'm organizing myself, mostly. And thinking." I squirmed at the lie of omission. "We'll need to talk, soon, about Barb and the night Rosemary was killed."

"Is it urgent?"

"It can probably wait."

"You sure?"

I hesitated, changed my mind, and quickly summarized what Barb had revealed.

"I'll need to question her again."

"She was trying to protect a friend."

"I know." He sighed. "Don't worry. I doubt there'll be any repercussions. She can say that she got her facts wrong. Happens all the time."

As we said our goodbyes, I stared at the wall, recognizing that what I'd been doing had served a secondary purpose: a distraction. I knew that it was Mac's duty to assist firefighters, to be right in the thick of things. Still, I wished he was back at the parsonage, safe and sound. If we were to try for some kind of long-distance relationship, just as he'd need to accept me for who I am, I'd need to come to terms with the risks he took every day.

I added the last photos to the wall, smoothing out wrinkles. It was helpful to have a replica of the restoration, but the colours were muted, and texture was missing. I stood back and let my gaze wander, resisting the pull of the darker images, their ruthless undercurrents. But what if I fully submerged myself? Would I suddenly see what Boyland wanted to show me?

I often slip metaphysically into fine art. While in Naples, a fellow conservator had bought me a ticket to the Van Gogh Immersive Experience, an exhibit which uses virtual reality, so that visitors can "step inside the painter's works." I'd enjoyed the night, but I have always been able to project myself into paintings. I am not a synesthete. I do not hear colours or see sounds, but I can integrate myself into a work of art. Sometimes, this happens involuntarily when I'm overcome by the talent or abilities of an artist. Other times, I prompt the merger, so I can better engage with a piece, but this commission rattled me to my core, so I'd kept my distance.

It was mid-afternoon. Earlier, I'd opened the window to air out the room, but I'd had to close it again, as a breeze kept rattling the papers. I took a step back.

At last, I could see the entirety of the duplicate I'd fashioned. I needed to drop my defenses, to let the madness touch me. I broke down each barrier I'd carefully erected, inviting the past into the present and the present into the past . . .

Rosemary is contented. She has no idea what is about to happen to her. Her eyes are full of trust. Her smile is sweet, and her cheeriness is like a lamp, casting a soft light. She has her back turned, cannot see her slaughtered pet. Beside the dead pony, apples grow on a birch tree. Birch trees symbolize rebirth and protection. But why the apples? Forbidden fruit or fairy tale? Snow White? Had Misty been fed a poisoned apple? The poor animal. Its eyes are shut. Meanwhile, the owl stares and stares. The bird is stranded, hungry and alone.

I home in on the candy-coloured lights and cringe, knowing they are bait.

The thought pulled me out of the makeshift poster and back into the room. Rosemary's life had not been an easy one; she'd been taunted by classmates who'd been schooled by gossiping parents. I imagined her snuggling against her mother, asking for just one more story about those mystic lights. The killer knew of Rosemary's love of fairies, her fondness for all things magical. They must have been friends, or at least acquaintances.

I slipped back into the copy by focusing on Beverly O'Dwyer, forcing myself to gaze at her petrified expression. She is drowning, but her screams for help are not heard. She, too, is only a little girl. Her doll is lost, but not so far away, lies a baby boy with blue lips. Poor Edmond, dead in his cradle. *"Never mind, Baby, Mother is near."* Delphine hangs from a tree like a marionette angel, leaving young Jane motherless and Boyland a widow.

His pain radiates from the work, corrupts each corner, enflaming the greenery with gore. The mural seethes with his anguish. In his grief, he gently ferries Rosemary across the river so that nothing and no one can ever hurt her again. All the horror is now behind her.

How many children were touched by the violence? I count four: Rosemary, Beverly, Edmond, and Barb, hiding in the background. No. Wait. The seed-eyes . . . in the window . . . the invisible person looking out must be Barb. Barb is inside the parsonage! There are not four children. There are five!

What had Barb said? *I've always loathed white. From the time I was a tot, I refused to wear it.* I studied the girl in the white dress, mapping her location. Rosemary is the mural's subject, but the other child is a secondary focal point. The white draws the eye to the center of the mural. All the elements orbit around her, not around Rosemary. I wrenched myself free from the integration. Sweat covered my brow, but I was shivering. I stepped closer to the wall and squinted, but the photo of the girl in white stayed flat and muddled. Why was she there? Why was she wearing a white dress? The church wasn't Catholic, so it couldn't be a First Communion gown. A nightgown? Maybe the child was a sleepwalker, or she represented lost innocence.

I thought of pulling up a JPEG, but enlarging the image would make it even blurrier. Copies make piss-poor substitutes. The mural had more to tell me, and I knew what I had to do.

≈∽

After my morning outing, the blackened parlour appeared all the more disturbing, and its atmosphere

overwhelmed me. I shook off the feeling as I crossed
the gutted room, reminding myself what was at stake.
Charred hardwood crunched under my feet, though
the floor was cushioned by tarps. I'd always found the
silence in the parsonage to be layered, as if the stillness
were a veil that could be lifted. High ceilings or not, the
space closed in on me.

Rosemary remained behind her smoky shroud. I was
glad we'd left the supplies where we had, but I wasn't
sure it there was enough of everything to thoroughly
clean even five inches. I'd use what I had. I rolled swab
after swab, dropping them to the floor. As I worked,
I kept replaying Barb's words. *Reminds me of maggots.*
There were three white objects in the mural: the pony,
the owl, and the long-sleeved dress. The images kept circling in my brain as I feverishly worked on cleaning the
small zone. My palms ached and the pain radiated to my
fingertips, but I refused to stop.

I lost track of time. Without windows or a clock,
it was hard to say how long I'd been working on the
mural. I removed the layer of soot from the small witness. I ignored her blond hair. Instead, I focused on her
oddly pale features, her gaping mouth, protruding eyes.
I retrieved the head magnifier, thankful it had been
secured in another room during the fire. I studied her
clothing, deciding it wasn't a dress; could it be she was
wearing a sweater and skirt, or a suit? I needed to get
closer.

I went to the kitchen, grabbed a stool, and dragged
it behind me. The scraping sound echoed in the hallway,
sounding like nails on a chalkboard. I had to lift the
chair over the tarps. Finally, like a woman possessed,
I heaved the scaffolding out of the way and shoved the

chair against the mural. I cautiously stepped onto the soft seating and had to put my hand against the mural to balance myself. Though I was in a precarious position, I managed to put on the magnifier. I leaned into the mural, got as close as I could and zoomed in on the sweater, noticing the tiny anonymities, barely discernible under the surface, miniscule rectangular shapes which had been over-painted. Boyland had added something onto the sweater, but he had changed his mind, hiding whatever it was under more white paint. Carefully, painstakingly, I removed just one pea-sized stroke of paint and studied what I'd revealed: a buckle.

Her top had buckles . . . and straps . . . and then I knew. It wasn't a white sweater.

It was a straitjacket.

CHAPTER

28

MY KNEES LOCKED, and the stool wobbled. I fell against the fireplace, smashing my forehead against a corner brick so hard that the room spun and as I dropped to the floor, I stretched out my hands to lessen the impact. The skin on my palms cracked open. I curled onto my side, gritting my teeth as I held in a scream. Both my hands and my head were throbbing.

I pulled myself to my feet by grabbing the hearth and steadying myself. My vision blurred for a moment, and I thought I was going to be sick. I touched my face. It was sticky with blood. I'd deal with it later. Desperate to reach Mac, I dug my phone out of my pocket, groaning when the call went straight to voicemail. He was in danger— we were all in danger. Johnston could use his radio to tell Mac that I'd needed him to return to the parsonage immediately because I'd identified the murderer.

I turned on my heel, unsteady on my feet as I headed toward the front door. But I heard it open, heard Mac calling for me. He sounded as panicked as I felt.

"Back here!" I shouted, walking toward him. "I'm in the parlour!"

He barreled toward me, his weapon drawn. "Johnston's been—"

The sound of the gunshot is something I will never forget. His face contorted, and he mouthed something as he collapsed. His gun slid across the floor. He lay there, horrifically still. I cried out his name and ran toward him, slipping on his blood and landing by his side.

"No! Oh God! No!" His breathing was shallow. Frantically but as lightly as I could, I ran my hands from his neck to his abdomen. I found the entrance wound near his waistband. I stripped off my sweater and pressed it against him, trying to stem the flow of blood, pleading with him to stay with me, to just open his eyes.

Where was Johnston? Surely, he must have heard the blast.

My heart felt ready to burst from my chest. I held Mac's life in my hands. His survival was dependent on what I said and did in the next few minutes. I could not imagine a world without him in it, and if I didn't act quickly enough, Grace would become an orphan. My mother's devastated face flashed before me. She'd already lost three daughters and her husband. My death would destroy her. I couldn't let that happen. I wasn't going down without a fight.

"Jane!" I called out. "I know it's you."

She emerged from her hiding spot behind the door, keeping her handgun aimed at my chest. She didn't take her eyes off me as she stooped to pick up Mac's revolver.

"This is your fault," she calmly said. "Poor, poor Mac."

"It's not too late. You don't have to do this."

"There is no other recourse. I'm afraid we've both run out of time."

"The police will be here any minute. There's a cruiser right outside."

"Constable Johnston has been temporarily incapacitated. I zapped him." She shrugged. "The voltage I used was high, but he'll recover. Mac, however, . . ."

My sweater was sodden. Mac was alive, but she was right. He wouldn't be for much longer. "If your father was here, he'd beg you to stop."

She flinched. "We all make mistakes. He buried his, and I will bury mine."

"Jane, if I figured it out, so will the authorities."

She stood straighter. "I'll fix this. Everything can still be fixed."

"Is that what happened to Edmond? Were you trying to fix him?"

"It had a heart defect. Daddy prized it, even though it wasn't going to live long. Crying, crying all the time. I put it out of its misery."

It. Her words sickened me, but I did my best to keep my expression neutral. Even if Johnston was unconscious, someone must have heard the shot. I needed to keep her talking, but Jane's psychosis was far worse than I'd suspected. I tried to reason with her anyway. "The neighbours are home."

"They'll assume it's Larry's tin lizzie. All that backfiring." She moved further into the room. "You had to keep prodding. Then you showed Len the mural."

"I didn't want him to see it. But when he did, he became upset."

"Len recognized my brooch. My father had it cus-tom designed. The Celtic father's knot with our birth-stones and the claddagh at its heart."

Keep her talking. "How did he recognize it?"

"I still have it." Her nostrils flared. "I wore it often."

"What did Len say to you?"

"He was going to betray me. Even though I'd housed him, rallied around him." Her voice broke. "What I did on that bridge is the hardest thing I've ever done in my life."

How long did I have 'til Mac bled out? "Was it hard to watch Beverly Dwyer drown?"

"Beverly? She went back on her word. I just wanted to scare her. She was so light, so puny, that when I heaved her off the dock, she went sailing like a paper airplane." She smirked. "She sank like one too."

This time I didn't hide my revulsion quickly enough.

"Don't look at me that way! I was a child. I didn't know any better."

"You were a teen when you killed your sister." I immediately regretted my words.

"That Green girl was never my sister! She was a secret Daddy hid from me. I followed him one day. Pretty, little Rosemary. Sweet, funny Rosemary. She was pitiful and low class. I have no idea why my father loved her."

Tell her what she wants to hear. "But he loved you more."

Jane blinked rapidly. "Did he?"

"What would he say, now, to you if he were here? Even though my father is gone, sometimes, I can hear him. Can you hear yours?"

Her face went bright red. "Stop it! Shut up!"

I hid a surge of hope as Mac squeezed my ankle. He squeezed it again; I knew he was warning me. *Careful.* I was feeling woozier by the minute. There was a ringing in my ears and my vision hazed. We were running out of time.

I said, "He'd be proud of you. Look at what you've accomplished."

"I'm a pillar in this community. I'd redeemed myself until Len . . . it was dreadful."

"Shooting Floyd must have been dreadful too."

"Floyd was disturbed. When I shot him, all I thought was, like fish in a barrel."

I cringed and Mac squeezed my ankle harder. *Easy now, easy.* "It was smart of you to set that fire. It took care of most of the evidence, didn't it?"

"I knew that weasel would be found, but the fire did what I wanted it to do."

"And the other fires?"

"Kept everyone guessing. Who'd suspect me of setting fire to my own coach house? But I knew our fire brigade would rise to the occasion. They always do. But it was hard to let go of the old summerhouse. The place held hundreds of good memories. Better days."

"James didn't much look after the place, did he?"

"My ex didn't look after much of anything," she snipped. Then, her expression softened. "I truly loved him, once, but when he found out about my girlhood . . . misfortunes . . . Daddy had to pay him to keep quiet."

"Did James know you were hospitalized, that you received care?"

She barked. "Care! They did unspeakable things in that institution! Daddy learned how bad it was and promised me I'd never go back." Her voice shook. "After he passed away, James became more demanding. He insisted I model for him. Finally, he showed a modicum of talent. And, by God, he got his revenge. His intention had been to humiliate me. And he did."

"He treated you horribly." *Somebody help us!*

She nodded. "At least, he kept his word. Until the mural was found and Len saw it. He told Floyd and James. They wanted me to get a lawyer, to confess everything. So I did what I had to do. And I warned James, if I'm going down, you're going down with me. After all, he was an accessory after the fact. He even made a tidy profit."

"James should have known better than to try and strong-arm you."

"He was weak, but he knew exactly what he was doing. If he'd turned me into the police, he'd have had to admit to decades of extortion. My ex was too much of a coward to kill me, but he wanted to make me suffer. So, he hung himself just like my mother hung herself. He knew her death shattered me."

"Delphine—"

"Stall tactics. This isn't personal. You and Mac are collateral damage." She pressed her lips together. "I can't go to another hospital."

"Your father felt responsible for—"

"Daddy allowed himself to be tricked by gold-diggers and whores."

"The mural says as much about him as it does about the people he could not protect." I played my last card. "Look at it, Jane."

She yelled, "No! I won't! I won't look at it!"

For a moment, I wondered if my mind had snapped too. Behind her, the mural began to shimmer, and light seeped around its edges. It felt like my skull was splitting open.

"I like you. I really wish there was another way." Jane aimed the gun at my chest.

Rosemary's figure quavered, and her button nose surfaced, as if she were arising from murky water. Horror-struck, I watched as her forehead and chin broke free from the filth, and then her entire face emerged from the wall. Those long eyelashes fluttered, twice. My heart pounded as Boyland's masterful brushstrokes, all that texture, simply . . . vanished. Her skin began to glow, and her hair flew about her shoulders. She twisted from side to side, freeing herself from the plaster. She looked from Jane to me. Her eyes widened and her mouth opened. The floor vibrated and air pulsed. Like the walls had been immersed in the river, soot began to stream from them, floating, flowing up to the ceiling, where it undulated above us, a seething black cloud.

Jane recoiled, turned her head, and screamed. Rose-mary stared down at her, her gaze piercing and full of anguish. She seemed to get larger. Jane's shrieking increased as Rosemary pointed to the door and mouthed the word "Go."

Music began to fill the room, piano music, somewhat discordant but recognizable, an arabesque that was deso-late, impassioned, simmering with sorrow. Jane heard it too, and she began to whimper. Mac's hand moved to cover mine, and I swallowed a sob.

Jane's face lost all colour and she swayed on her feet.

Rosemary began to speak. I couldn't hear what she was saying, but Jane became hysterical. She shouted incoherently at the mural and repeatedly fired her gun at the phantom she'd released. In response, Rosemary sadly shook her head, and tears streamed down her face as she lifted her hand again and turned it over. A small blue light appeared in her palm. She cupped its glow, and it intensified. A red spot appeared in a corner, and a soft pink light suddenly gleamed through the soot on the ceiling, a solitary star.

One after another, lights began to bloom around us, shimmering and flickering as if the room had been strung with a thousand bulbs. The music grew louder and louder and louder. It felt as if my ear drums would rupture. Mac had become still again, and his hand fell away from mine. For the first time in a very long time, I began to pray.

Jane shrieked for it to stop! Her screams blended with the jarring notes of the arabesque and the keening intensified, became a wail of pure anguish. She was a cornered animal—snarling, eyes bulging. Her corded neck looked ready to snap as she clawed air. The lights descended, swirling around her in a frenzied vortex, so bright they were almost blinding.

Jane turned toward me, her expression tortured. She backed up to the painting, until her heels hit brick. She lifted the gun higher.

I shouted, "Please, no! Just go!"

Jane sneered and stuck the nozzle into her mouth. I squeezed my eyes shut. One bang, a thud, then complete and utter silence.

I tried to prepare myself, but my stomach lurched when I saw the body crumpled on the floor. All the lights had disappeared. Gone, too, the swirling dark cloud.

I turned to Mac. "Don't you dare die!"

He didn't move, even when the wail of sirens replaced the terrifying stillness. He needed to hold on for one more minute. Just one minute.

"C'mon, Mac! Scot! Scottie MacGowan, open your eyes!"

He stirred under my hands, and I sobbed with relief.

I let myself believe he'd live and clung to that belief as I glanced at the mural. Rosemary was no longer encased only in soot. Like James, Jane had known what she'd been doing. Nothing and no one would ever get the mural clean again. I blinked back blood and collapsed against Mac's chest. The last thing I heard was his heartbeat slowing and people running down the hall toward us.

29

A MEMORIAL SERVICE HAD been carefully planned, and anyone who wished to pay their respects was welcome. The event was held along the river, behind the library. Townies came and went throughout the day, leaving flowers at the water's edge. Many congregated around the bonfire that Mig vigilantly tended. Easton from the local paper had discreetly snapped a few shots while Daniel took dozens of commemorative photographs as unobtrusively as he could.

Constable Johnston and others from Mac's detachment bowed their heads as Sawyer gave a moving eulogy. Barb openly wept. We'd stood side by side as if we were family, and she'd reached for my hand more than once. I needed a few moments alone, but people wanted to thank me, and I didn't want to be unkind or rude.

Lilith lowered her voice. "Where did you get that dress? You look lovely."

Less than a month had passed since that nightmarish day when he had been shot and Jane had taken her own life. I'd stayed in Bliss River, refusing to leave, using up most of my emergency savings while turning down two juicy job offers. The centennial celebration had been cancelled. The town was in shock, still reeling from all that had happened.

Mac was on extended medical leave, which he hated. All the restrictions were getting to him. After his surgery, he'd meticulously followed his doctor's orders; he didn't lift anything, rested periodically, ate healthy meals, changed his dressings often, and even kept his appointments with the police psychiatrist. He walked with a cane, but he insisted that he'd be back to his old self in three months. He argued this point, despite his surgeon cautioning him that his recovery could take a year or longer. Meanwhile, he called *me* the ornery one.

We were so much alike, ignoring anyone who told us to slow down, to take it easy. At times, we were so like-minded that I knew what he needed without him saying a single word. At other times, we were incompatible, flying off the handle at each other, two battleships passing in the night.

I struggled with a new guilt: my hands had fully healed, and I no longer felt pain, but Mac suffered horribly and was only starting to convalesce. Our roles had reversed. I understood all his moods, his boredom, his resentment.

Lilith and Mac were discussing tuition fees when Kate approached us. "Mom, where did you put my coat? I'm freezing!"

"I told you not to leave it in the car," Lilith muttered. "Remember?"

"Can you go get it for me?"

"I didn't lock the hatch and you know where we parked."

Kate pouted, flipped her hair, and trudged up the hill.

"She's having a hard time with the separation." Lilith sighed. "But Parker adjusted quicker than I'd expected. I thought it would be the other way around."

Mac gave us some privacy and hobbled toward Daniel and his sister, Eileen. We'd spoken twice since she'd arrived. She was sweet and thoughtful. She offered Mac a chair, insisted he sit down, and then handed him a mug of hot chocolate.

I turned toward Lilith. "So, how's John?"

"He joined AA. We may try couple counseling." She cleared her throat and lowered her voice. "I ended things with Mark, by the way. I need to go in a new direction. Actually, I'm writing, again. A mystery novel, a cozy set on Manitoulin Island."

I noticed her nails were longer and manicured. "You're happy?"

"I'm happy-er. We'll see what the New Year brings." Someone waved and she waved back. "Come spring, the parsonage will be torn down. Town council's agreed it's time to put that building to rest."

I didn't say anything, though I had much to say.

Lilith raised her hands, blew onto them, and rubbed them together. "The Boyland Estate will become the Bliss River Art Gallery and Museum. The Boyland collection will be on permanent loan, of course, and we're planning for six exhibits a year."

"The family hasn't contested the will?"

"They're already dealing with a media circus, trying to protect their children from the ugliness of the whole thing. This is not how I want Bliss River to be remembered. And all those stupid headlines make my blood boil: *"Famous Painter's Daughter Toasted the Town"*. Like it's all a joke." Her voice became gruff. "How could she fool us for so long?"

I'm a pillar in this community, Jane had said, then talked about redemption.

"I think she even fooled herself, Lil."

"A part of her wanted to confess. She could have destroyed that locket years ago. I can't imagine what her son must have felt when he found it in the safe."

I shivered. "We should try to focus on Rosemary today."

She agreed and changed the subject, enthusiastically describing a memorial garden being planned to honour Rosemary. It would feature a mix of perennials and statuaries. One donor—who wished to remain anonymous—would provide a substantial gift, a custom-designed water fountain shaped like a piano.

As she described the fountain, goosebumps rose on my arms. I was again in that parlour, thunderous notes shaking the walls while ghost lights spun like a cyclone in an ocean of soot. I'd stopped sleepwalking, but I was still having nightmares. I'd wake in a cold sweat, a crescendo ringing in my ears.

While Mac was in surgery, Constable Patel explained that Jane's screams had been heard, and three neighbours called 911, concerned someone was hurt. They hadn't heard any music. At the hospital, once we were finally alone, I asked Mac if he'd heard the piano. He said all he remembered hearing was my voice.

Severe concussions could cause hallucinations, I'd been told. I wasn't wholly convinced. It had all seemed

so real. I liked believing that Rosemary had saved my
life and the life of the man I had grown to love. But I
kept these thoughts to myself.

Mig had snuck up behind me. "Ten minutes 'til we
release the lanterns."

"She'd have loved those, wouldn't she?" *A parade of
floating fairy lights.*

"They will guide her to The Land of Everlasting
Happiness, Gaagige Minawaanigozigiwining."

They began to talk about the specifics of a Missis-
saugi youth art exhibit, so I excused myself and wandered closer to the river. Torches flickered here and
there, casting just enough light so that nobody lost their
footing. The sun had set an hour earlier. More and more
townsfolk arrived for the ceremony. The water lanterns
had been Barb's idea.

The Bliss River OPP Marine Unit would be following behind the lanterns, acting as a police escort for the
procession of lights and ensuring nothing went amiss.
Lilith had thought of everything; a collection barrier
had been placed at the river's mouth, and a dozen volunteers would retrieve the lanterns in the morning. The
lanterns were made of rice paper and wood, and they
were deemed eco-safe, but the community wanted to
minimize the environmental impact.

I hoped the memorial service would do what it was
intended to do: provide closure and offer peace. Mac
clumped toward me. "It's time."

A large crowd of people had gathered by the boat
launch. Many had decorated their lanterns. I had
drawn fairies on the one that I held. Other lanterns had
been inscribed with her name and words like "Angel,"
"Heaven," and "Child of Nature."

Daniel released the first lantern. He whispered something only his sister could hear. They held each other, watching as other lanterns joined theirs setting the water aglow. Tiny rafts drifted into the darkness, a hundred blessings hallowing the night.

Barb gasped. "I might change my mind about white. Oh, my! It's like a river of stars."

Serendipitously, the Northern lights lit up the sky. Mig openly wept, tears streaming down his weathered cheeks as spirits joyfully danced above us. *The Land of Everlasting Happiness. Gaagige Minawaanigozigiwining.* I thought about my sisters and my father, up there, sending me a sign. Mac put his arm around my waist, and we stood with the others, stayed long after the lanterns had disappeared around the bend.

I'd be leaving in the morning. I'd accepted a commission in Montreal. Mac and I had rarely been apart in weeks. We'd already booked a stay at a posh Toronto inn—the city is a halfway point between our homes. The room we chose has a fireplace and an enormous tub. I'd mercilessly teased him about the hearts he'd drawn around those three days on his desk calendar, but the truth was I felt the same way. I had no idea what was in store for us, and the future seemed as clouded to me as the art I restore. As if he'd read my mind, Mac gave my hip a gentle squeeze, and I tried to stay in the moment, to not worry about the months ahead, but the lights above us started to fade. Chilled, I pressed myself against his side, looked up, and made a wish.

EPILOGUE

MY SEX LIFE was in a temporary state of limbo, but my career was thriving. I had mixed feelings about the commission. Lady Drummond, the philanthropist, had believed in charity but shamed those who requested it. Her portrait was not aging well and required multiple treatments to stabilize it. Each morning I'd greet her with a "Chin up. Time for your facial."

The McCord Museum was just a short drive from my condo. I picked up Indian food on the way home—curry, naan bread, and samosas. I'd be staying in for the night, but I'd be meeting up with friends on Saturday at the Cinéma du Musée to take in an art house flick. Grace had recommended it, said it was a tearjerker. I promised to let her know what I thought.

I checked my mailbox. I was surprised it was full and excited to see a small package from Mac. He and I had started a mail game, sending each other small gifts. We'd decided on a ten-dollar limit. Knowing he was a Maple Leafs fan, I'd wickedly sent him a Canadiens hockey card I'd scored on eBay for five dollars: Larry

Robinson, 1978–79. "Canadiens win the 3rd Stanley Cup."

"Cute," he'd quipped. "Freaking adorable."

I salted the wound. "When you visit, I'll take you to a game."

"And when you visit, I'll take you line-dancing."

As curious as a cat, I rushed upstairs. I kicked off my boots, tossed my coat on a chair, and dropped the food onto my kitchen counter. I set the rest of the mail down, then plopped onto my sofa. Feeling stupidly giddy, I ripped off the brown paper, tore open the box, and burst out laughing. It was a vintage Limoges egg cup—a scowling face—chipped and too ugly for words. His cheeks were red, apparently from annoyance. The note that came with it read: *Egghead, I found this in a discount bin at the Salvation Army for a Toonie. It needs a good home. Handle with care. Much Love, Mac*

I opened the rest of my mail. There was a postcard from Mig with a simple message of "Town's not the same without you." Barb had sent me an early Christmas card and a tea cozy she'd knitted. Sawyer's thank-you card featured a panoramic shot of the Bliss River. His penmanship was barely legible. I managed to decipher that he'd appreciated the Montreal musical snow globe I'd sent him—another flea market find.

The large, padded envelope was from Daniel. I opened it carefully, discovering it was full of photographs. His note was brief: *Annora: I promise, nothing was retouched. With deepest gratitude for your help, courage, and friendship.*

I poured myself a glass of wine, then slowly went through the pictures of the memorial service. He'd done a wonderful job of capturing the mood and atmosphere.

I winced at the photo of me. I looked wan, a bit gaunt. Then, I saw something by my waist, a small bubble of light. I skimmed through the other photos, noticing the orb seemed to be following me.

I stared at the group shot. It had been taken just before the lantern release. Daniel had set up a tripod. He'd managed to squeeze himself between Eileen and Barb. Mig stood beside Lilith; Johnston stood behind them. Mac was smiling at me, instead of the camera.

Beside me, there was a short, thin ribbon of light. An anomaly. As a scientist I know a lens flare would have caused the phenomenon, but my eyes misted as I gently touched the photo.

I slipped the photos back into the envelope, then phoned Mac. "I got your package."

"Wow. That was quick. And?"

"It's perfect, my little cup of cheer."

"I'm going to refill that cup. Often." His voice warmed as he said, "So, I've added more hearts to my calendar. Glitter stickers. A dozen of 'em."

"Mac?"

"Yeah?"

"Go ahead. Add even more."

AUTHOR'S NOTE

Though Bliss River is a fictional town, it does resemble Blind River, Ontario, in its location and geographical characteristics. I would like to acknowledge that both the wilderness and populated land I describe in this novel is the traditional territory of the Anishinabek, specifically, Mississauga First Nation, as well as the Huron Regional Métis Community.

Vandals continue to desecrate indigenous pictographs, located on sacred lands, in various parks. It must stop; these strongholds to the past must be protected and preserved, or one day, soon, there will not be a single one left.

Also, Joseph Šíma's *Return of Ulysses* was actually restored by David Frank of Atelier Frank Painting and Paper Conservation, a private studio in Prague. I hold the deepest admiration and respect for all those who safeguard art.

ACKNOWLEDGMENTS

I T TAKES A village to nurture a book into being.

First, I'd like to thank the entire crew at Crooked Lane Books, especially my editor, Tara Gavin, who believed in me from the get-go.

I am indebted to art conservator Christine Adams, MAC, for all her wonderful advice. I could not have written this book without her guidance.

A great deal of what I learned about writing I owe to author Melodie Campbell. Years ago, I took her fiction writing course at Sheridan College. I'm still very much in awe of her.

I would also like to thank those who have read and commented on my manuscript, including beta readers extraordinaire: Debbie Guzzi (sister in spirit), Jennifer Hughes, Dario Ortellao, and Francine MacKenzie Roberts. A shout-out to the members of The Squirrel Writers' Group for the second set of eyes and suggestions.

And finally, thank you to my sister—my fellow Phoenix who is rising from ashes—Dawn Gordon, for her loving support throughout the years. *Je t'aime.*